D0482685

river angel

also by a. manette ansay

Sister
Read This and Tell Me What It Says
Vinegar Hill

river angel

a. manette ansay

William Morrow and Company, Inc. | New York

This is a work of fiction. The events and characters portrayed
are imaginary. Their resemblance to real-life counterparts, if any, is
entirely coincidental.

Copyright © 1998 by A. Manette Ansay
Photo on title page by Jake Wyman/Photonica
Map © 1998 by David Cain

All rights reserved. No part of this book may be reproduced or utilized in
any form or by any means, electronic or mechanical, including
photocopying, recording, or by any information storage or retrieval system,
without permission in writing from the Publisher. Inquiries should be
addressed to Permissions Department, William Morrow and Company,
Inc., 1350 Avenue of the Americas, New York, N.Y. 10019.

It is the policy of William Morrow and Company, Inc., and its imprints
and affiliates, recognizing the importance of preserving what has been
written, to print the books we publish on acid-free paper, and we exert
our best efforts to that end.

Library of Congress Cataloging-in-Publication Data

Ansay, A. Manette.
River angel / by A. Manette Ansay.
p.   cm.
ISBN 0-688-15243-0
I. Title.
PS3551.N645R58   1998
813'.54—dc21   97-31006
                                                    CIP

Printed in the United States of America

First Edition

1 2 3 4 5 6 7 8 9 10

BOOK DESIGN BY CHRIS WELCH

www.williammorrow.com

This book is dedicated to Stephen Hall Smith.

acknowledgments

I would like to thank the Ragdale Foundation, the MacDowell Colony, the Virginia Center for the Creative Arts, and the Vanderbilt Research Council for their support. Thanks to the folks at William Morrow and Company, especially my editor, Claire Wachtel, and also to Katherine Beitner and Sharyn Rosenblum, those angels of publicity. And thanks to my agent, Deborah Schneider: You are awesome.

Heartfelt thanks to Denise and Luby Chambul; to Janis May; to Paul Cody, Kim Dionis, and Stewart O'Nan; to John and Elizabeth Grammer and their joyful daughter, Zoe; to Dick Ansay; to Jake Smith, whom I admire beyond words; and especially to Sylvia J. Ansay for postponing her own work to help with mine.

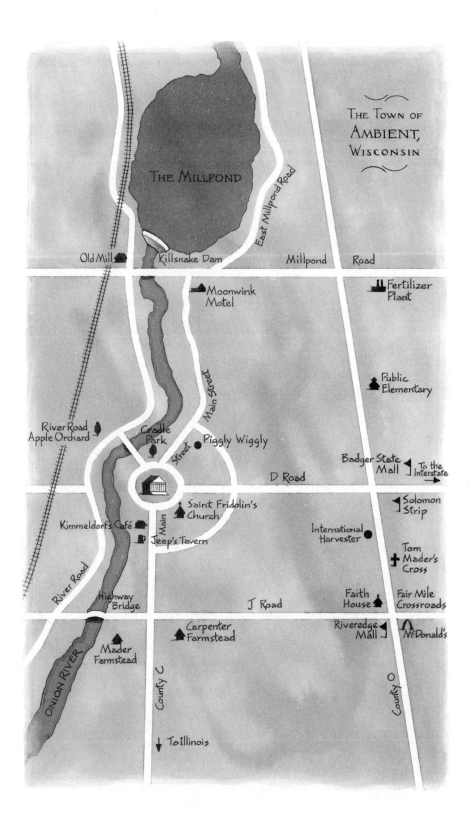

And Jesus said unto them . . . If ye have faith as a grain of mustard seed, ye shall say unto this mountain, Remove hence to yonder place; and it shall remove; and nothing shall be impossible unto you.

—MATTHEW 17:20

author's note

River Angel is a work of fiction, the best way I've found to tell the truth. It is less the story of an individual than the history of a community; it is less about what did or did not happen in a town I have chosen to call Ambient than it is about the ways in which we try to make sense of a world that doesn't.

In April 1991, in a little Wisconsin town about a hundred miles southwest of the town where I grew up, a misfit boy was kidnapped by a group of high school kids who, later, would testify they'd merely meant to frighten him, to drive him around for a while. Somehow they ended up at the river, whooping and hollering on a two-lane bridge. Somehow the boy was shoved, he jumped, he slipped—accounts vary—into the icy water. The kids told police that they never heard a splash; one reported seeing a brilliant flash of light. (Several people in the area witnessed a similar light, while others recalled hearing something "kind of like thunder.") All night, volunteers walked the river's edge, but it was dawn before the body was found in a barn a good mile from the bridge. Investigators constructed this unlikely scenario: The boy had drifted downstream, crawled out of the water, climbed up the slick embankment, and crossed a snow-dusted pea field. But if that was the case, then where were the footprints? The evidence of his shivering scramble up the embankment? And how could he have survived the cold long enough to make it that far?

The owner of the barn had been the one to discover the body, and she said the boy's cheeks were rosy, his skin warm to the touch. A sweet smell hung in the air. "It was," she said, "as if he were just sleeping." And then she told police she believed an angel had carried him there.

For years, it had been said that an angel lived in the river. Residents flipped coins into the water for luck, and a few claimed they had seen the angel, or known someone who'd seen it. The historical society downtown had a farmwife's journal, dated 1898, in which a woman described how an angel had rescued her family from a flood. Now, as the story of the boy's death spread, more people came forward with accounts of strange things that had happened on that night. Dogs had barked without ceasing till dawn; livestock broke free of padlocked barns. Someone's child crayoned a bridge and, above it, a wide-winged tapioca angel. Several people reported dream visitations by the dead. There were stories about the boy himself—that he frequently prayed in public places, that he never once raised his hand against another, that a childless woman conceived after showing him one small act of kindness.

Though both church and state investigators eventually deemed all evidence unsubstantiated, money was raised to build a shrine on the spot where the boy's body was found. I have been to the River Angel shrine, and to others. I have traveled to places as unlikely as Cullman, Alabama, and as breathtaking as Chimayo, New Mexico. I leaf through the gift shop books about angels, books about miracles, books filled with personal testimonies. Books in which supernatural events rescue ordinary people from the effects of a world that is becoming increasingly violent, dangerous, complex. Though I myself am not a believer, I understand the desire to believe. I live every day with the weight of that desire.

Ultimately, I have found it is meaningless to hold the yardstick of fact against the complexities of the human heart. Reality simply isn't large enough to hold us. And so the sky becomes a gateway to the heavens. Death is not an end but a beginning. A child crossing a pea field into the indifferent, inevitable darkness may be reborn, raised up by our longing into light.

Holly's Field, Wisconsin

Thank you, Saint Martha, for favors granted. The following prayer is to be said for nine consecutive Tuesdays: Saint Martha, I resort to your protection and faith. Comfort me in all my difficulties and, through the great favor you enjoy in the house of my savior, intercede for me and my family. (Say three Hail Marys.) I beseech thee to have infinite pity in regard to the favor I ask of thee, Saint Martha, (name favor) and that I may be able to overcome all difficulties. Amen. This prayer has never been known to fail. You will receive your intention on or before the ninth Tuesday, no matter how impossible it might seem. Publication must be promised.

    B.D.

—*From the* Ambient Weekly
    December 1990

one

The boy, Gabriel, and his father stopped for the night somewhere north of Canton, Ohio. Around them, the land lay in one vast slab, the snow crust bright as water beneath the waxing moon. The nearest town was ten miles away, unincorporated, and there was nothing in between except a handful of farmhouses, Christmas lights burning in each front window; a few roads; fewer stop signs; a small white crossroads church. High above and out of harm's way were the cold, gleaming eyes of stars, and each one was so strangely iridescent that if a man in one of the farmhouses had risen for an aspirin or a glass of warm milk, he could have been forgiven for waking his wife to tell her he'd seen—well, *something*. A glowing disk that swelled and shrank. A pattern of flashing lights. And she could have been forgiven, later, for telling people she'd seen something too as she'd stood by the bedroom window, sock-footed and shivering, her husband still pointing to that place in the sky.

But a wind came up in the early morning hours, scattering the stars and moon like winter seeds, so that by dawn the sky was empty, the color of a tin cup. It was the day before Christmas.

The air had turned cold enough to make Gabriel's nostrils pinch together as he stood in the motel parking lot, listening to his father quote figures about the length of time human skin could be exposed to various temperatures.

"It's not like this is Alaska, kiddo," Shawn Carpenter said, clattering bright-yellow plastic plates and cups from the motel's kitchenette onto the floor of the station wagon. The old dog, Grumble, who was investigating the crushed snow around the dumpster, shuddered as if the sound had been gunshot. The previous day, she'd ridden on the floor between Gabriel's legs, her face at eye level with Gabriel's face, panting with motion sickness. There'd been nowhere else to put her. Behind the front seats, the space was packed with all the things that hadn't been sold or lost or left behind: clothing, cookbooks, a color TV, a neon-orange beanbag chair, snowshoes, a half-built dulcimer, two miniature lemon trees in large lemon-shaped pots, and Shawn's extensive butterfly collection, which was mounted on pieces of wood and enclosed behind glass plates. Whenever she'd started barking crazily, they'd been forced to stop and let her outside. The last time, it had taken over an hour of whistling to coax her back.

Shawn peeled off one of his gloves and held his bare hand out toward Gabriel. "One one thousand," he said, counting out the seconds. "Two one thousand. Three one thousand."

They were on their way to Ambient, Wisconsin. An oily light spread toward them from the edge of the horizon, and now Gabriel could see I-77 in the distance, a thin gray line slicing through the snowy fields, unremarkable as a healed-over scar. A single car crept along it, and he imagined it lifting into the air as lightly as a cotton ball. He imagined it again. If you believed in something hard enough, if your faith was pure, you could make anything happen—his fifth-grade teacher, Miss Welch, had told him that. Miss Welch was born again. Still the car kept moving at its careful speed, and Gabriel knew he must have doubted, and that was the only reason why the car kept dwindling down the highway to a point no brighter than a star.

"You see?" Shawn said, and he wriggled his fingers. "If this was Alaska, my hand would be frozen. If this was Alaska, we'd probably be dead."

Grumble had found a grease-stained paper bag. Her tail moved rapidly to and fro as if she believed something good was inside it. Yet Grumble wagged her tail just as energetically at snowplows and mailboxes, at the sound of canned laughter on TV, at absolutely nothing at all.

"A dog, on the other hand, is a survivor. Warm fur, sharp teeth. A survivor!" Shawn said, and he must have enjoyed the sound of that word because he said it again as they pulled out of the parking lot. Gabriel stared back at Grumble, hoping she would look up, hoping she would not. Then he faced front and kicked the plates and cups aside, making room for his feet against the vent. He pulled off one of his mittens and picked up a cup, which he held in front of his glasses. Peering through the oval handle, he watched the land compress to fit into that tiny space. "She'll find a nice family," Shawn assured him. "She'll forget all about us."

Noreen had been much harder to leave behind. Shawn still owed her money from the camper, which they'd bought with money she'd saved from years of work at a small insurance company. That was when they still had plans to travel cross-country— Noreen and Shawn, Noreen's son, Jeffy, and Gabriel—to Arizona, where the weather stayed warm and dry. Noreen had a soft Southern accent that made the things she said seem original and true, and she knew how to do things like make biscuits from scratch. It had been five months since Shawn and Gabriel moved into her one-bedroom apartment in Fairmont, West Virginia, and sometimes, during that first charmed month, when it was too muggy to sleep, they'd taken their blankets onto the tiny balcony and lain there beneath the stars, talking about the future—even Jeffy, who was only four and didn't understand what anyone was saying. But the camper had brought one thousand dollars, money that would get them to Wisconsin and feed them until Shawn found work. He handed Gabriel the thick wad of fifties and hundreds, letting him feel its weight. "You'll have to help out with expenses for a while," he said. "A paper route, kiddo, how do you feel about that?"

Gabriel imagined slogging through the snowdrifts, dragging a wet bag of newspapers behind him. "Maybe I could work in a restaurant," he said, although he wasn't sure a ten-year-old could do that kind of thing, even if he was *big-boned*, the way people said.

"A paper route would be better for you—exercise, fresh air, all that."

"OK," Gabriel said warily—was his father going to start in on his weight?—but Shawn stuffed the money back into the deep pocket of his coat and turned on the radio. More soldiers were arriving in Saudi Arabia; aircraft carriers had moved into striking range of the Gulf. "Listen up, son," Shawn said. "There's going to be a war." The sun was gaining strength, bloodying the hoarfrost that clung to the shrubs and the tall wild grasses that poked up through the snow crust at the edges of the highway. They passed an intersection boasting the world's largest collection of rocks, a car dealership with its necklace of bright flags, a nursery selling Christmas trees beneath a yellow-and-white-striped tent. The land was flatter than any place Gabriel could imagine except, perhaps, heaven, with its shining streets of gold. Miss Welch had told the class all about heaven and Jesus Christ, and how, if they had faith the size of a mustard seed, they would be filled with the power of God and could perform any miracle they wished.

"You mean," Gabriel said, "if I had a glass of white milk I could make it chocolate?"

"That's right," Miss Welch said. "But you'd have to believe with all your heart. Most people can't do that. Most people have a little bit of doubt that they can't overcome no matter how hard they try. Otherwise it would be easy to make a miracle happen. Anyone could do it."

Gabriel picked up the rest of the cups and fitted them into a towering stack. He tried not to think about Grumble. He tried not to think about Noreen, who must be waking up to an empty apartment and a bare spot on the lawn by the parking lot where the camper had been sitting. He reminded himself there would be other girlfriends and dogs and Jeffys, although his father had assured him that this time things would be different because Ambient was the place where Shawn had grown up. This time, Shawn said, they were really going home.

In the past, when Shawn had talked about Ambient, it was to make fun of the people who lived there. Hicks and religious fanatics, he called them. Local yokels married to cousins. People with six fingers and bulging foreheads. Now he was talking about how much Gabriel was going to like *country living*. He talked about the way the sown fields around the town looked like a green and gold checkerboard, split by sleepy county highways where you could drive for an hour without seeing anything except meadowlarks, sparrow hawks, and red-winged blackbirds, and perhaps a sputtering tractor. He described the millpond, how on hot summer days you could dive off the wall of the old Killsnake Dam and float on your back beneath a sky so blue it seemed like a reflection of the water itself. He talked about the Onion River, which ran all the way from the millpond smack through the center of Ambient, where there was a park with a little gazebo and swings, and an old-fashioned town square with a five-and-dime, a pharmacy, and a café with an ice cream soda counter. An angel lived in the river, he said. In fact, he'd even seen it once: small and white, about the size of a seagull, hovering just above the water. But the absolute best part about Ambient was that both Gabriel's grandfather and his uncle—Shawn's older brother, Fred—lived in a farmhouse big enough so that Gabriel could have his own room. At night, he could lie in bed and listen to the freight trains passing through, just the way Shawn had done as a boy, imagining he was a hobo, a stowaway, rocked to sleep inside one of the cars.

Gabriel raised the stack of cups so the top cup touched the roof of the station wagon. He wondered if the angel was real, or if it was just something his father had made up so he would want to live there.

"Ambient," Shawn announced, "is the perfect place for a boy like you to grow up, don't you think?"

The station wagon swerved a little, and Gabriel let the cups collapse, a shattering waterfall of sound. Shawn jumped and accelerated into the breakdown lane. There was the raw hiss of tires spinning on ice, and for a moment, Gabriel saw the long fingers of the weeds reaching for him, close enough to touch. Then they were back on the highway.

"Goddamn it!" Shawn said. "See what you made me do?"

Gabriel picked up a cup that had fallen into his lap.

"You blame me for everything, don't you?" Shawn said. "This is your way of getting back at me. This is your way of getting under the old man's skin."

He turned up the radio and they drove without speaking as the red sunrise dissipated into the steely morning. People were arguing over what the war was going to be about, if there even was a war at all. Gabriel tried to topple a thin stand of trees. He tried to make himself invisible. When nothing happened, he searched his soul for the blemish of doubt that, somehow, he must have overlooked. Noreen had been born again just like Miss

Welch, and she said that Miss Welch was right: Pure faith made anything possible. She told Gabriel stories of people who'd had cancer and been completely cured without surgery or drugs, leaving the doctors mystified. She told Gabriel about modern-day people who'd seen Jesus sitting beside them on a bus or in a cafeteria or even walking along the road, plain as day. She told him about one time when she'd been broke and she'd prayed really hard for a lottery number. The number 462 appeared in her mind as if God had painted it there with His finger; she'd won five hundred dollars. Noreen was younger than Shawn and she wore red lipstick that stuck like a miracle to the complicated shape of her mouth. She loved bright colors and soft, sweet desserts. She was good to Jeffy, and she would have been good to Gabriel if he had let her, if he had not known in his heart that someday soon his father would decide he didn't love her anymore.

Just before noon, Shawn pulled over at a rest area and parked the car at the edge of the lot, away from the kiosk. He moved the seat back as far as it would go. "Tired?" he asked Gabriel tenderly. They were at the edge of a tiny strip of woods. The frosted ground was merry with soda cans and candy wrappers and bags of garbage people had dumped from their cars.

"A little," Gabriel said.

"You'll feel better after a catnap. Ten, fifteen minutes, and the world will be a brighter place." He took off his woolly cap and tucked his gloves inside it, making a small round pillow. Then he wedged it between the seat and the door, put his head against it, and slept.

For a long time Gabriel waited, staring at the broad, blunt shape of Shawn's chin, the fine hairs outlining his ears like an aura. He divided his father into parts and let his gaze move slowly, deliberately, over each of them. The lean, rough cheek. The neck with its strong Adam's apple and the finger of hair curling out from the collar. The sloping shoulders beneath the dark coat, the long narrow thighs. He looked at his father's crotch—there was no one to tell him not to—but then he made himself stop. An eyelash clung to the side of his father's nose and, breathless, he reached over and flicked it away. When Gabriel was still a little boy, his father would occasionally allow him to comb his curly black hair, and afterward Gabriel would smell his fingers, the bitter mint of dandruff shampoo, the oily musk of his father's skin. He'd make up his mind to concentrate harder, to stop daydreaming, to do better in school and make his father proud. He'd lie in bed imagining scenes in which he rescued his father from some terrible danger, and—over and over again—he'd imagine his father's gratitude.

Shawn Carpenter was so handsome that people, women and sometimes men too, would stop on the street and turn their heads to look as he walked on. He had robin's-egg eyes speckled with green, a dimple in his chin so deep you wanted to heal it with a kiss. He was an accomplished welder and electrician; he could fix cars and photocopiers; he was a natural salesperson, an elegant waiter, a creative and indulgent chef. And when he met another woman he wanted to fall in love with, it was hard for Gabriel not to be jealous. He watched him for the early symptoms of a crush like a parent alert for fever. There were sudden bouts of giddy playfulness, late suppers, a rash of practical jokes. Raw eggs in Gabriel's lunch bag instead of cooked. A fart cushion under his pillow. Next came splurges: take-out pizza, television privileges, a toy that had been previously forbidden. There were professional haircuts for them both and, for Shawn, a trip to the dentist. Soon a woman's name would ring from Shawn's tongue too often, too brightly, an insistent dinner bell, and then would come the first awkward meal all together in a restaurant, with candles and fancy wine and a waiter quick to mop up any spills. One night, Shawn would *step out for a good-night kiss* and not return until the next day, and tears would glaze his eyes in that moment before he shouted at Gabriel for forgiveness. "It's hard," he'd say, "raising you alone. Every day of my life since I turned eighteen I've spent looking after you."

Eventually, they'd start moving a few things from wherever they were staying into the woman's apartment or trailer or house or camp, and sometimes these places were elegant and clean, and sometimes they smelled of dog or fried potatoes, but ultimately none of that mattered because, eventually, they became the same. Shawn unpacked his butterfly collection and his beanbag chair, his dulcimer, his snowshoes, his cookbooks. He hung the butterflies on the living room wall, worked a little more on the dulcimer, and prepared chilled soups and golden puff pastries and fish baked inside parchment paper. He'd get to work on time each day and, at night, cut back on his drinking. He was charming and energetic; when he spoke, he waved his hands in the air. But it was always during these optimistic periods that he started to look at Gabriel with a shocked, critical eye, the way that Gabriel himself had looked at the world the first time he was fitted for his thick eyeglasses. "Kiddo, you were blind as the proverbial bat," Shawn told him. "Things must look pretty good to you now," but the truth of the matter was that everything had looked much better before, and sometimes Gabriel still took off his glasses to enjoy a stranger's smooth complexion or a soft gray street, its velvet sidewalk lolling beside it like a tongue, the slow melt of land and sky at the horizon. "Where are your glasses?" Shawn would say. "I didn't spend that kind of money for you to decorate your pockets." Then everything jumped too close and filled with complicated detail: acne and scars and colorful litter, painfully double-jointed trees, clouds with their rough, unsympathetic faces.

Suddenly Shawn would decide that Gabriel needed more exercise, less TV. Perhaps it would occur to him that Gabriel should learn French, and then every night he'd have to listen to a tape that Shawn had ordered from a catalogue. Sometimes it was cooking lessons, Shawn standing over him as he tried to make a smooth hollandaise. It could be his posture, or his attitude, or his ineptitude at sports, and sometimes it was all three. He'd always remember one endless autumn, when they'd lived in Michigan with a woman named Bell, her three sons, and their basketball hoop. Every night, Gabriel had to practice jump shots and layups and free throws with the other boys. Every morning, he'd cross his fingers and stare up at the sky, willing winter to blow in early and leave the driveway slick with ice.

Eventually, Shawn would give up on Gabriel and turn to the girlfriend they were living with. At first, there were only a few small things, and he'd bring them to her attention reluctantly, sweetly, and always with a remedy: a permanent wave, adult ed classes, a more functional arrangement of the living room. He'd sit up late in the orange beanbag chair, drinking from his flask and writing scraps of poetry, and he'd sometimes oversleep in the morning. Around that time, the fights would begin, secretive at first: a hissed exchange in the bedroom; sharp voices from the porch. One night, Gabriel would awaken to find Shawn sitting on the edge of his bed. "What was I thinking?" Shawn would ask, his breath golden with Jack Daniel's. "Next time," he'd say, "warn me, kiddo. I'm pushing thirty. That's too old to be making big decisions with the wrong damn head," and he'd lie down on top of the covers beside Gabriel, and if Gabriel threw an arm over his chest, his father didn't shrug it away.

It was always best between them just after they'd moved back into a place of their own or, more likely, pointed the station wagon toward a city or town where they hadn't lived before, some place where Shawn still had a friend or two, somewhere he knew he could find work. Together they'd bask in the afterglow of leaving, and it was during these times that Shawn always brought up the possibility of moving back to Ambient. Maybe he'd find a job doing piecework for the shoe factory on the River Road, something that would leave him time to write a novel, a thriller; he was certain it would sell. Or maybe he could start a little business, run it with his brother—a landscaping company or, perhaps, a used-car dealership. "Kiddo," Shawn would say, "I have got to get a grip on myself. I've got to get things together." At times like these, with Shawn's face flushed and open and hanging too close, Gabriel thought he might die of love for his father. "Daddy, it's all right," he'd say. "We're fine, everything's fine." And when he thought about how fervently his father believed in those words, words that fell like manna from Gabriel's own mouth, he truly understood the power of faith.

But now his father was sleeping. They were on their way to Ambient. There was no need for Gabriel to say anything. He dug down between the seats, looking for loose change, and when he'd collected enough dimes and nickels he got out of the car and went over to the kiosk. The vending machines were lined up in an outdoor alcove at the back, and he took his time before deciding on an Almond Joy. He ate the first section in one sweet, greedy bite; the remaining section he ate more slowly, licking off the chocolate to expose the clean white coconut beneath. Then he explored the small wooded area behind the kiosk. Finally, he sat down on a graffitied bench and flattened the empty Almond Joy wrapper, folded it into a fighter jet, guided it through barrel rolls and screaming dives and bombing runs. He wondered if his uncle and grandfather would really be glad to see him. He wondered if he really could have his own room, or if he'd be sleeping on a couch until Shawn found them a place of their own. His butt was getting numb from the coldness of the bench. His nose was running. His toes hurt. He decided that even if there was an angel in the Onion River, his father had never seen it.

A thin winter sunlight trickled through the trees, and he let his head fall back, thinking about the shapes the branches made against the sky. If an Iraqi plane flew over, he'd make it disappear, leave all those soldiers hanging like cartoon characters in midair. He imagined them falling to earth. He imagined their souls rising like milkweed, like dandelion seeds. Though he felt the thump of Shawn's hand on his shoulder, it took him a moment to respond to it.

"Like an idiot," Shawn was saying, "with your mouth hanging open and chocolate all over your face. How old are you now? Eight? Nine?"

"I'm ten," Gabriel said.

"Almost grown up," Shawn said. "Almost a goddamn man. What do you think about when you sit there like a ninny? Girls?" He plucked the candy wrapper airplane out of Gabriel's lap and threw it at the ground, but the wind caught it and sent it wafting away into the woods. "I hope to God it's girls," he said. "Christ." He pulled Gabriel up by the shoulder. "Where did you get the money for that candy?"

"The car."

"A thief, on top of everything," Shawn said. "Well, maybe your uncle and grandfather will have some idea what to do with you. Because I do not. Because I simply have had it up to here," and he made a slicing motion across his throat.

They walked back to the station wagon. As soon as they got inside, Gabriel's teeth chattered stupidly. Shawn glared at him, then started the engine and turned the heat on high. "Scared me half to death," he said, and he raked his hands through his hair. "What possessed you to get out of this car?"

"Hungry," Gabriel said. His toes burned. He shifted them carefully, trying not to rattle the cups and plates and risk drawing further attention to himself.

"Hungry!" Shawn said, as if that were the most outrageous of possibilities. He pulled back onto the highway, and they drove for another hour, listening to talk radio. Now and then there were bursts of static, which made the people sound far away, as if they were calling from the moon. A man said the hell with the UN, the United States should drop the bomb. A woman said that if people over there wanted to kill each other, let them. They passed billboards advertising an adult bookstore, a barn with SEE ROCK CITY! painted on its roof, the carcass of a deer and, less than a mile beyond it, a hitchhiker, his face hidden by a multicolored scarf. They passed a low brick church decorated with a banner that read: PUT THE "CHRIST" BACK IN CHRISTMAS. They passed two white crosses at the mouth of an off-ramp, each decorated with a small green wreath. At the end of the ramp was a bullet-ridden stop sign where a van idled, as if the driver was uncertain, exhaust drifting lazily through the air. But all the county roads met at ninety-degree angles. There was never any question which way was left, which was right, which was straight ahead.

When Shawn finally spoke to Gabriel, his voice was softer. "You frozen anywhere?"

"Maybe my feet."

"Kick your shoes off. Get them up against that vent. Does it hurt?"

"Yeah."

"That's good, kiddo," Shawn said. "Pain is the way we know for certain that we're living. If you only remember one thing your old man tells you, try and remember that."

A truck passed them, traveling too fast, splattering their windshield with icy slush. Gabriel pictured it rolling over, bouncing off the guardrail, bursting into a perfect globe of fire. But though he believed without reservation, just the way Miss Welch had said, the truck slipped into the dark eye of the horizon. They were coming up on an exit. A McDonald's sign floated high above the highway, dazzling against all that gray and white.

"Look at that!" Shawn said heartily. "The answer to your prayers! What do you want, a hamburger? Fish sandwich?"

Help bring the Christmas story to life! Human and animal volunteers needed for Ambient's annual Living Crèche to be held in front of the railroad museum from noon till three on Christmas Eve Day. Costumes and hot chocolate provided. The manger will be heated this year! Participants and visitors alike are invited to warm up in the museum lobby where the Christmas Ornament Collection of Mr. Alphonse Pearlmutter will be on display.

    —From the Ambient Weekly
    December 1990

t w o

You could ask anybody in Ambient: Fred Carpenter's new wife, Bethany, wasn't the type to bend her own rules. But that Christmas Eve, she allowed the men to bring their whiskey inside the house. Later, she'd say she'd had a feeling all along that *something* was about to happen, and it drove her to such distraction that when Fred asked her if just this once, for the holidays, they might have a round before supper, she nodded before she realized what he'd asked, what she'd done. The telephone rang, but when she picked up the receiver, a giggling child asked if her refrigerator was running. A lightbulb blew in the foyer and then, only minutes later, in the bathroom off the hall. For no reason whatsoever, a jar of sweet pickles slipped from her hand and shattered on the linoleum floor. More than once, she caught herself checking the sky above the field where, just last August, the legs of two tornadoes had stumbled, knock-kneed, toward the highway.

But on this day, the winter sky was plain and pale as her own face, and at six o'clock sharp, Bethany called everyone to the table: her boys and Fred and Fred's father, Alfred, whom everybody called Pops. Pops was well known around Ambient; since losing his driver's license for DWI, he'd been driving his tractor to Jeep's Tavern each weekend, parking it on Main Street, forcing traffic to squeeze by. Now he wore the nice dress shirt Bethany had given him last Christmas, fresh from the box, all the creases intact. His beard—once dark and thick as Fred's—had grown in pale and patchy since the night he'd accidentally set it on fire, heating up a pan of SpaghettiOs. Still, it brushed the clean surface of his plate as he hitched his chair up to the table. The water in the glasses shivered and danced.

"Already a few sheets to the wind," Bethany complained, not bothering to lower her voice.

Pops said, "Hell, I only had two."

Bethany said, "Language."

The boys nudged each other and grinned.

"Well, *heck*, then," Pops mumbled, cracking his knuckles as if he wanted to fight the Christmas ham. But the electric company had cut his lights again, and even Bethany could see he was pleased enough to be sitting under her bright chandelier. Outside the dining room window, not ten yards beyond the edge of the gravel courtyard, the farmhouse he'd occupied for sixty years loomed like a pirate's ship—all it needed was a skull-and-crossbones to replace the tattered American flag that drooped from a boarded-up window, stripes faded pink. The yard was a carnival of discarded chairs and mattresses, tires, tractor parts, buckets of paint; the porch sagged beneath two mildewed couches where, in summer, Pops and the boys from Jeep's gathered to talk dirty, to swap outrageous lies. Each year, the whole place leaned a little more to the right, and though Fred had spent the better part of one summer jacking up the central support, the house still looked like it wanted to slide off its foundation and slip away, embarrassed, into the fields.

"Now, Beth," Fred said from time to time, twisting at his beard until it formed an anxious point. "It seems to me we might have Pops over for a hot meal now and again." But Bethany refused to pity Pops. She figured he made his bed each time he headed for the liquor store. After all, he had his social security, plus whatever he earned doing odd jobs for Big Roly Schmitt—that is, when he made up his mind to work. She had him to supper on holidays, of course; beyond that, she drew the line. Otherwise, she knew, he'd be crossing the courtyard every night of the week to eat her good food and stink up her nice furniture, to mistreat her house the way he'd done his own and infect her boys with his laziness.

Back when Fred had first proposed, Bethany saw he had some idea about her moving into those cat-piss-smelling rooms, looking after his father, imposing some order on their lives. Even then Fred's beard was thick enough to hide his mouth, but Bethany saw the smug pride in his eyes, how he expected her to leap for that ring like a cat for a bird. After all, at the time she was a thirty-something waitress, mother to two boys who'd never had a father's name. But Bethany told Fred, "Listen once. We're not kids so we can be straight with each other. If you marry me, you are getting two fine sons and a wife who will cook you the best meals you've ever eaten, and keep a nice garden, and make sure your clothes are tidy-looking, and don't forget I'll be out there earning money too. When the lights go out I'll never say no, provided you keep yourself clean. So that's a good deal for you and well worth the cost of a house I'll be proud to live in."

She'd surprised him, but Fred was quick on his feet. He said, "There are gals who'd take it as a challenge to fix an old farmhouse into a showplace."

"I guess you should propose to one of them," she said.

He set his beer down on the coffee table; she nudged it onto a coaster. It didn't take much to leave a ring.

"I guess you should take another look in those magazines

you're always reading," he said. "Half those ladies' fancy places are old farmhouses somebody smart bought cheap. I'd give you a thousand dollars," he said, and he paused to let that sink in. "You could spend it however you pleased."

She took a *Better Homes and Gardens* from the magazine rack and held it out to him. "Show me," she said, "where one of these fancy places comes furnished with a half-crazy drunken old man."

She knew he had money for a decent house—a thirty-six-year-old bartender who sleeps in his childhood bed can save a pretty penny—but he said, "I have to do some more thinking on this," and walked out, taking that ring along with him. Her mother said, "Oh, Bethany, look what you did, those boys will never have a father now." And Bethany said, "Ma, these boys live in a two-bedroom apartment with carpet on the floors and cereal in the cupboards, which is more than any father ever gave them." True, she was lonely, but if it came down to a choice between a man who'd have them live dirt cheap and dirty, or her own waxed floors and freshly scrubbed windows, Bethany was proud to choose door number two. Why marry if it didn't improve your standing, make things a little easier on yourself? Why lose control of the few things you'd finally managed to get a firm grip on?

She would never forget how she and her sister had had to walk on tippy-toe around Pa, how Ma was always saying, *Now don't upset your father, now leave your father be*, like he was some wild animal they'd lured in with table scraps. They'd lived in a duplex, rented their side from a man named Mr. Shuckel. When he came to the door to ask about rent, Pa always sent little Rose to say nobody was home, but Mr. Shuckel hollered at her just like she was a grown-up. Now Pa was long gone and Ma had moved in with Rose and her three half-grown kids. She lectured Rose and Bethany both about how *her* children always had a father, how'd they been a real family, not like *you young gals today*. Bethany ignored her the same way she ignored the politicians on TV.

She'd never voted, hadn't even bothered to hear George Bush when he stopped to give a stump speech in Cradle Park. What did this politician, or for that matter any other, care what *she* had to say? *She* could have told them that a happy family didn't start with the right church or a fancy school or *x* many cops on the street. It started with a nice place to live. And when Fred returned three months later, that same ring hooked to a house key, Bethany married him right there in her heart—Father Oberling's ceremony at Saint Fridolin's Church had little to do with it. It was a home that cleaved two into one, and it was only their second Christmas together when Shawn Carpenter showed up to spoil it all.

They had just said grace, something they did only on holidays—Bethany saved prayer for special occasions, the same way she saved her good china. "Everything looks great," Fred said, and he stood up to carve the ham, which was wrapped in a pineapple-and-cherry necklace Bethany had copied from the cover of *Good Housekeeping*. There were side dishes of scalloped potatoes and carrot salad piled high in a Jell-O ring and squash with marshmallow topping. There were baby canned pear halves spread with cream cheese, garnished with a dab of mint jelly. *A perfect Christmas dinner*, Bethany thought. *A perfect family to enjoy it*. She silently challenged Ma or the tight-lipped ladies she cleaned house for or even George Bush himself to say it wasn't so. Then her heart froze at the sound of somebody pulling into the driveway. "Who's got a big brown station wagon?" she said. It stalled on the ice, slipped back, lurched ahead so that it spun a cookie in the courtyard, crashing into the drift along the snow fence.

"What the hell," Pops said, standing up to look.

"Language," Bethany said.

"What the hooey," he corrected himself.

"It's two of them," Bethany said. "They're headed over to the farmhouse."

"Maybe it's Santa and Rudolph," Pete said sarcastically.

"Ho ho ho," Pops said.

"Maybe it's Saddam Hussein," Robert John said.

"Hush," Bethany said. "That's not table talk." Fred finished off the last of his whiskey; Pops wobbled slightly as he followed him to the door. "Hullo?" Fred called, and Pops hollered, "We're over here!" Then the cold air sucked all the good food smells out into the night and, in exchange, presented them with Shawn Carpenter.

Bethany knew from the get-go who he was—she'd heard all about his good looks and bad habits from Lorna Pranke, the police chief's wife, one of the nicer ladies she cleaned house for. Fred himself didn't talk about Shawn much, just said he had ways of making bad ideas sound sensible. But Lorna had told of how he'd stolen and scammed and disturbed the peace and generally made a nuisance of himself, how for years you couldn't open the *Ambient Weekly* without finding his name under "Citations." The chief lost many a good night's sleep before Shawn graduated from high school and left town for good. Whenever Bethany asked Fred about the things Lorna told her, he'd neither confirmed nor denied them. "Now, now," he'd said. "You want to dig for skeletons, you keep to your own closet."

"Surprise!" Shawn yelped, and he grabbed Fred and thumped him on the back right where it was always sore from standing at the bar. That spot, if you pressed your hand to it, would bring tears to his eyes, and Bethany felt that pain all the way up her own spine. But Fred only moaned and grabbed his brother harder, and the two of them hugged like no two men she'd ever seen, the way women hug, or lovers.

"Shawn-O!" Pops said, and the three of them wrestled around like kids instead of the grown men they were. Bethany and Pete and Robert John just sat there, and what Bethany felt at that moment was jealousy—jealousy and an odd twinge of fear. For this was something else Lorna Pranke had told her: Shawn Carpenter drew people to him, made them do whatever he wished. He was like a magnet, like that iron ball inside the world that holds everything together, whether things want to be held or no. He had those good looks you couldn't look away from; he moved like whole milk poured smooth out of a bottle. Fred, her own husband, loved him so much he was weeping like a child, and yet she'd never known until now. He'd kept it a secret, too painful, too sweet to share even with his own wife.

"Who's that?" Robert John said. A fat little boy was standing on the threshold, letting out the heat. His weight made it hard to guess his age. His nose was running. There was a flu going around, and Bethany hoped he didn't have it.

"Don't let the cows out, Gabriel," Shawn said, and the boy quickly shut the door. Bethany was the afternoon crossing guard at Solomon Public Elementary, and she could already see he was the sort of kid the others wouldn't want to sit with. She could tell anybody might copy off his homework or pick on him at recess. "Whew," Shawn said, swinging an arm around the boy's shoulder. "Some Taj Mahal your grandpa's got—huh, kiddo?"

"Pops still lives at the farmhouse," Fred said, and he pulled Bethany forward by the hand. "I built this place for Bethany when we married."

"Married? You?" Shawn said. "Freddie, you old dog!"

"Yes, sir," Fred said proudly. "These are my new sons, Pete and Robert John."

Shawn ignored the boys. "Bethany," he said, as though her name tasted creamy in his mouth. "A pleasure to meet a woman who could make an honest man of my brother." His incisors were so sharp and white she wanted to touch one with her finger, the way you'd test a good kitchen knife. It was clear he wanted something from her, though what that was she couldn't say. She remembered Pete's father, and Robert John's father, how their smiles had wrapped around her, held her close; Shawn's smile was trying to do the same. He said, "You got room at your table for a couple of weary travelers, Bethany?" beaming like he'd done her a favor. But a pretty smile didn't work on Bethany the way it used to. She'd set the table for five; there wasn't room for two more people. Anyone could see the whole arrangement would be ruined.

"Well," Bethany said. She saw the boy looking hungrily at the ham, at the hot, fresh dinner rolls. His hair was tangled as a wind-blown field.

"If there's not enough to eat," Shawn said quickly, "we're happy with a sandwich. We don't want to put anybody out."

Which was a lie. You didn't show up uninvited for Christmas supper to beg a sandwich. "You're welcome to what we have," she said. "It's just that I'm wondering where to seat you."

"Oh, we can sit on the floor," Shawn said, as if a decent person would allow something like that. So Bethany ran to the kitchen to find more plates, while Fred dragged the twin wing-backs in from the living room. The boy sank into one, still wearing his coat, and took the plate Fred filled for him. Then, to everyone's surprise, he put the plate on his lap, folded his hands, and lowered his head.

"Gabriel's on a religious kick," Shawn explained. "Teacher at his last school brainwashed him. So much for separation of church and state."

"A little religion never hurt anyone," Bethany said firmly. "I'll be taking my boys to Mass tonight, and we always go on Easter."

"This isn't just Christmas and Easter," Shawn said. "This is morning, noon, and night." He laughed, but the child's face was radiant with concentration. Pete and Robert John stared. The room ticked with silence. Finally, the boy blinked, opened his eyes.

"Did you remember to pray for your old man?" Shawn teased, and with those words, Gabriel began to eat, steadily and noisily,

like an animal at a trough. Robert John let loose with a soft pig
snort; Bethany cut him a warning look. "How old are you, Gabriel?" she said to be polite, but Gabriel didn't answer, didn't
even look up.

"He's a big fifth grader this year," Shawn said, and he smiled
again, that slick, wanting smile. "How old are these handsome
boys?"

Pete said, low as he could, "I'm at Solomon High," and Bethany could tell he wanted to put as much distance between himself
and Gabriel as possible.

Robert John said reluctantly, "I'm in fifth."

"Hear that, Gabey?" Shawn said. "You're the same age! You'll
probably see each other at school."

Bethany put down her fork uneasily. "So you intend to stay in
Ambient?"

"Thinking in that direction," Shawn said. "Of course, we need
to find a place to stay."

"I got plenty of room at the farmhouse," Pops said. There was
mashed potato in his beard. Bethany signaled Fred, who leaned
over and tenderly wiped it away with his napkin.

"The thing is," Fred said to Shawn, "Pops is having another
dispute with Wisconsin Electric."

Gabriel's fork moved from his plate to his mouth, from his
mouth to his plate.

Shawn said, "Then maybe Gabriel could stay here for a bit, let
his cousins show him the ropes."

At last, Gabriel's fork fell still. Pete and Robert John looked at
each other as if the only rope they planned to show Gabriel was
a noose. And it was all Bethany could do to conceal her rage. She
cleaned fourteen houses each week, plus her own. Weekday afternoons, she met the buses at Solomon Public. She had no time
for the child of a man too lazy to look after his own.

"You need to understand something," she said. "We keep our

households separate. I've got all I can handle with my own two
boys.''

"Now, Bethany,'' Fred said. "It's just a night or two.''

But if she'd learned anything over the years, she'd learned how
to stand up for herself. One night would stretch out into a week,
and then a month, and once Gabriel got the run of her house,
Pops and Shawn would soon follow. And it wouldn't take long
for squalor to take root, settle in to stay. A few stray cups could
collect overnight into a dried-on sinkful. Some newspapers left
on the couch might slide across the floor, pile up beside the arm-
chair, snag the dust bunnies that had materialized the moment
you looked away. And when you turned back to deal with them,
you'd forget the laundry you'd meant to start, so the beds
wouldn't get made for a night that stretched into a week because
Mrs. So-and-so called and she needed *her* house cleaned special
for a party, or because you caught cold or your back went out,
or because it was already time to take out the garbage and vacuum the living room carpet and rinse the teapot with vinegar.
Suddenly the house would seem smaller and voices would seem
louder and supper, again, would be Van Camp's pork 'n' beans.
She could see the clutter building up already in the twin crystal
balls of the boy's thick glasses.

She said, "I'm sorry, but it's more than I can do.''

"Now, Beth.''

"I won't be sending him *my* boys to care for.''

"It's OK,'' Shawn said, but that smile was finally wavering. "I
don't want Bethany to put herself out on our account.''

"I assure you that I won't,'' she said. "That's what I'm telling
you.''

"Of course I'm happy at the farmhouse,'' Shawn said. "And
Gabriel will be too. I just thought he'd like to spend a little time
with boys his age.''

"I want to stay with *you*," Gabriel said to his father. It was the first time he'd spoken.

"For Pete's sake, kiddo," Shawn said, too heartily. "I bet you could survive a night or two without me. How old are you now anyway, twelve? Thirteen?"

"I'm *ten*," Gabriel said, and he broke into silent, shaking sobs.

"Old enough for a super-big slice of pie," Bethany said to quiet him, to quiet them all. But tears kept bubbling up in the corners of his eyes, and the sleeve of his coat was shiny from wiping his nose, even though, twice, she offered him the Kleenex box. He ate three huge pieces of pie, bite after bite, wedge after wedge, in the same helpless way she remembered Ma eating cookies right from the bag. By that time Pa's late nights had stretched into lost days, and she weighed over two hundred pounds. Even today she was a big lady, and she'd be living with Bethany instead of Rose if Bethany hadn't hardened her heart. There'd be a yellow stain on the ceiling above the chair where she smoked her cigarettes, butts toppling out of whichever clean plate she chose for an ashtray, burn holes scattered across the upholstery like flecks of dirt. And then Fred would start lighting up his after-dinner cigar in the house instead of going next door, and maybe he'd have one after work, seeing it was so convenient for him to do so. That was how easily it started. You had to be on your guard. As soon as somebody balled up a handkerchief, left it lying on the end table, there'd suddenly be a couple of pennies, a pen, a scrap of paper beside it.

"Rosie," Bethany had told her sister, "you've got yourself and those kids to think of. Don't let Ma go bullying you if you don't want her living with you."

"I just think you ought to take a turn for a while," Rose said. "Just give me a break from her, that's all."

But that kind of thinking was the beginning of the end. It was the beginning of Ma and those dresses she couldn't be bothered to wash, and that stinking little dog she'd adopted last year and doted on more than she ever did on Bethany. It was the beginning of forgetting where you drew the line. For by the time you were in a particular situation, that line got hard to see because there were people stepping all over it, waving their arms, hollering and crying and making demands. The thing was to keep yourself clear of those troubles. The thing was to understand your limits, to put your foot down with a boom. Bethany had known before she'd married Fred that he had his family's taste for booze. But she also knew he had a kind heart and a yearning for better things, and she'd designed the house to feed those inclinations.

After supper, Fred led everybody into the living room to play cards around the coffee table as Bethany put the leftovers away, did the dishes and wiped down the cupboards and washed the floor. By then it was nearly eleven, time to leave for Midnight Mass—if you didn't get there early, you'd end up standing at the back. Bethany had taken the boys each year since they were old enough to sit up in a pew. Religion, like a spoonful of cod-liver oil, was an easy ounce of prevention, even though some might protest its bitter taste. She stuck her head in the living room. The Christmas tree cast a warm light over the crèche in the big bay window, and Bethany admired the faces of the shepherds, the wise men, the little drummer boy. Even the animals' dull expressions were made human in the presence of the Baby Jesus. Mouths parted expectantly. Eyes solemn with hope. She'd draped the top of the crèche with red ribbon that matched the ribbons on the gifts beneath the tree, and these matched the tiny red bows she had glued to each of the golden ornaments. The angel she'd seated at the tree's tippy top, a white bulb illuminating her dress, looked down upon everything with pleasure—except for the bottle of Wild Turkey, the men hunched over their cards. Pete and Robert John sat beside them; Gabriel dozed on the love seat, his river angel

35

mouth open on one of her nice throw pillows, his coat tugged carelessly over him.

"Pete, Robert John," she said. "Time to get ready for church."

The men had cigars tucked in their shirt pockets; Bethany saw Pete had one too. And perhaps it was that cigar which made him decide to feel his oats a little. "Oh, Ma," he said. "I'm too old for that sort of thing."

"Me too," Robert John said.

"Then I guess you're too old for what Santa brought you," Bethany said.

Pete sighed theatrically; Robert John popped to his feet. In the fall, Fred had taken the boys out to look at snowmobiles, and they suspected, rightly, there was something waiting for them in the milk house under a tarp. But then Fred said, "Aw, Beth, don't you think Pete's old enough to make up his own mind?"

And before Bethany could reply, Pete said, "Dad's right. I'm not a kid anymore."

Dad. She'd been after the boys to call Fred that since they were married, but this was the first time either one had done so. Fred beamed, knuckled Pete's shoulder; Pops cackled vengefully. What could she do? She said, "Whatever your father thinks is best," hoping he would say, "Go along with your ma," or maybe even, "Let's all go to Mass together this year," which, of course, he didn't. Robert John sat back down and announced he wasn't a kid either, but she had him by the ear so fast he yipped like the pup he still was. "We leave in five minutes," she told him, anger masking her hurt. "March." She turned to follow, saw Gabriel clumsily working his arms into his coat. He said, "May I go to church too?"

"Now, son," Shawn said, "we don't want to impose." He was looking at Bethany when he spoke, but the easy, oily smile was gone. Maybe she'd been too hard on him. Clearly, he cared about the boy. And she knew firsthand how difficult it was to raise a child alone.

"Beth?" Fred said. "Honey?"

But the truth was that she didn't want to take Gabriel to church, to have him sit beside her with his uncombed hair and unwashed smell, that jacket sleeve stiff from wiping at his nose. She wanted her own sons sitting right beside her, where everyone in that congregation could see what big, fine boys they were, how she was raising them right, how she was keeping herself up, how Fred Carpenter was one lucky man. "You sure you can be good for one whole hour?" Bethany said. "Because if you fidget, I'll send you out to the car."

"Gabriel's always good," Shawn said, and the boy smiled at him gratefully. Robert John sulked back into the room, his feet crammed into unlaced boots. His coat was unzipped. His clip-on tie was crooked. He shot Pete a clean, cold look of hate.

Pete said, "Hey, this'll cheer you up! Gabriel's coming with you."

Robert John mumbled, "Will he fit in a pew?"

Fred said sharply, "That's enough of that."

"Take your cousin out to the car," Bethany told Robert John, and as soon as the younger boys had left the room, she plucked the cigar from Pete's shirt pocket. "If you're going to be treated like a man," she said curtly, "you'd better start learning to act like one. I expect you to set an example for both your brother and your cousin." She flipped the cigar at Fred and walked out to the foyer. To her surprise, he followed; he even helped her on with her coat. "Aw, don't be mad," he said. "He'd just sleep through the service anyway." He was cuddling up behind her, his beard tickly against her neck. *"Dad,"* he said, and he leaned his chin on her shoulder. "Did you hear him say it, Bethie?" His hands locked over her stomach like the buckle of a belt. And Bethany forgave him, leaned back against him—just for a moment—before unbuckling his hands, kissing each rough palm, and hurrying after the boys.

Robert John had claimed the front seat; Gabriel sat in back. The angel in the big bay window winked and blinked as they drove away, dwindling down to the small, still light of a distant star. Bethany thought of Pete, alone with the men, their whiskey, their ways. The fact was that both her boys were growing up. She hoped Fred's example would keep them from being like their fathers and her own, the walk-away types, the sort of men she didn't even pretend to understand. As she turned north, following County C along the river, she wondered how it could be that Pa wasn't even the least bit curious to see how she and Rose turned out. Ma, for all her dislike of them, wouldn't have left them any more than she would have left behind an arm or a leg. Maybe, Bethany thought, that was why she'd treated them so mean. Because she couldn't leave. Because they'd been a part of her once and her body still remembered them, claimed them, the way Bethany's body claimed her boys somewhere just below the breastbone.

"Is that the river where the angel lives?" Gabriel asked in his clear, child's voice.

"Angel?" Bethany said. It had started to snow, a light sparkling haze that shattered the moonlight into millions of pieces and skipped them across the narrow strip of water still untouched by ice.

"My dad said there was an angel," Gabriel said, and his voice was less hopeful now.

"That's just an old wives' tale," Bethany said.

"No it's not," Robert John said. "This kid at school? Davey Otto? Some other kids dared him to jump off the Killsnake Dam and he did it? And he—"

"Nearly drowned," Bethany said.

"His mom says the angel saved his life."

"I don't ever want to hear about you playing at the dam."

"Pops saw it once. By the highway bridge," Robert John said. "He says it jumped out of the water like a fish!"

"Have *you* ever seen it?" Gabriel said.

Robert John twisted in his seat to stare at him. "Maybe," he said mysteriously.

They were coming into Ambient. All the houses were outlined with lights, and some were capped by glowing reindeer, sleighs and snowmen, Santa Clauses wired to the chimneys. That afternoon, there'd been a living crèche in front of the railroad museum, and all the props were still in place: the manger with its cradle, the shepherds' staffs, the post where the Farbs' pet pony had been tied. Downtown, every other parking meter boasted a red-ribboned wreath, and the tall pine tree in front of the courthouse was decorated so beautifully, its star shining so brightly, that a stranger might barely have noticed the empty storefronts: the boarded-over windows of the Sew Pretty House of Fabric, the close-out sale banner at Fohr's Family Furniture, the old brick bank where first a bridal shop and then a shoe store had started up and failed. The pharmacy was gone, and so was the five-and-dime. But there were a couple of new gift shops that catered to the millpond people—weekenders and summer vacationers who thought nothing of buying a perfectly fine little bungalow overlooking the Killsnake Dam, then ripping it down and putting a great big house up in its place. Cheddarheads sold cow T-shirts and German dolls and cheese; The River Stop sold cards and books, expensive kitchenware. And some of the old businesses were doing just fine—Roland Schmitt's real estate company, Kimmeldorf's Family Café, the bowling alley around the corner and, of course, Jeep's Tavern. The sad thing was, if you wanted a can of paint or a new blouse, a slice of liverwurst or a refill on your prescription, you had to drive to Solomon, which, just a few years earlier, had been no more than a couple–three hundred houses upwind from the fertilizer plant, a dance bar called the Hodag and, down the road a mile or so, the Badger State Mall.

Sometimes Bethany couldn't believe how fast everything had changed, even since she and Fred were married. But she had no problem with the newcomers, the way some people did. You couldn't blame others for moving in from the cities. Who wouldn't want to live somewhere like Ambient? At the town square, Cradle Park was as lovely as any picture postcard she had ever seen, especially now that the Onion River had finally begun to freeze over, the ice beneath the bridge glistening like spilled cream. You could forget all about how crowded it was in summer, how the trash cans spilled over, drawing flies, how several women had had their purses snatched in broad daylight last July. There was talk of the city buying land on the outskirts of town for a larger park, setting up a boat ramp, dumping sand for a beach. Bethany didn't care what they did, as long as it didn't raise her taxes.

Saint Fridolin's parking lot was full, so she parked illegally—on Christmas Eve you could. Inside, she took off her gloves and swatted the snow from the boys' hair and shoulders; she straightened Robert John's tie, mopped Gabriel's nose with her handkerchief. Joe Kimmeldorf, wearing an usher's red carnation, was handing out thin white candles. He gave one to Bethany—ignoring the boys' longing looks—then led her to a side pew at the back of the church, as she'd known he would. But the moment he was gone, she got up and dragged them toward the front. What was the point in coming to church if all you could see was a wall of backsides?

"Ma," Robert John whispered, his head hung low with embarrassment, for the choir had begun to sing and people were turning their heads to stare. *Stille Nacht, heilige Nacht.* In the pews, men let their knees fall open and women set their purses beside them, daring her to crowd in. From the corner of her eye,

Bethany saw Joe Kimmeldorf coming back down the aisle. Then she heard someone whisper her name—Ruthie Mader, her neighbor to the west. "Over here," Ruthie said, and she motioned for her daughter, Cherish, to scoot over. Cherish Mader was a high school senior and more beautiful than any fashion model. Everybody said she took after her grandmother Gwendolyn, who'd run off to New York in the 1940s and come home with a wicked tongue and a toddling baby—Ruth. But Cherish wasn't wild like her grandmother had been. You never saw Cherish Mader stray very far from her mother's side.

"Thanks," Bethany said, pulling the boys in after her. She ignored the pop-eyed looks of parishioners crushed in the middle of the pew. Wasn't that what being a Christian was supposed to mean—doing unto others, even if that meant inconveniencing yourself just a little? Ruthie Mader was a Christian in the best sense of that word. Only days after Bethany's marriage, she'd stopped by with a plate of brownies and an invitation to join the Circle of Faith, the prayer group she'd started after her husband's death. "It's a social club, mostly," Ruthie said. "A way to get to know other women." Lorna Pranke was a member, and she had only good things to say about it. Of course, Bethany had no time for that sort of thing. Still, it had been nice to be asked, and she thought of Ruthie every time she passed the small white cross on County O that marked the spot where Tom Mader had been killed by a hit-and-run driver. Seven years had passed, but Ruthie had never remarried. She still wore her wedding ring. Sunday afternoons, you'd see her with Cherish in the cemetery, pulling the weeds from around his grave.

The choir finished "Stille Nacht," launched into "Die Kinderlein Kommen," and Bethany settled back to enjoy the sound of the choir, the stained-glass colors, the various perfumes that rose from the coats of the women around her. Ruthie wasn't the type to hold it against someone if she didn't join prayer circles or go

to church each week. Others were more particular. No doubt
Father Oberling would remark on what he called "Christmas
Christians," trying to make people like Bethany feel bad because
they didn't come more often—it had been the same at her old
church in Dodgeville, where she'd lived before she and Fred
were married. But over the years, Bethany had trained herself to
ignore that part and concentrate on what was good. And what
was good was when the priest first came in at the back of the
church with his candle and everybody rose. And he touched his
flame to someone's candle, and that person lit someone else's, on
and on, until the light spread over everyone like sunrise. What
was good was the story of Mary and Joseph, the shepherds, the
wise men bearing gifts, the story of Baby Jesus in the manger
with the cows and donkeys and sheep. *Not my will but Thine be
done*, Mary had said, and of her own free will. Now she was forever blessed.

Bethany glanced at the boys and saw that Robert John was
sleeping, his head rising and falling with each deep breath. But
Gabriel was wide awake, hands folded high on his chest like a
child in a First Communion picture. Candlelight danced off his
thick glasses. His mouth was open, a perfect plump O.

"Who's Robert John's little friend?" Ruthie whispered, and
Bethany said, "Fred's brother Shawn's boy."

"Devout little one," Ruthie said, nudging Cherish, and when
it was time for the Sign of Peace, they both leaned across Bethany
to offer Gabriel their hands. Gabriel smiled, bewildered but
pleased, and Bethany seized his hand too. For suddenly she loved
him, loved even his handsome, wayward father, loved everyone
in the church and the whole wide world beyond. She approached
the altar for Communion with such joy she couldn't help smiling
at Father Oberling, who did not smile back but glanced at her
uncertainly, as if trying to recall just who she was. But it didn't
matter. She loved him too. And she left the church feeling as if

God was guiding her home, the same way that she guided Robert John and Gabriel, an arm around each of their shoulders.

Yes, God was her chauffeur. It must have been so, for the car started without complaint, and she weaved her way out of the parking lot and through the downtown just ahead of the crowd. In the country, beyond the lights of Ambient, He stretched out His mighty hand, and she found that she could love even the cold, black waters of the Onion River, the silent fields with their chilly fringe of weeds, the quiet blossom of light that marked each distant house. Nowadays, there were people who said the star shining over Bethlehem was nothing but a comet, but who was to say it couldn't have meant something else as well? Perhaps it became whatever you believed. Perhaps you controlled the thing that it was, the way you controlled your own destiny. She recalled the first time she came to Ambient for the summer festival, how Fred had followed her all around Cradle Park on that hot Fourth of July. If she bought a diet Coke, he bought a diet Coke; if she rode the Hammer, he rode the Hammer. Later, he introduced himself and bought her and the boys each a fish fry, which they ate standing up in the polka tent, next to the gazebo. The accordion players cheered as the dancers skipped and spun so close that Bethany caught her breath. "They look like they're going to crash into each other," she said.

"Don't you polka?" Fred said, and when she shook her head, he said, "I'll show you, it's easy," and it was, especially when she closed her eyes and stiffened her spine and let him swing her around and around.

She recalled the times he drove all the way to Dodgeville to court her, and how she'd always sent him home at sundown, no matter how tired he claimed to be. She recalled the time she thought he'd left for good, taking his ring, and his return three months later on a Sunday morning in fall. "Let's go for a drive," he'd said, "all four of us, Beth, what do you say?" It didn't take long before she saw they were headed for Ambient. Halfway there, Robert John had to relieve himself. There was nothing but fields for miles, and Bethany told him, "You're just going to have to hold it." But Fred pulled over to the side of the road and said, "Looks like a good spot to me."

It was a sunflower field. By that time in the season they'd all turned brown, their faces shriveled up. They looked like the walking dead, all facing the same direction, and you could see how there might be some privacy a few rows in, but not much. Not to mention it was trespassing.

"Here?" Robert John protested, and Bethany was pleased. After all, he hadn't been raised to go beside the road like a dog. But both he and Pete followed Fred out of the car and into that raggedy field. She had time to think while she was looking in the other direction, and her thought was that Fred had made up his mind to break things off, and he wanted one last spat to make it permanent. Right there, she decided he would not get it. No matter what, she'd turn her smooth cheek, and later on its memory would light up his nights like a moon, like a sweet ripe peach. So when he and the boys got back into the car, she just looked out the window, admiring the scenery. The boys seemed awfully fidgety, and when she turned around she caught them grinning. Fred was grinning too, though he was trying to hide it. She was mad as a yellow jacket, them laughing at her just because they'd flashed their peckers in the weak autumn sunshine.

"What is it?" she said, keeping her voice steady.

"Nice day, ain't it?" Fred said.

"Yes, it certainly is," she said, and the boys snorted and choked, kicking the back of the seat, but she just closed her eyes and kept them closed, as if she were resting, as if she hadn't a care in the world, until they finally turned onto the J road, crossing the railroad tracks with a jaw-popping *bump*. Bethany pretended to study the billboards all along the highway: SCHMITT

REAL ESTATE; KIMMELDORF'S FAMILY CAFÉ; SOLOMON INDUS-
TRIAL PARK; RIVEREDGE MALL; and the newest one: MCDONALD'S,
2 MILES AHEAD!

"Home sweet home," Fred said as they turned into the driveway, spraying gravel and dust. They passed rusted-out cars and
farm equipment, an old washing machine and hand wringer, a
tireless bicycle, a low pyramid of busted TVs, the gangly remains
of a patio umbrella—every kind of waste you'd care to think of.
The boys were cutting up again, and as she turned to give them
a look, she saw the spanking new ranch house across the courtyard from the farmhouse. Fred angled toward it and parked by
the corncrib, where a neat concrete sidewalk led right up to the
front door. Everything was mud all around it, but leveled. A tiny
staked tree shivered in the middle of where the yard would go.
"Open the glove compartment," Fred told her, and there was
both a key and a wedding band on a yellow smiley-face key ring
that said *Property of Bethany Carpenter.*

"Surprise, Ma, it's ours," the boys screamed, both at once.
"Can we go in?"

"It's a double-wide," Fred said. "Two bedrooms, one and a
half baths. I ordered it stone empty so you can fix it up however
you want."

She let the boys run ahead. The house was the same cheery
yellow as the key ring, and she knew it would be beautiful even
before she went inside. Ever since she was a bitty girl, she'd
wanted a house of her own, where no Mr. Shuckel could come
in and say, Do this, Don't you dare do that, Get out. In high
school, when they got evicted, they'd moved to another duplex,
south of town. Ma cut hair in the kitchen, and you'd find clumps
of it everywhere—blond and red and black—hair you knew was
not your own, and when you'd sweat, you could smell the stink
of perm solution oozing out of your pores. Bethany shared a bedroom with Rose, and while Rose let every piece of clothing lay

where it fell, Bethany kept her side shiny as a licked-out pot. She filled up a scrapbook with decorating ideas; she had it to this day. Ma made fun of it every chance she got. "Miss Fancy," she called Bethany. "Miss La-di-da."

Now, as Bethany turned off the J road and started up the drive, she recalled how she'd clung to those keys and wept, and she gave thanks to God for His goodness. Home sweet home. She parked in her usual spot by the corncrib, listened to the boys' quiet breathing, for Gabriel, too, had fallen asleep, slumped across the backseat. The Christmas tree lights winked and blinked in the front window, but the house lights were out, which surprised her. Fred and Pete must have gone to bed, left Pops and Shawn to stumble back to the farmhouse, following the round yellow stepping-stones cast by the old man's flashlight. Robert John stirred, sensing the sudden stillness. Gabriel sat up. Yet Bethany waited, steeped in warm feeling, reluctant to disturb the mood.

"We're home," she finally said. "Let's get you both to bed."

"Where am I going to sleep?" Gabriel said.

"With your father," Bethany said, eyeing the dark farmhouse. "I'll walk you over. He's probably waiting up." But she couldn't see the slightest glow of a candle or kerosene lantern, and then Robert John said, "How come his car is gone?"

Bethany stared at the empty line of sky above the snow fence. She got out of the car. Gabriel came around to stand beside her, and she felt her peace of mind torn away like a beautiful scarf caught in a cold snap of wind. It wasn't so much a feeling of shock as it was the feeling that she'd been deceived. That she should have known better. That all the beautiful candlelight services in the world were of no use whatsoever when it came to the practical logic of living. This, then, was what Shawn Carpenter had wanted from her. She did not have to go over to the farmhouse to understand that he was truly gone.

The boy was clinging to the fabric of her coat. He had wrapped his arms tightly around her hips. Robert John said, "Is he going to live with us now?" and for the first time, Bethany thought of Mary in a whole new way. *Not my will but Thine be done*, she'd said to God, but what else could she have said? The Almighty staring down upon her. The favor on His mind already taking shape.

"I suppose he is, for a while," Bethany said.

Robert John groaned. Gabriel said nothing at first, but as she led him into her house, he asked her, "My dad's coming back, isn't he?"

"Of course," she said automatically, shooting Robert John a look in case he planned to contradict. "He loves you very much. Now let's get you to bed. Things are bound to look brighter in the morning."

But she was startled by a memory she'd all but forgotten: her own father digging through the freezer for a Popsicle. It was July, and there was only one left—grape, the best kind—and he split it with her carefully. As their tongues tasted that simple sweetness, he winked at her and smiled. She was twelve or thirteen, and she thought to herself, *So he loves me*. He probably did.

But the next day, he was gone.

YOU KNOW WHO YOU ARE: If you are the thief who took a wooden bird feeder from the front yard of 462 River Road PLEASE *do the right thing and return it, no questions asked. It has no monetary value but is greatly sentimental as my Dad made it, before he died. Surely you must know how it feels to lose something you love. The bird feeder is painted to look like a gingerbread house, if anybody sees it hung out someplace, call John Grosshuesch at 555-1424.*

—*From the* Ambient Weekly
January 1991

three

Anna Grey Graf—Mrs. G. to her fifth-grade students—was driving to work at Solomon Public, smoking a cigarette from the pack she kept hidden in her glove compartment and wondering what to do about Gabriel Carpenter. She'd been fighting her gut dislike of the boy from the moment Principal Johns first led him into her classroom. The poor child's face was shaped like a pie, and he had skin the color of raw pie dough. His eyes looked bleary behind his glasses, as if he had a cold, which, in fact, he did most of the time. At recess, he walked by himself along the chain-link fence that bordered the highway, and if other kids shouted *Hey!* to him, he wouldn't look up, no matter how many times they tried. Instead he'd bow his head and pray, the way he did in the cafeteria before lunch, the way he did in the middle of class, lips moving silently as if he were reading.

For a while, the other kids were nice to him, partly because his aunt was the afternoon crossing guard, but mostly because of rumors that his father had left behind an envelope of money with Gabriel's name written across the seal. Nobody knew exactly how much money the envelope had contained. Kids speculated that it was at least a million dollars and that Gabriel was so rich he could buy a house with a swimming pool. But Bethany Carpenter had told Anna Grey that it hadn't been very much money at all and that old Pops Carpenter had gotten to it first and used it to pay his electric bill. She said that, at home, the boy was silent, distant. Her own boys teased him, and he often slipped away to the river, where he walked along the banks for hours. Or he went next door to his grandfather's house to rummage through Shawn's old boyhood things. Sometimes he'd explore the derelict barn, where Pops kept the tractor he drove to town as if it were a car. Sometimes he simply disappeared, and did not return until well after dark. Bethany said, "There's something about him, I don't know. Something not quite right—" She didn't finish her thought, but Anna Grey knew exactly what she meant.

There were children one simply disliked on sight. It didn't happen often, thank goodness. The only other time it had happened to Anna Grey had been twenty-odd years earlier, in a suburb of Indianapolis where she'd lived before she married Bill and moved to Ambient, Wisconsin. How she'd loved that little school! The teachers had done everything from serving lunches to cleaning lavatories to minding the infirmary, but the workload hadn't bothered her. She'd been young, and she'd liked the people she'd worked with, and there was something about walking down the tiled hallways and hearing the warble of the children's voices as they lined up outside, eager for the bell—even now she couldn't explain it, but it made her happy in a way she'd never felt since. Euphoric, even. She was so excited to be living up north, over five hundred miles from her hometown of Skylark, Georgia. She believed she was doing something important. She believed these children would take the knowledge she gave them and carry it with them to the sixth grade and the seventh, on to high school and maybe college, to places in the world she'd never see, and this somehow made her bigger than she was, better than she was, a good person. And then, in the fall of 1968, she walked into her classroom and saw Sandy Shore—her parents had really named her that—poking her cheek with the eraser end of a pencil, not hard or anything, just an absentminded gesture, and all of Anna Grey's warm feeling was snuffed out as if a cloud had passed between her body and the sun.

Sandy Shore was a twitchy-looking girl, with pale-yellow hair so fine that it had clumped to her sweater with static. One sock drooped around her ankle; the other was stretched as high as it could go. Already she had her hand in the air, and when Anna Grey got to her desk, it took every ounce of self-control she had to keep her voice level as she said, "Yes?"

What the girl wanted to know was, could she write in pen? Her teacher last year had insisted on pencil. "I'm sure I don't care what you write with," Anna Grey said with such venom that the child blushed and the restless rustlings of the other children dried right up. Silence, at least ten beats, before Anna Grey found the presence of mind to begin taking role. At the end of the day, she went home to her efficiency apartment above the hardware store. She'd fixed it up to look bright and cheery—red and white checkered curtains she sewed herself, a matching oilcloth for the table, a framed Sears print on the wall. Suddenly she saw it for what it was: the linoleum faded around the kitchen sink, the couch with its shameful cigarette burns—she'd lied to the landlady, told her she'd quit smoking—the odor of mildew seeping out past the rose-scented air freshener Anna Grey favored back then. Outside her small window, the Indianapolis sky was getting dark. Three weeks from now, there'd be frost on the ground, and then the long winter would slap everything flat beneath its palm. People were starting to hurry along the sidewalks, heads down, hands jammed in pockets, hard faces set against the growing chill. It was all Anna Grey could do to heat a can of soup, open her lesson planner, prepare for the next day. She knew Sandy Shore would be waiting, that dirty eraser pressed to her cheek. Anna Grey tried to reason with herself. Sandy Shore was no different than a hundred other little girls, anxious, eager to do things right—a student who needed the sort of reassurance Anna Grey's supervisor claimed she had a knack for. But it had been no use. An irrational feeling can't be remedied with reason. If it were that easy, the world would be a different place.

She crushed out her cigarette, checked her watch. It was only ten minutes till the first bell. At the Fair Mile Crossroads, she rolled through the four-way stop, and as she turned onto County O, she saw a hitchhiker waiting on the shoulder. A Styrofoam cup of coffee from the McDonald's steamed in his gloved hand. At first, she thought he was smiling at her, a wide, ragged smile. Then she realized he had a harelip. His stare was blank, unyielding. She wanted to stop, to offer assistance or, at least, a dollar and a friendly word. But she was late already, and besides, who in this day and age would stop to help a stranger? Anna Grey accelerated onto County O, her mouth flat with regret.

She thought about the story she'd heard a few weeks earlier from Maya Paluski, the art teacher, who'd heard it from Ruthie Mader at a meeting of the Circle of Faith. It went like this: An older couple west of the Killsnake Dam were moved to pick up a hitchhiker, something they'd never done before. The hitchhiker was a young man, long-haired, unshaven; it was downpouring rain, and he was soaked to the bone. The couple offered him what they had: a blanket, lukewarm coffee in a Styrofoam cup, a fruitcake they'd planned to give to a friend—no, take it, they said, take the whole thing. They were goodhearted people and they told the hitchhiker how they could see he was goodhearted too, and they hoped he would get wherever he was going and find the happiness he was due. They wrote their names down for him on a scrap of paper, and their address, and they gave him twenty dollars, which was everything the woman had in her purse.

Two weeks later, they got a letter postmarked California. The hitchhiker thanked them for their kindness. He told them he'd had a semiautomatic and planned to kill the first person who stopped to offer him a ride. "I pushed it under the seat," he wrote. "I had a change of heart. I know Jesus has forgiven me and I hope you'll forgive me too." They found the gun where he'd said it would be, and for those who don't believe, there is the cold steel fact that the couple wrested from underneath their seat. A person can see it, reach out his or her hand, slip a doubtful finger into its small round mouth.

Anna Grey liked to think of herself as a caring person, a compassionate person. She admired the couple from Killsnake, but she also thought they'd taken a terrible risk. The world wasn't what it used to be. Even people in small towns like Ambient had started to lock their doors at night, post Neighborhood Watch signs in their windows, keep handguns in the clutter of nightstand drawers—and still one heard reports of vandalism, break-ins, even sexual assault. Lawn mowers and snowblowers and power tools disappeared from garages. Windows and streetlights got shot out in the fancy neighborhoods around the millpond, and every now and then somebody's tires were slashed. Recently, there'd been two drug-related arrests at the high school, and last year's senior prom, which was held at the Knights of Columbus hall, had resulted in so much property damage the Catholics voted not to rent out the facility again—it was said that this year's prom would have to take place outside, beneath a canvas tent. And how many times had Anna Grey walked to the foot of her driveway to get the morning paper and discovered her mailbox lying in the ditch, the post snapped like a spine? Then, for days, she'd wonder if it was the work of some former student, now grown and avenging a long-ago slight. Or if it was a lunatic, or worse. Or if it was just a random thing, like what had happened to Ruthie Mader's husband. Tom Mader had worked for the post office, farmed sheep on the side. Even then, Cherish Mader had been a lovely girl, obedient and hardworking, with a talent for art—a pencil sketch she'd done of Saint Fridolin's still hung above Maya Paluski's desk. Cherish had been in Anna Grey's fifth grade the year somebody broadsided Tom's little green Bobcat in front of the Neumillers' mailbox. The impact knocked him into the ditch; he died right there on County O as letters fluttered like doves across the wet spring fields. Even now no one knew who had done it. It could have been anybody, perhaps someone everybody knew. You simply couldn't be sure of anyone anymore.

Still, at night, as Anna Grey lay beside Bill's silent, sweating body, she sometimes imagined slowing, stopping, opening her heart to a man like the one she'd just seen, except that this man was good-looking, educated, someone who was just a little down on his luck. He'd climb into her Taurus, balance his backpack across his knees, and the slow burn of his smell—cigarettes, dampness, wind—would fill her throat. "If you hadn't stopped," he'd tell Anna Grey, "I guess I don't know what I would have done," and his voice would be gentle, apologetic, warm with the same Georgia lilt that still softened her own words. Such a man would agree that even well-meaning Northerners had a way of talking that made them sound impatient, superior. His teeth would be as white and square as buttermints. His eyes would hold a complicated mix of brown and gold and yearning.

But where were these thoughts coming from? What was all this nonsense about a stranger's eyes and yearnings? She slowed behind the line of cars piling up at the entrance to the school. Enrollment had swollen to an average of thirty-five kids per class, and class sizes continued to increase, despite periodic additions of "mobile classrooms"—trailers that circled the original structure like settlers' wagons under Indian attack. The trailers were painted in lively colors—lime green, cobalt blue, pink—and as Anna Grey turned into the parking lot, the ugliness of the whole place struck her afresh. The asphalt playground. The bare wallows beneath the swings, where the snow and ice had been worn away. The faint, sour tang of the fertilizer plant that was always present, regardless of which way the wind blew. The children, bundled like cumbersome dolls into snow pants and heavy coats. Half of them were catching the same coughs and colds the other half still hadn't quite gotten over. And there, pacing the fence, was Gabriel Carpenter. His arms were wrapped around his books, mashing them to his chest. His hands were bare—Bethany said he kept losing his mittens—and as Anna Grey walked from the parking lot to the Main Building, she tried not to think about the way he picked and picked at his chapped knuckles. For weeks, he'd had a sore at the corner of his mouth; every now and then, he'd moisten it with his tongue. Yesterday, during social studies, Anna Grey couldn't help but excuse herself to the teachers' lavatory, where she checked her own lip in the mirror. Of course, there was nothing there. Of course, it was only her imagination making her taste a swelling against her gum. She'd stared into the mirror, her face jaundiced by the overhead lights. Her eyes were wide apart, her eyebrows plucked in high, surprised arcs, each one as thin as a torn fingernail. Deep lines creased either side of her mouth, but it was a kind mouth, an easygoing mouth, a mouth that wanted to smile. Surely all the crow's-feet narrowing her eyes were evidence of that. It was just that the child brought out the worst in her, the same as Sandy Shore. He made her realize all her limitations. He made her realize she should be doing more.

The hallways of Main were empty, quiet, though she could hear laughter coming from the teachers' lounge. Cigarette smoke listed from the open door. Inside, multicolored couches were arranged around a low, square coffee table. There were some magazine racks, a wobbly coat stand nobody used, a sink that had been dry ever since the pipes froze up last year. A few valentines were already posted on the bulletin board, covering the New Year's decorations no one had bothered to take down. A small group of teachers had gathered around Marty Klepner, the guidance counselor, who was telling jokes so bad he must have learned them from the kids. Anna Grey filled her coffee cup with bitter decaf and tucked her sack lunch (fat-free-cheese sandwich, celery sticks, an overripe pear) into the fridge. She longed for another cigarette, but everybody thought she'd quit.

"What's Wisconsin's state flower?" Marty asked.

"The satellite dish," Anna Grey said, half under her breath but still loud enough for him to hear. It was an old joke, a stupid joke. Her daughter, Milly, had told it to her last year.

Marty smiled at Anna Grey across the heads of the others, a friendly, apologetic smile that made her long to haul off and slap him as hard as she could. She turned away without a word, imagining the reddening imprint of her hand against his chalk-pale skin, and then how she'd kiss each fingertip. His forehead was freckled and beautiful; the shape of his skull showed beneath his thinning hair. She noticed he seemed bulkier through the chest, less hunched—had he been lifting weights? It wouldn't have surprised her. She'd heard he'd found a steady girlfriend, younger, a single mother with a six-month-old baby girl. Why should it matter to Anna Grey? It didn't. She'd married Bill for better or worse, and of course there was Milly to think of. A couple of long kisses one day before Christmas, a loose-limbed walk down the hall to his office, half an hour on the counseling couch beneath the field of construction-paper sunflowers kids had stapled to the ceiling—these things meant nothing when you held them up against the light of a husband and child. A home. A stable, sensible life. When she and Bill went to sleep without so much as a peck on the cheek, she told herself they were both just tired, that they'd been married too long for foolishness. When Bill sat silent at the table, night after night, she kept up the conversation for them both.

The first bell sounded. She picked up her coffee cup, walked down the hall to her classroom. Seniority had earned her a permanent room in Main. Of course, she felt sorry for the younger teachers, who had to pick their way out to the trailers, hopping frozen puddles, high heels sinking into brown patches of snow, but she herself had spent several years assigned to North Trailer, the worst of them all, known unofficially as the North Pole. Her permanent room was a palace by comparison: well heated and spacious, with two chalkboards, windows she could open when the weather turned warm. Yet it was all she could do to hang her coat behind the door, to set her coffee cup on the corner of her desk already stained by dozens of overlapping rings. Maya Paluski said that she used to feel that way before she'd joined the Circle of Faith. She said that the Faith meetings had given her a new lease on life.

"We hold open meetings on the first of each month," she often reminded Anna Grey. "You ought to come, Anna. It would do you a world of good." When she spoke, she played with the plain gold cross all Faith members wore around their necks. "We're a family. We don't always agree, but we look out for each other."

The Circle of Faith put Anna Grey in mind of the Skylark Bible Circle, a Baptist organization her mother had belonged to and enjoyed. Faith members did charity work, scheduled afternoon picnics and winter cider parties. They sponsored guest speakers and visited each other's churches, went on nondenominational retreats, explored faith healing and women's spirituality, and helped each other with everything from child care to tax preparation. But Anna Grey didn't want to air her troubles in front of Ruthie Mader, who lived on an idyllic hundred-acre farm overlooking the river, whose husband had been, by all accounts, a truly wonderful man, whose daughter had gone on to become so popular and pretty she'd been crowned Festival Queen last Fourth of July at Cradle Park. Cherish Mader wasn't sitting home every weekend like Anna Grey's Milly, rereading her collection of science fiction novels. Besides, Anna Grey had her own church home, Christ the King Lutheran—she'd converted when she married Bill. She could always make an appointment with Pastor Floyd if she wanted someone to talk to. Pastor Floyd spoke against the Circle of Faith, which he said was a feel-good kind of thing with no spiritual basis. *People taking God into their own hands,* he'd said. *Well, God isn't like Play-Doh you can shape into anything you want. Man is the Play-Doh. God is God. And tradition teaches what he expects from us.*

Anna Grey sighed, checked her lipstick in the compact mirror she kept inside her desk. It was probably just the weather. She hadn't gotten used to Northern winters, the chill that never left her hands and feet. The children thundered in, and she smiled at them vaguely, but she did not come around from behind her desk. In September, it had been announced that teachers shouldn't touch the children anymore, because of liability. Some of the teachers were outraged, but Anna Grey herself hadn't touched a child in years. Strange, because she remembered hugging the children at her school in Indianapolis: the surprising cold of their cheeks after recess, the various shampoo smells of their hair. Gabriel's hair was uncombed and oily. That awful sore glistened—would it ever heal? He sat down at his desk as if he had no idea where he was; his expression was the same one the hitchhiker had worn as he stood beside the highway, watching or not watching Anna Grey drive by, untouchable, untouched. It was the same one Bill wore at night as he sat at the supper table, the flat line of his mouth rippling as he worked his roast like a cud.

The principal's voice came over the intercom, and Gabriel rose with the other children, pressed his hand over his heart. *I pledge allegiance—to the flag—of the United States of America—*

Anna Grey had neglected to rise, to put her hand over her own heart, and when they finished the pledge of allegiance, the children looked at her curiously. "You may be seated," she said. "Open your math books to Chapter Fourteen."

When Gabriel opened his book, Anna Grey could tell he was in the wrong place. His reading and writing skills were far behind the other children's. "Chapter *Four-teen*," she said, but Gabriel wasn't listening. His hand was in his desk cubby, and Anna Grey thought she heard the irritable crackle of his lunch bag. Bethany packed him plenty of food, but the child was always hungry. All morning, he'd sneak bits of crushed Ding-Dong, a corn chip, a peanut butter cracker—that slow hand moving from his cubby to his mouth. By lunchtime, most of it would be gone; still, he prayed before he ate, seemingly oblivious to the mimicking gestures of the kids all around him. Looking for attention, Anna Grey knew, like the second-grade boy who always fell down or the girl—thank heavens she'd moved away—who kept taking off her underwear. *Poor child*, the other teachers said, and inevitably they'd ask, *Why isn't he in Living and Learning?* Living and Learning was Marty's pet project, a special class for special kids that met three mornings a week. But Anna Grey couldn't admit she was failing with Gabriel, especially not to Marty, especially not now. She wasn't the same green teacher who'd encountered Sandy Shore. She planned to surprise everyone, discover a special talent in Gabriel—art or, perhaps, music—and encourage him until he grew to trust her, blossomed like a flower. She imagined how he'd start making friends, play kickball and softball at recess, look boldly out at the world—but the fact was that, nearly a month into the term, Gabriel still was staring at the ground.

What made it worse was that Marty himself had approached Anna Grey about Gabriel just last week, surprising her as she sneaked a cigarette in the teachers' lounge after the first bell had already rung. "I think he needs more than you can give him," he said matter-of-factly.

"My recommendation is to keep him mainstreamed," Anna Grey said firmly. "You know how the Living and Learning kids get ostracized."

"Gabriel is already ostracized," Marty said. "Tortured might be a better word. Let me help the kid, Anna."

"I'm late," Anna Grey said, crushing out her half-smoked cigarette.

"Can we schedule a meeting to discuss this?" Marty said. "It would be, I mean, strictly professional."

He blushed with the sincerity of those words, and Anna Grey blushed too, but angrily, because even as he spoke she was imagining the scrape of his beard against her cheeks, the edge of his teeth against her tongue. Strictly professional—of course, that December afternoon had been a mistake, a weak moment after his separation, her only infidelity, ever. Until that day, affairs had been something that happened only to other people, and even now, after the fact, it was unthinkable that she had fallen into such a thing herself. She almost wished she were a Catholic so that she could confess, receive her punishment, leave her sin in the care of someone bound by God's law not to repeat it. Maya assured her that the Circle of Faith meetings worked the same way—members took a vow of silence so that whatever was said between Faith walls was sure to stay there. "I know something's on your mind, Anna," she'd said more than once. "You just don't seem yourself lately." But Anna Grey could not imagine admitting something like this to anyone, though the fact was that she longed to tell Bill, to make a clean breast of everything. Her fear wasn't that he'd be angry, or hurt, or even that he'd leave her. Her fear was that he wouldn't care one way or the other.

She'd first met Bill on the IU campus during the terrible fall of Sandy Shore, when it seemed to Anna Grey that her life had changed, that nothing was satisfying anymore. She and another teacher were there to see a football game. Bill was sitting next to them, and they all got talking during the halftime show. As the cheerleaders kicked their pretty legs, Bill told Anna Grey how his father owned a funeral home in Ambient, Wisconsin (*Where?* Anna Grey had said), and how he'd offered Bill a junior partnership when he'd graduated from high school. But Bill was worried about the draft, and he had an idea about becoming a veterinarian, so Bill senior gave his blessing, even paid Bill's tuition on the condition he spend his summers at the morgue. Now, three years into his undergraduate degree, Bill was failing all his science classes. The army had stopped drafting people, and Bill wished he had the guts to drop out and go home. If he'd taken his father's offer, he said, he'd be out in the real world, making money, instead of studying abstract ideas that meant nothing. As he talked, Anna Grey kept looking at the curious gray streak in his hair. (Later, his mother would tell Anna Grey he'd been born with it. The devil's kiss, she said.) She wrote her phone number on a corn dog wrapper, and the other teacher giggled about it all the way home. "Imagine all the dead people he's touched," she said. "Imagine him combing some dead person's hair." In spring, when he bought the ring with his fall tuition money, the other teachers teased Anna Grey that he'd taken it off a dead woman's finger. They said that on her wedding night, he'd ask her to hold her breath, tell her not to move.

Opposites attract: That was what people always said about Bill and Anna Grey. She was short, fair, talkative, while he was the quiet type, tall and dark. Back in those days, she was interested in politics. She supported environmental causes, hunger drives, and women's rights. It was true that Bill seemed to have no opinions whatsoever on any of these subjects. But she'd grown bone weary of her life in Indianapolis, and she was still young enough to believe that change could only mean something good. Bill had a solid future; he loved her, he wanted a family. At the time, it had all seemed simple enough.

Math period ended; science began. Anna Grey divided the students into task groups, ignoring the groans of the three girls who got stuck with Gabriel. Their assignment was to design an ecosystem. All parts of the food chain were to be represented. If they didn't finish their ecosystems today, they could work on them again during science period tomorrow. She gave each group a poster board, tracing paper, and a stack of *National Geographics*; they already had glue and scissors and markers in their desks. "Plan the whole thing out in *pencil* first," she warned, and then she went back to her desk, where she took three Tylenol caplets with the gritty dregs of her decaf. She thought about Bill undressing for bed, his spare tire spangled with varicose veins. How last night, again, she'd laid a warm hand on the small of his back and he'd twisted to look at her curiously. "What?" he'd said. *"What?"* She thought about Marty, how he'd fumbled with the front of her bra until she guided his hands to the back. How she looked away, shy, when he kicked off his trousers and how then— too quickly—he'd slid up inside her so that she never actually saw him, and this left her even more unsatisfied than his odd, staccato rocking. *He'd* looked at *her*, afterward, spreading her with his fingers to blow cool air on the place that didn't want cooling, and yet she had held his head between her hands until he had blown the last of her desire out.

The lunch bell rang. Half the day down. At noon recess, a group of boys led by Bethany Carpenter's own Robert John—a troublemaker if Anna Grey had ever seen one—pinned Gabriel down and made him eat chunks of dirty slush that shot through the fence from the highway. The teacher on recess duty was Maya Paluski; she called Bethany at home, but Bethany had to clean house for someone in Killsnake and couldn't come in before her crossing guard shift started at three. "Call my husband at Jeep's," she said, but Fred was unloading stock and couldn't leave. "Handle it however you see fit," he said. "I'll talk to Robert John again when I get home." So Maya brought Gabriel back to Anna Grey's classroom, interrupting her half-hour planning period, the only break she would get all day. Gabriel's face was raw and wet, streaked black around the mouth. He didn't look at Anna Grey, but he didn't *not* look at her, either. Gabriel just *looked*. That was what always got to Anna Grey. "Maybe you should keep him here," Maya said. "I mean, instead of sending him outside with the others. They're worse than wolves."

Anna Grey imagined spending the rest of the term's planning periods under Gabriel's absent stare. "He has to learn to stick up for himself," she said, perhaps a little more crossly than she meant to. "He won't always have teachers to look out for him."

"Well, OK," Maya said. "But if I can help, Anna, let me know."

After Maya was gone, Anna Grey wiped Gabriel's mouth with a Kleenex from her desk drawer, careful not to let her fingers touch his sore. "You're *bigger* than those boys," she said. "It's *silly* to let them do this to you." She poked the Kleenex into his hand. "Here. You can wipe your own mouth, don't you think?" Suddenly he leaned over and spat into the wastebasket, a dark stream that made Anna Grey's stomach turn.

"Gabriel!" she said.

"It tasted bad," he whined. "It still tastes bad."

"Then don't let them bully you next time."

He stared at the floor, unresponsive. It was as if she were talking to the air.

"Do you hear me?" she said. "Do you?" Then abruptly, cruelly, she knocked on his head with her knuckles. "Hello? Anybody home?"

He lifted his head to look at her, eyes brimming, an innocent child. Appalled by what she'd just done, Anna Grey turned and walked away, down the hall and out the school's back entrance, where she inhaled deep, burning gulps of cold air. On the asphalt, a group of boys chased a red rubber kickball, slipping and sliding over the ice. Younger girls jumped rope, while the older ones floated in groups. Maya was right. She wasn't herself lately. The truth was that she wanted to go home—not home to Ambient, but to Skylark, where her sister still lived. She wanted to hear people speak her full name—Anna *Grey*—instead of shortening it to just plain Anna, the way Northerners automatically did. She wanted true heat that lasted more than a week or two in August, and she wanted humidity that left a person not knowing where her own skin ended and the air began. She wanted country music on the radio instead of rock 'n' roll, and she wanted to order a glass of tea in a restaurant without having to say *iced* tea. She wanted to open her mouth without somebody telling her, "You're not from here, are you?" And she wanted to walk down a street where people looked you in the face; but the thing was, Anna Grey's sister said that Skylark had changed. People who worked in Atlanta lived there now; it was more like a suburb than a town. It had been seven years since Anna Grey had gone back, though her sister had come twice to Ambient. "You don't want to see it, really," her sister said. "It's one big parking lot."

But the same sort of thing was happening to Ambient. Once, Solomon Public had stood alone on County O, the only building north of the D road. To the south was the school bus parking lot and repair shed; farther down the road, well out of sight, was an International Harvester dealership. Now the IH stood empty, but new homes were sprouting up haphazardly as mushrooms, and the D road, which continued out past the Badger State Mall toward the interstate, had been transformed into what was now called the Solomon strip: outdoor malls and fast-food restaurants, gas stations and minimarts, video stores, electronic shops, outlets. The couples building homes in the developments around it weren't rich weekenders like the millpond people: They had to commute to Milwaukee, or even Chicago, five days a week, morning and night. If you asked if the drive didn't bother them, if the smell of the fertilizer plant didn't get into their hair and clothes on days the wind was wrong, they said it was worth it to own their own house, to live where the money went further, to have their kids grow up in the country, away from guns and drugs.

The bell rang. Anna Grey blew her nose into the tissue she kept tucked inside her sleeve. The truth of the matter was that what she really wanted, more than anything, was a cigarette. She could *see* that pack of Salem Lights tucked between her car registration and an emergency box of Kotex. But there simply wasn't time to walk to her car. Besides, somebody might catch her smoking.

Inside, Gabriel was sitting at his desk. His hands were folded; his eyes were closed. The child was praying, and this time, the image twisted like a hook in Anna Grey's heart. Hating herself all over again, she got her purse from her desk, dug through it until she found a half-eaten roll of cherry Life Savers.

"Here," she said. She meant to let her fingers touch his hand— an apology—but instead she dropped the roll on his desk. It landed with a hard, metallic sound. "That'll get the taste out of your mouth." Kids were coming in from recess now, bringing with them the mildewed odor of wet wool. Anna Grey swallowed three more Tylenol before calling them to order; still, by the end of the afternoon, her headache clutched her skull like a heavy knit cap. And perhaps the headache could have been blamed for the peculiar thought that bobbed to the surface of her conscious-ness as she drove home from work: Why not just keep on driving? Why not just?

Milly, a responsible voice replied, but Anna Grey ignored it and lit a cigarette. She had her checkbook, credit cards, a map if she chose to look at it. Maybe she'd just drive until she got good and hungry; then she'd stop at an all-night diner, where she'd buy more cigarettes from a machine and order steak and eggs. If she wanted pie, she'd damn well have that too; the hell with her spreading thighs. In her mind's kind eye, a man—the hitchhiker with the buttermint smile—took the stool beside hers. "Coffee," he told the waitress. "Just coffee." And then, seeing the concern in Anna Grey's face, he revealed to her that he had nothing in the world but what he carried with him on his back. "I'll help you," she told him. "I'll take you wherever you need to go," and his windburned face flushed darker as he realized his good fortune. Together they discussed the possibilities—Atlanta, Florida, Mexico, Baton Rouge—but even as they tried to choose, Anna Grey was startled by the sight of Bill's car parked in its usual spot in the driveway, the Graf Funeral Parlor logo stamped on the driver's-side door. Habit had brought her home.

Inside, Bill was watching TV. He did not turn around as Anna Grey hung her coat in the hallway closet. President Bush was being interviewed by reporters about the effects of environmental terrorism; he looked ten years older than he had when he'd given his speech in Cradle Park. Anna Grey stared helplessly as images of the Persian Gulf flashed on the screen, the terrible black smoke of the oil wells rising, unchecked, into the sky. Experts said it would affect the level of air pollution worldwide, and some even predicted increased incidents of cancer, birth defects, and infertility. There was nothing anybody could do about it, just like there was nothing anybody could do about all the civilians who were dying in the aftermath of the bombings with no drinking water, no medical care. But if Anna Grey said anything, Bill would say, "OK, OK, can't a fella watch the news?" He liked things quiet when he came home. He was tired. He wanted some peace.

"Look at 'em burn" was all he said now. The fine hairs tangling above his balding head were haloed with light.

Anna Grey went into the kitchen, where Milly already had the table set and was now chopping tomatoes for a salad. She was tall and plain, painfully shy, the sort of girl the Cherish Maders of the world never gave a second thought. It broke Anna Grey's heart to think about it. Suddenly she lifted her daughter's pony-tail and kissed the soft, sweet skin beneath it.

"*Ma.*"

"You're a good kid, you know that?" Anna Grey said. She started browning the ground beef while Milly emptied the dish-washer. "Anything new?" she asked, expecting Milly's usual shrug. But when Milly spun around and beamed, Anna Grey realized she'd been waiting for the question.

"I tried out for the summer play."

"You did?" Anna Grey was shocked. Every summer, the Ambient Community Center put on a musical, but Anna Grey could no more imagine Milly climbing onto a stage than she could imagine her skydiving. Still, Anna Grey had surprised Milly singing around the house, and what a beautiful voice she had! Anna Grey quickly learned not to mention it, though. If she did, Milly got embarrassed and was careful not to sing for a while.

Milly nodded. "Actually, I tried out last week."

"How did it go?"

"Pretty well." She was trying to be nonchalant. "I got one of the leads."

"Congratulations!" Anna Grey said. Her voice rose with emotion, the way Milly and Bill both hated. "Why didn't you tell me? Mercy, Milly, I can't believe it!"

"Don't have a heart attack, Ma," Milly said, but she was smiling. "I can't believe it, either, OK?"

The ground beef sizzled and popped. Too late, Anna Grey pulled it off the burner. A cloud of smoke enveloped them both before she could turn on the fan. "It's all right," Anna Grey said, turning her head so she wouldn't cough into the meat. "It's just a little singed. Tell me about your play."

The musical was *The Music Man*, and Milly told Anna Grey all about it as they spooned the burned bits out of the ground beef. "Rehearsals start this Saturday," she said. "We're just going to do a read-through first: That means everybody sits in a circle and says their lines so we all get a sense of the characters. I'm the young teacher the music man falls in love with, and—"

The kitchen was open to the living room, and suddenly Bill appeared in the doorway.

"Could you keep it down in here?" he said. He fanned his hand through the air. "Good grief, what's going on?"

Before Anna Grey could say anything, Milly jumped up as if she'd been slapped. "We were talking—what's so bad about talking?" she screamed. "All—we—were—doing—was—*talking!*" Then she ran down the hall to her room and slammed the door. Anna Grey stared at the familiar lines of Bill's face: the soft chin with its velvet stubble, the shaving scar on his left cheek, the eyes that could be green or gray or blue, depending on what he was wearing, held in place by crow's-feet neat as fancy-sewn pleats. She stared at his sloping shoulders, the way his worn jeans hung low on his hips beneath the bulk of his belly. His hair, which was still full and curly in the front. That streak of gray. *The devil's kiss.* His feet were long and slender, graceful; as always, they pointed slightly out. She removed his shirt, his undershirt, his jeans and socks and Jockeys. She removed the silver four-leaf clover that had hung from his neck since he'd turned sixteen, a gift from his mother. She turned him around, spun him over and over like a piece of meat on a giant spit, and still—the thought came to her with the rush of a sparrow fluttering in through a window accidentally left ajar—she knew nothing about this man. And she wondered if it was truly possible to know anyone in the world.

"What?" Bill said to her, clearly bewildered. "All I did was ask a question." And then he sniffed at the air near her forehead. "You've been smoking, haven't you?" he said.

That night, she went to bed early, and when she lay down in the double bed that had once belonged to her grandmother, she imagined having all that space to herself for the rest of her life. She opened her arms, spread her legs, until her hands and heels hung over the edges. As a child, she'd always worried that something might come up out of the darkness and sink its teeth into her dangling limbs. She'd slept with her arms at her sides, her legs tucked against her stomach, and even as she dreamed, some part of her stayed alert, watching with a parent's eye, keeping her aligned in the center of the bed. Now, try as she might, Anna Grey could not close her eyes until she'd pulled her arms and legs back in and turned on her right side, facing the place where Bill should have been. She dreamed she was walking along an unfamiliar highway. In the distance, she could see the figure of a man; it was the hitchhiker, the real hitchhiker, the one with the harelip. "What do you want?" she asked, and he said, "One small act of kindness will appease me." But she knew one kindness would lead to another, and then another, and it would never, ever be enough. And then she saw he held the semiautomatic in his hand.

The alarm woke her. She felt confused, cotton-headed, as if she hadn't slept. Bill had already come and gone, and when she went downstairs to fix breakfast, she saw he hadn't even bothered to close the cover of the cereal box, let alone clear his dirty bowl and coffee cup from the table. She fixed two more bowls of cereal, buttered toast, poured orange juice, hoping routine would salvage the day. When Milly came into the kitchen, she gave her a cheery "Good morning!" But Milly had retreated into her usual silent shell.

"How late will your rehearsal run on Saturday?" Anna Grey asked.

Milly shrugged, sipped her juice.

"Are you nervous?"

Another shrug.

"Maybe I could come watch you rehearse sometime," Anna Grey said, and Milly said, softly, angrily, "Ma, it's no big deal, OK? It's just a stupid play."

Still, when the bus came, Anna Grey waved from the doorway as if nothing whatsoever were wrong. Then she threw Bill's coffee cup across the kitchen and into the sink, enjoying the splash of broken china, the crisp, charred, ringing sound.

At school, the children sensed her mood, stayed on their best behavior. Midmorning, she set them back to work on their eco-systems and stepped out to reserve a movie to carry them through the afternoon. So far so good, she thought. I can handle this day. But at lunchtime she remembered she'd been scheduled for recess duty weeks earlier, and no sooner did she get outside than she saw Robert John and his gang backing Gabriel up against the school wall. How she hated Gabriel for his weakness, that passive acceptance of all that befell him, so much like her own. She hated him fully and purely, in a way she would not have dreamed possible. She blew her whistle and marched over to where the boys had assumed postures of fearful defiance, gloved hands wedged into their pockets. Gabriel stood with his head down, waiting for whatever was going to happen next to happen. He didn't even seem to notice when Anna Grey grabbed the shoulder of his coat.

"I don't have the patience for this," she screamed at the boys. "If you're still here in three seconds, I'll slap your goddamn little punk faces bloody, do you understand English?"

They did. After they'd dispersed, she spun Gabriel around and slammed him hard against the wall. He didn't even blink. "What's wrong with you," she shouted, "that you don't stand up for yourself? Do you want to live this way all your life? Is that what you want?"

Gabriel didn't answer. What child could answer stupid questions like that?

She kept her hand on his shoulder, took a few deep breaths. She could feel the bones in his shoulder all the way through his coat, through his fat: the V of his clavicle, the flat patch of scapula. For all his bulk, he was a very small boy. If she squeezed hard enough, she could crush everything in her fist like a handful of potato chips.

"Trouble?" someone said. It was Marty Klepner. Without saying anything, Anna Grey let go of Gabriel and walked back to her classroom, leaving her section of playground unattended. She opened the coat closet, and her red eyes fixed on the mess of toys and games and random supplies that were always threatening to spill out onto the floor. By the time the kids came in from recess, she had everything stacked in piles along the wall and was wiping down the shelves.

"Spring cleaning!" she announced. "Everybody empty out your desks!"

It was barely February, but what else could they do? Even Gabriel lifted the lid of his desk and began scooping the contents onto his seat. They scoured every surface with Comet. They washed every window, soaped every blackboard, organized the bulletin boards. They finished just as the librarian arrived with the antiquated film projector, and Anna Grey let *The World of Volcanoes* carry them right up to the three o'clock bell, when the kids—Gabriel included—flew out of there like buckshot.

She didn't know how much time passed before she heard a knock at the door. "Come in," she said. Of course it was Marty, the last person in the world she wanted to see. She started packing up the projector so she wouldn't have to look at him.

"What's going on?" Marty said.

Anna Grey tucked the film into its box, held it out to Marty. *"The World of Volcanoes,"* she told him.

"Can I help with anything?"

"Oh, you could return this to the library, if you're headed that way," she said airily.

"That's not what I meant," Marty said. "I mean, we're still friends, aren't we, Anna? Is there anything I can do?"

"Anna *Grey*," Anna Grey said. "My name is Anna *Grey*." And then she grabbed her purse from her desk, lifted her coat from its hook, and ran down the hallway toward the parking lot, hating the hard, frantic sound of her heels on the tiled floors. Outside, the air was thick with the odor of the fertilizer plant, but it smelled worse than usual: oilier, sharper. She thought of the smoke boiling up from the fires in the Gulf, the pale sky opening to receive it, and at that moment she felt the bump forming at the edge of her lower lip. In the car, she flipped down the vanity mirror, stared at her reflection. Nothing. Yet she could *feel* something with her tongue. The most terrifying things were the ones you couldn't see, the ones you harbored inside yourself. She remembered how, after Chernobyl, she'd listened to reports that said the cloud of radiation would reach America in four days, then two days, then one. That day, nothing had seemed different on the surface, but in the middle of the afternoon, a faint shadow passed over the sun and she felt the radiation settling into her bones, sparkling like diamonds, waiting for a chance to make the right cell blossom.

CURIOUS ABOUT US? We'd love to meet you! The Circle of Faith holds open meetings the first Saturday of every month. Healing Prayers, Practical Advice, and some Good Laughs too. For women of all ages—nonjudgmental, supportive. Stay for a spaghetti supper with garlic bread, green beans, and choice of dessert. Fair Mile Crossroads, 4 P.M. Free child care provided by Cherish Mader and Lisa Marie Kirsch.

    —From the Ambient Weekly
      February 1991

four

Circle of Faith meetings were held at the Fair Mile Crossroads in a building that had once been a Pump and Go, and sea-
soned members still talked about the work it had taken to
conquer the odor of gasoline and mildew. But Janey Fields had
joined only last year, and it was hard for her to imagine the Faith
house as anything other than the cozy place it was, with comfy
castoff couches and homemade curtains, card tables, a refrigerator, and an interpretive mural of the Resurrection, which Ruthie's
daughter, Cherish, had been working on under Maya Paluski's
supervision. Jesus' body was complete, but he still had no face or
feet or hands. Cherish said she'd finish them as soon as she'd done
more preliminary sketches. In the meantime, Maya had started
painting angels all around him, ordinary-looking women dressed
in business suits, lab coats, aprons, maternity dresses. One was
holding an artist's palette; Maya said that was for Cherish. She
said that Cherish Mader was the most talented art student she'd
ever had. Cherish wasn't a member of the Circle—she was only
seventeen—but she often helped out around the Faith house. To-

day she'd made the coffee and set out cups and saucers before heading back home to work on a paper for school.

Beyond the wide display windows, the razor lines of the plowed county highways sliced the snowy fields into precise geometric shapes. *Like ice cream sandwiches*, Janey thought. Snow had been falling steadily since morning, but nine Faith members had shown up for the Saturday meeting in spite of the weather: Ruthie Mader, of course, and Janey; Margaret Kirsch, whose daughter Lisa Marie was Cherish's best friend; Maya Paluski; Lorna Pranke; Jolena Carp; Shelley Beuchel; Tabby and Mary Smoot, who were sisters; and finally the newest member, Anna Graf—no, they were to call her Anna *Grey*. Last week's meeting had been a spaghetti supper, open to any woman who wanted to come, more of a social event than anything. But today's meeting was closed, which meant that only full members could attend. Anna Grey had just been initiated; she kept reaching for her gold Faith cross as if she were afraid she might have lost it. Her eyes were puffy and red, and when Ruthie asked, she said she'd had a fight with her husband. He didn't like the idea of her joining a women-only prayer group, and everyone smiled sympathetically when she told them that.

"My husband was the same way," Shelley assured her, "until he started seeing the difference in me." Shelley had just finished her last round of chemo; her head was wrapped in a pretty floral scarf the Circle had given her to celebrate.

Anna Grey said, "I'm sure I could set myself on fire and Bill wouldn't see any difference in *me*." You could tell she was trying to be funny, but her smile was more like the wince of someone who'd just stepped on something sharp.

"Look at it this way," Ruthie said. "He's noticed *this* change in you, hasn't he? You decide to take some time for yourself, just once a week, just to pray with friends, and suddenly you're on his mind. It's a start, really, if you think of it that way."

For the first time, Anna Grey looked directly at Ruthie, and Janey remembered how it had been when she herself, new to the group, first looked into Ruthie's deep-set eyes. Ruthie wasn't exactly what you'd call pretty, but there was something about the way she gave you her full attention when she spoke, and the plain, old-fashioned way she pulled back her hair—she didn't have a permanent, like the others—and the loose dresses she always wore, which seemed to change direction about a quarter second after she did . . . it was hard for anyone to explain. You just had to see her, and once you did, you were forever changed. When Ruthie took your hand during a Circle of Prayer, it was like nothing you'd ever felt before. It was leaving the misery of the body. It was going out beyond yourself so you saw all sides to everything. It was loving what you saw and carrying that love back with you so that, when you opened your eyes again, people glowed with a fresh, whole light.

Lorna put her hand over her mouth, the way she always did when she wanted to speak. "Stan looks forward to my meetings," she said, "because he gets the house to himself. We never realized how rarely that happened all those years, with him working and me at home. Now he plays around in the kitchen, invents sandwich combinations. He calls them his *Stanleys*." Lorna laughed. "He offered to make us a dozen for today. I put him off this time, but, ladies, you've been warned."

Everybody was laughing now, if a little ruefully. These days, they were all praying for the chief, whose mind simply wasn't what it used to be. They were praying for Lorna, whose health had been poor ever since her hysterectomy. They were praying for Shelley's cancer cells to melt away. They were praying for Jolena Carp's retarded son, Lovey, who was twenty-two years old and unable to speak; for Tabby and Mary's ailing dog, Buster; for Maya Paluski's diabetes; for various troubled marriages, lost jobs, problems with alcohol. They prayed that Ruthie would find a way to pay the back taxes on her farm so she wouldn't have to sell out to Big Roly, as so many others had done. Technically, Big Roly owned the Faith house; he'd let Ruthie fix it up and use it for next to nothing, hoping to soften her up. But all of them knew that try as he might, Big Roly would never get Ruthie's land. For when they joined hands in that comfortable room, a constellation of gold crosses shining at their throats, no one could doubt that her prayers would be answered.

Ask and ye shall receive; seek and ye shall find; knock and the door shall be opened to you. These were the words Faith members lived by, and one only had to look at Shelley, now in a second remission against every medical prediction, to know that God was listening. Jolena Carp's Lovey, still unable to speak, had started to crayon beautiful pictures; Maya was managing her diabetes through diet and exercise. Last fall, when it looked as though Ruthie wouldn't come up with her minimum tax payment, the Circle met at night to join hands, and the next day, she won nine hundred dollars at bingo, the largest pot in Saint Fridolin's history. Sometimes it seemed to Janey as if everyone's prayers except her own were being answered. But it was wrong to think that way, for God revealed His glory in His own good time. Infertility might have left her devastated, cost her a marriage, shaken her to the core; still, she had to believe that this, like all things, was a part of God's plan. If she only had faith the size of a mustard seed, He would focus His healing power upon her.

Now they began the meeting by asking for God's blessing. Today's topic was the story of the Good Samaritan, and after Ruthie had finished reading from the Bible, she invited them to share encounters with Good Samaritans they had known. Anna Grey talked about Maya's persistent concern over her unhappiness at work; Shelley told about a woman from her church who'd brought supper to Shelley's family for two weeks while Shelley was in the hospital. Tabby and Mary talked about the time their car broke down coming back from Madison and a man and his two young boys had stopped to help. While he fixed their car, the boys sang a duet they had been practicing for a play at school. "There we were on the interstate," Tabby said, "all these semi trucks roaring by and the boys just singing away. We tried to pay their father, but he wouldn't take our money. Wouldn't even let us give those boys a dollar."

"Though we slipped them a little something while his back was turned," Mary said.

And so it went, and as the women talked, they found themselves recalling times they'd tried to help someone and been rebuffed, or needed help themselves and had not received it, or themselves walked on past another soul in need. They talked about their children, their husbands, parents and siblings and friends. They talked about their jobs, books they had read, places they had visited or hoped someday to go. They gave advice, laughed, and listened. And then, as the meeting drew to a close, they all joined hands to form a Circle of Prayer for Good Samaritans everywhere. Angels, Ruthie called them. Though it was rare to encounter a spirit angel, there were many human angels in the world, ordinary people just like any one of them. One person *could* make a difference. One person had the *power* to change the way things were, to transform the events of daily life into multiple blessings. The meeting ended with each woman in turn reaffirming her Vow of Silence, a vow which assured that whatever had been said within Faith walls would remain there.

Afterward, there was always punch and cookies, a little bit of sweet wine. So it was late in the afternoon by the time Janey finally headed home on County O, passing Tom Mader's memorial cross, its crisp plastic necklace of roses. Behind it, the Neumillers' Holsteins were confined to a single icy pasture, and it seemed to Janey there was wistfulness in the way they stared past the electric fence at the unspoiled whiteness of fields. She remembered making snow angels with her brothers, how they'd visit friends in the country and spend an afternoon making a chain of angels stretching as far as the eye could see. It was a happy memory, and Janey gave thanks for this small gift. She always felt good after Faith meetings. Perhaps, when she got back to her parents' house, she'd do some more work on her résumé. Tabby Smoot managed a Pizza Hut, and though she had no job openings at present, she'd encouraged Janey to apply in case something came available. There was also a job at the Badger State Mall, which Ruthie had seen in the *Ambient Weekly*. It had been a year since Janey had moved home from Green Bay, and all the Faith members said she'd feel better once she was earning money again, getting out of her parents' house.

The snow had let up, and now the sky cracked and bled, releasing its pale yolk of sun. Farther up the road, the fields were spotted with new ranch houses, crisscrossed by snowmobile tracks as savage as welts left by a whip. Something in the distance caught Janey's eye—three snowmobiles making lazy buzzard circles not twenty yards from the edge of the highway. As she approached, she saw they were circling someone. The figure floundered in the deep snow as the snowmobiles went round and round. At times, they cut so close that he disappeared in a powdery plume—she could tell it was a boy; they were all boys—but when the snow settled, Janey saw he was still there.

She slowed reluctantly. All she wanted to do was keep on driving until she reached her parents' house, go up to her room, turn on the little typewriter that Mary and Tabby had loaned her. Perhaps she could finish the résumé today, have it ready to mail out on Monday—a small step, but more than she'd felt able to accomplish in months. The boy probably lived nearby anyway, in one of those ugly ranches that were going up left and right. Developers like Big Roly bought the old farmsteads for nothing, subdivided them into residential lots, and sold them to people nobody knew. Or maybe the boy's own snowmobile had broken down somewhere, and the others were going to help him fix it. Or perhaps this *was* a spat between kids. In that case, what right did Janey have to meddle? All of these thoughts were going through her mind when, beneath her thick wool scarf, she felt the weight of her Faith cross tapping lightly against her collarbone. Once, she would have overlooked the significance of such a thing, but Ruthie had taught her to recognize God's nudge, His whisper in her ear.

She pulled up alongside the shoulder, as close as she could without getting stuck. It took a while before the boys noticed her; when they did, they darted a few yards farther into the field and waited, engines idling. The boy they'd been tormenting stared at the ground. She could see his shoulders moving, as if he were breathing hard, or crying. "You want a ride?" she called, stepping off the shoulder. The snow was deeper than she'd realized, and she promptly sank to her knees. One of the boys cut his engine, motioned the others to do the same. "C'mon," he hollered. "We'll take you there this time."

"Yeah, we promise," another boy said.

"Let me give you a ride," Janey called again, and when the boy turned his face toward the sound of her voice, she saw the blood on his chin. Who knew what might have happened to him had she hardened her heart and driven on by? The boy hesitated briefly, looked back at the others. They all were younger than Janey first thought—twelve, maybe thirteen, tops. Too young to be playing on snowmobiles unsupervised. When the boy began trudging toward her, they started their engines again, hooted and jeered. Janey couldn't hear what they were saying. It was probably just as well.

"Where did you want to go?" Janey said, leading him back to her mother's Buick. "I can take you there." She wasn't sure if she should drive him to the hospital or what. Maybe he needed stitches. Or a tetanus shot. As they pulled away, the boys rode off into the fields, shrank to dim specks, vanished like demons.

"Are you lost?" Janey said. "Where do you live, near the Crossroads?"

"Do you have anything to eat?" the boy asked.

"No," Janey said. It was an odd question, though reassuring. If he was hungry, he couldn't be badly hurt.

"Oh," the boy said. "What about gum?"

"Gum isn't good for you. It rots your teeth."

"Not sugar-free gum."

"That's bad for your kidneys," Janey said—she remembered reading that somewhere. Or maybe her father had told her. At any rate, the boy certainly didn't *look* like he needed something to eat. In fact, he carried quite a bit of extra weight. But thoughts like that were judgmental, wrong. She tried to think of what Ruthie would do in a situation like this. She tried to see the boy through Ruthie's eyes, to open her mouth and let God move her tongue, which Ruthie said was just a matter of having faith that all the right words would be there.

"What's your name?" she said. "What were you doing in the field?" But the boy simply repeated that he was hungry, using his coat sleeve to wipe at his chin. Janey's father was a retired GP. Perhaps the best thing was to take him home, let Dad check him out.

"I guess I could take you to my house," she said. "You could have a sandwich or something."

"What kind of sandwich?" the boy asked.

"Tell me your name," Janey said, "and I'll tell you what kind of sandwich."

The boy considered this seriously. He shivered, and Janey turned up the heater, aimed the vents at his face. What kind of parents let a child this age go out without a scarf or a proper pair of mittens? And instead of a hat, all the boy had was the hood of his coat. No wonder he was freezing. It struck Janey, as it often did, how unfair it was that such people could have children and she could not. Three miscarriages, then eight years of ovulation charts, hormone injections, mood swings and bleeding, and, finally, the loss of bleeding altogether. She and Harper looked into adoption, but it was too expensive; besides, the wait would have been years. "I'm sorry," Harp had finally said. "All I've ever wanted was a family of my own." And though Janey's friends had all sided with her, in her heart she knew she'd have done the same thing.

"My name," the boy said, startling Janey from her thoughts, "is Shawn."

"Well, Shawn," Janey said, "we have bologna, or peanut butter, or cold meat loaf with ketchup."

"Meat loaf," the boy said, "but I don't want any ketchup on it."

"OK," Janey said, slowing for her turn onto the D road. Her parents' house was behind the Solomon strip on the Saw Whet Road, in one of the few original neighborhoods that remained in Solomon. Janey had grown up with a best friend who lived next door, and each of them had dated the boy across the street, Danny Hope, all elbows and shins. Tonight was the night of the neighborhood block party Danny's parents hosted each year. It was always held in the dead of winter, and in recent years it had gotten pretty wild. Men wore their wives' sundresses, summer gowns, and bikinis; women wore their husbands' short-sleeve bowling shirts, neckties and boxers and skimpy tees. There were summery foods and tropical drinks; the Hopes turned up the heat and set out fans and buckets of ice. The *Ambient Weekly* took pictures. At midnight, members of the Polar Bear Club stripped as naked as they dared, rushed out of the house, and rolled in the snow until Chief Pranke arrived to hustle them back inside. Both Mum and Daddy had been trying to get Janey to go to the Hopes' party, especially now that Danny, a successful chiropractor, had divorced his wife and come back home from Houston to think things over.

"You don't even have to dress up," Daddy had said at lunch. "You can be the chaperone."

"And once you see the dress Daddy's going to wear, you'll know he's going to *need* a chaperone," Mum said, and she waggled a scolding finger at Daddy until he kissed it, kissed it again. They were worse than newlyweds. They took classes in ballroom dancing at the community center. They were planning a Carnival cruise. Nights, they watched TV on the couch, cuddled up under the afghan like teenagers. If Janey came downstairs, they'd sit up quick and make room, Mum patting the space between them. "Come join the old folks," she'd say. *Wheel of Fortune* was their favorite show. They'd yell at the contestants, urge them to spin, buy another vowel, while Janey slumped deeper into the cushions, feeling like an intruder. Her brothers had gone into insurance: Lee had an Allstate office in Minneapolis; Matt had one in Saint Paul. They came home with their wives and children twice a year.

Janey was the only one who hadn't made good. After ten years of marriage, she was right back where she'd started: single, childless, dependent on her parents. At first, she'd seen doctor friends of Daddy's, who prescribed hormones to start her monthly bleeding, pills to cure her sorrow. But her sorrow deepened, her bleeding still did not return, and some days she wept for hours on end. Things might have gone on this way if Mum hadn't thought of the Circle of Faith. Mum had attended meetings herself before Daddy retired and they'd fallen in love again. Janey would never forget the day that Ruthie came to the house like an old-fashioned doctor, her black satchel filled with gifts: a journal for Janey to record positive thoughts, a small china angel that was also a night-light, three white candles she asked Janey to light whenever she felt the dark thoughts closing in.

"What's the matter?" the boy asked. They were parked in the driveway, but Janey didn't remember pulling up to the house. When the dark thoughts came, she'd lose time that way—not a lot, not like that TV girl with all the personalities. Just a blip. She'd drive to a Faith meeting, and when she arrived, she'd realize she couldn't remember a thing she'd seen along the way. Or she'd be doing something like folding laundry, and then it would all be folded.

"Nothing's wrong," Janey said. "This is where I live."

She led him through the garage and brought him through the back door into the sudden warmth of the house. Mum was vacuuming; the cord stretched down the hall and disappeared into the living room. She'd used the same Hoover for twenty-five years, and it sounded as if she was driving a tractor back and forth.

"Hello?" Janey shouted, and when Daddy called back, "Down here!" she led the boy downstairs into the basement den, where the noise was absorbed into the wall-to-wall carpet. The den was spanking new, one of Daddy's retirement projects.

"A visitor!" Daddy said, clearly delighted. He was busy combing Rusty. Rusty woofed once when he saw the boy, but he was even-tempered and never barked at anyone for long.

"I found him along County O," Janey said. "His name is Shawn, but that's all he'll tell me."

"What did you do to your face there, pal?" Daddy said, as if Janey brought stray children home every day. He let go of Rusty, who wagged his tail so hard it made his whole backside swing to and fro.

The boy shrugged. "Got beat up."

"Oh, yeah?" Daddy said. He took the boy's face in his hands, tipped his chin up to the light. "By who?"

"Just some kids," the boy said. When Daddy released his face, he let Rusty lick his hands. "This is a very nice house."

"Thank you," Daddy said, pleased. "Tell you what. Why don't you tell me your dad's name, and we'll just call him up and have him give those kids a talking to."

"Can I have something to eat?" the boy replied.

Daddy looked a little surprised. "Sure, why not?" he said, and he turned to Janey. "Wipe him down with Merthiolate and then bring him up to the kitchen. I'll see if Mum knows where he belongs." He headed for the stairs, Rusty dancing happily underfoot. *Kitchen* was one of the words he knew, like *walk* and *treat* and *Rusty*. Janey often thought it would be wonderful to be a dog like Rusty, with so few words to be responsible for, all of them pleasant and promising.

She led the boy into the utility bathroom, gave him a washcloth from the linen closet, then opened the medicine chest, where Mum kept first-aid supplies and a collection of tiny wrapped hotel soaps. Janey's antidepressants and hormone tablets were on the bottom shelf, in full deliberate view, so Mum and Daddy wouldn't suspect she'd stopped taking them. Every night, she'd flush another batch down the toilet. Only God had the power to heal, and Janey was determined to put her faith in Him. Still, she couldn't help but wish for a sign, some small thing that would let her know that He was watching. Ruthie said God spoke to people nowadays as often as He had during Bible times—it was just that the modern mind wasn't trained to understand. Janey wondered if she'd recognize a sign if it came. Upstairs, the sound of the vacuum cleaner stopped, and suddenly all the little sounds around her seemed too loud: the closing of the cabinet, the scuff of her feet on the tile floor, the boy's thick breathing as he lathered his face and hands.

"What were you doing with those boys?" Janey said. "Where

were they taking you? You can tell me. You don't have to be afraid.''

She handed him a towel, and he patted his face dry. His chin was still a little puffy, but with the blood washed away, it didn't look too bad. There was only one small cut, more of a scratch really, under his mouth.

"I don't want any of that stuff on me," he said, eyeing the Merthiolate.

"Just on the cut," she said. "To keep it from getting infected."

"It won't get infected," he said.

"It might," Janey said.

"No, it won't," the boy said. "God will make it heal. God can do anything if you believe He can."

His words took Janey by surprise. A strange thing happened: She felt the cross at her throat begin to move, tap-tapping like a heartbeat. She grabbed for it—dropped it! It was hot! Then the bathroom door swung open, clipping her hip. "Knock-knock," Mum said, which was what she always said whenever she came into a room. She wore one of Daddy's old baby-blue seersucker suits, and she'd darkened the space between her eyebrows, so it looked as if one long eyebrow stretched across her forehead. Her tie was fat and black, with the word DANGEROUS spelled down the front in red letters. "Daddy's upstairs doing his nails. Oh, goodness," she said, noticing the boy's wide eyes, "you must think I've escaped from the loony bin! It's just that I'm on my way to a party where everyone dresses silly. Do I look silly?"

The boy nodded hesitantly. Mum laughed, delighted. "There's an honest answer," she said. "I'm Kathryn. And you're Shawn?"

The boy didn't answer.

"Don't be afraid, love. Where do you live?" She turned to Janey. "Do we know anything about him?"

"He believes in the power of God," Janey said, and when Mum gave her a funny look, she wished she hadn't said anything. At lunch, when Janey had told Mum for the hundredth time that, no, she didn't want to go to the Hopes' party, Mum said she was concerned that Janey was getting too religious, that she spent too much time with Faith members and not enough with other people. Back in Mum's day, they didn't meet at the Fair Mile Crossroads—they just sat around in Ruthie's living room, played cards, and talked, and maybe they each had a splash of kümmel in a shot glass. "Of course, we prayed," Mum said. "And a few times we went on retreat. But there wasn't all this talk about angels and goodness and—I don't know—miracles."

"You and Daddy are a miracle," Janey said, "compared to how you used to be."

Daddy said agreeably, "So we are. So we are."

"And there certainly weren't any vows of silence," Mum continued, as if she hadn't heard. "What's so secret that you can't tell your own parents what you pray for?"

"Nothing," Janey said, trying not to sound irritable. "It's just that we pray for personal things sometimes. Like, if somebody has a problem, they bring it to a meeting and we talk about it and then we pray about it. Like, when it's time to pray for me"—Janey paused; it was OK to talk about your own requests—"we pray that someday I'll meet somebody again and have a family." She had to whisper to keep from crying.

"But, sweetheart," Mum said, her eyes filling with sympathetic tears, "how can God answer a prayer like that if you stay hidden away in the house?"

"Aw, she'll venture out again when she's ready." Daddy was trying to smooth things over; now he changed the subject. "Boy, would I love to be a fly on the wall during one of those meetings!" he said, nudging Janey's shoulder in a playful way. "Bet I'd learn a thing or two." Men were always saying things like that; it was just because they weren't invited. They thought that meant you were talking about sex. Or else that you were talking about them.

Now Mum took the boy by the hand. "I hear you've been asking for a snack," she said, and Janey followed them up the stairs. Mum had been cleaning since early this morning, and everything smelled of lemons. The curtains were freshly ironed, and the floors were waxed. She'd even raked the old shag rug in the living room. Janey hadn't offered to do anything, because no matter how carefully she washed or waxed or dusted, Mum would do it all over again. She said she couldn't help herself. "It's just that I have my routine," she said. "Relax, Pumpkin. Think of yourself as our special guest."

Daddy was in the kitchen. He'd changed into a peach muumuu splashed with yellow flowers. He had flip-flops on his feet. Rhinestone clip-ons hung from his earlobes. "What do you think?" he said, and he turned in a lavish circle. Rusty circled with him, toenails click-clicking on the linoleum.

"Darling," Mum said. "You'll be the belle of the ball."

The boy giggled.

They kissed, and in that casual gesture Janey saw everything her own life lacked. Harper had already remarried, and now he was the father of a baby girl. Month after month, when her bleeding did not come, she prayed the same prayer: *Only say the word, Lord, and I shall be healed.* Sometimes she watched *Praise the Lord!* on TV, listening closely to the testimonies of everyday people who'd witnessed the supernatural. Christ had appeared to one man in the form of a very young boy; another man had been in a plane crash and heard God's voice saying he would be OK. Even people in Ambient had experienced things that could not be explained. There was a family who saw the ghost of a girl in their living room every New Year's Eve. At the Faith house one time, as they'd prayed for Shelley Beuchel, a blue light had descended from the ceiling, slid down the walls and across the floor and up her body, where it rested on her forehead like a kiss.

"I'm going to find out what to do with our visitor," Daddy

said, and he headed down the hall toward the phone. Mum sat the boy at the kitchen counter and made him hold a washcloth of crushed ice against his chin while she fixed a meat loaf sandwich. The boy bowed his head before he took a single bite. Janey fingered her cross; it was still warm, though not the way it had been. *God can do anything if you believe.* "Tell me," she begged him. "Why were you out in the field with those boys?"

The boy shrugged. He seemed quite content now, the half-eaten sandwich in his hand. "They said I could see the river angel there."

"Oh, honey," Mum said.

"They said that when the water freezes, the angel comes up on land."

"But the river angel is a story," Mum said. "Like the Easter bunny."

"How do you know?" Janey said. "What about what happened to that kid last summer? Davey Otto?"

His picture had run in the *Ambient Weekly* under the caption "Believe It or Not!" He'd fallen off the Cradle Park footbridge and said that an angel, small and white as a paper plate, had pushed him back to the surface.

"Some people will say anything to get attention," Mum said.

"Some people aren't afraid to bear witness to the truth."

"Don't get upset," Mum said, and she gestured at the boy with her chin. "I just don't think you should encourage him, that's all."

"I've seen the angel twice," the boy said. "Maybe three times. The last time, I wasn't sure."

"You probably saw it," Janey told him when Mum turned back to the sink. The boy smiled at her gratefully. And Janey dared to believe he was the sign from God she'd longed for.

Daddy came back into the kitchen then, laid a hand on Janey's shoulder. "Apparently," he said, "the police know our visitor pretty well."

"Who is he?" Mum said.

"His real name is Gabriel," Daddy said. "Shawn Carpenter's son." Mum's face grew soft with sympathy, but Janey blushed hard, first with disappointment, then again with anger at her own stupidity. She stood up and walked over to the kitchen sink and stared out the small, square window at their neighbors' backyard, where two little girls were making a snowman. Gabriel Carpenter—it was only the child Anna Grey had talked about the first time she came to the Circle.

"Stan Pranke's on his way with a squad car," Daddy said. "I guess this is the fourth or fifth time the kid's run off."

The girls had finished the snowman's base; now they began his round white abdomen. How easily these might have been her own daughters. Janey could feel their small hands clutching her fingers. She smelled the backs of their necks, heard their squeals as she tickled them. She tasted their skin as she kissed them good night, tucked them into bed. But no, that wasn't true. What she really tasted was the emptiness of her mouth, the sourness working its way up from her stomach. Mum was right—she was getting too religious. Crazy, even. How could she ever have thought that the boy was anything more than he appeared to be? She pressed her index finger just above her upper lip to keep herself from crying.

Shawn Carpenter's son. It was adding insult to injury. She'd been one year behind him in high school and she'd had a terrible crush on him, just like all the girls. Once, he offered her a ride home from school, but he drove her down to Cradle Park instead. He lifted her skirt, put his hand underneath, all the while talking about classes and teachers and everyday things. She was fourteen, and she didn't understand what was happening. That's how innocent she'd been. Oddly, she couldn't remember what had happened next. Did he just take her home? Did she accept another ride from him after that? Maybe there was something wrong with her memory. Maybe she was getting old-timer's disease. Yet there were some things she remembered in such detail that they seemed more real than anything in the present. Like the time, just after her third and final miscarriage, when she woke up to see a little boy at the foot of her bed. Clearly, he was as curious about her as she was about him. He raised one hand, and she raised one hand back. She tilted her head; he tilted his. She stuck out her tongue and he grinned, mischievous, flicked his like a snake. Then Harper moaned in his sleep; the boy took a step back and disappeared. Janey could still see him in perfect detail—the broad, slightly flattened shape of his nose, so much like Daddy's; Harp's high cheekbones; her own soft brown eyes.

Gabriel had started to sniffle, and Mum said, "There, sweetheart, it's OK. Tell you what—I'll make you up a little care package." Without looking, Janey knew Mum was filling a Baggie with oatmeal cookies from the cookie jar.

"We shouldn't reward him for this," Daddy said, though his voice wasn't as stern as his words. "Looks like he's got the system down. You know where they picked him up last time, Mother? Kimmeldorf's, having a piece of Lucy's raisin-and-sour-cream pie."

There was a heavy knock at the door. Rusty rolled over, gave his single deep *woof*.

"Here you go, hon," Mum said, and she handed Gabriel his cookies. Janey did not turn around to see him go. She went over to the kitchen table, sat down, and stroked Rusty's smooth, broad forehead. There was something so steadfast and simple about the way Rusty looked at you. Rusty had no doubts about anything. Rusty just knew what he knew.

"You did a kind thing," Daddy said, "stopping to help that

boy." He took a six-pack of Miller from the fridge, started collecting bags of pretzels and chips to take along to the Hopes'.

Janey was too miserable to answer.

"Imagine," Mum said, coming back into the kitchen. "Stan says
the boy's been chasing the river angel all over the county."

"Poor little guy," Dad said. "It'll take more than an angel to
solve all his problems." Then he rattled the chips like tambourines. "All set?" he asked Mum. "Party started at six."

Mum sighed. "You *sure* you won't come along?" she said to
Janey.

"I'm sure." Janey tried to keep her voice steady. "I'm just going
to watch TV."

After they'd gone, she opened the refrigerator and stared at
what was in there without really seeing any of it. Her stomach
felt funny, and she decided to skip dinner altogether. Instead, she
went downstairs to the den and turned on the TV. She settled
herself on the couch, closed one hand over her gold Faith cross,
and laid the other on her flat, soft belly. Time passed. Her mood
blistered into despair. She knelt down beside the couch and imagined three white candles burning. Ruthie had promised her that,
someday, all of this would pass, that there would come a time
when she'd awaken every morning with her heart singing God's
praises. "Sometimes I miss Tom so terribly," Ruthie said, "and
when I think of taxes coming due, and how hard it's getting to
rent the fields, and the money I'm losing on the sheep, and all
the repairs that need to be done, my head gets racing and my
heart gets pounding and I lose my way completely. It is then I
remember God's love for me. I remember that when a child asks
for bread, the father won't hand her a stone. I remember that
faith the size of a mustard seed is all God asks of me, and from
that place of calm I say, Not my will but Thine be done."

How long Janey knelt there she did not know, but when she
opened her eyes, she felt as if something inside her had eased.

Not my will but Thine be done, she whispered, and she realized that, for the first time, she truly meant those words. Slowly, she got to her feet. She finally understood. No matter what happened, she would be OK. Her purpose in the world was to do God's will, *whatever* that might be. And if she never had a child of her own, so be it. *Thy will be done.*

It was a strange place for a revelation, the TV humming in the background. "God is never dull," Ruthie liked to say, and it was certainly true. Janey went to the bathroom, splashed her face with cold water. She could barely contain her joy. And it was no more than a few days later when she discovered the blood she'd prayed for, staining her white cotton underwear, beautiful as a rose.

AUCTION—DAIRY COWS * MACHINERY * EQUIPMENT * Joe and Edna Skrepenski are retiring—Everything must Go! Folks, there is a lot of fine Merchandise here, with more calls daily. Ten A.M. Saturday, March 1 (Snow date, March 8) with lunch on grounds. LIVESTOCK at 11:00 includes 41 head of Hi Grade Holstein Dairy Cattle. Majority sells just fresh and in their second and third lactation. Avg 41% butterfat test w/3.3% protein. MACHINERY AND EQUIP at 1:30 includes 10 tractors, combines (includes Gleaner #C2 G self-propelled, w/ cab), harvesting equip including Vermeer round baler, hay swather w/half cab, forage choppers, green choppers, hi-throw forage throwers, planting and tillage equip PLUS many special items including Gehl #309 Scavenger side slinger manure spreader and MUCH MORE! Household items plus some antiques, including weathervane, mixed in all day. Cash or good check day of sale. Location: Skrepenski Farmstead. Take County O South from the Fair Mile Crossroads, watch for Auction Arrows!

—*From the* Ambient Weekly
 March 1991

five

It was a cold, clear morning in March, sunlight skating across the sparkling surface of the snow, when Big Roly Schmitt's ten-year-old daughter turned to him and said, boom, out of nowhere, "Daddy, teach me to drive." They were on their way to the Fair Mile Crossroads, where Big Roly fetched his rents in person, the first Saturday of every month, going door to door the way his own daddy had done. Big Roly felt it was important to maintain personal contact with his tenants, to check on all properties, business and residential, with his own two eyes. Besides, he genuinely liked to visit with people. He looked forward to hearing the gossip, maybe telling a story or two of his own.

"Most kids wait on driving till they're a little older, Scoot."

She looked at him, dead serious. *Uh-oh*, Big Roly thought. She said, "I think it's a life skill everyone should have."

The kid just busted him up.

"Maybe. If I see a plowed parking lot."

"I'll be a good driver," Christina said.

"I know you will."

They were coming up on the International Harvester dealership, which had gone belly-up five years earlier. Big Roly had known the family who'd owned it; the parents retired to Florida, bought themselves a trailer right smack on a canal. Now there was talk of Toyota coming in, selling those zippy little cars. The area sure was changing fast, with so many people moving in, drawn by the millpond and the Onion River, the safe public schools, the affordability. For eighty thousand, a person could build a nice ranch house on a two-acre country lot—although that was changing too. It was just twenty miles from Ambient to the I-90/94 split, and from there it was only sixty to Milwaukee, seventy-five to Chicago, take your pick. Commuting was nothing these days for the corporates who worked via modem and fax. Big Roly ran ads in the big city papers: AMBIENT—WISCONSIN'S BEST-KEPT SECRET! The folks who responded were worth a little extra time, and Big Roly personally drove them around in his Lincoln to admire the town and countryside. The River Road shoe factory was said to be haunted; he'd pull into the parking lot to describe the ghostly woman more than one night watchman had seen. "They say she's dressed in an apron, carrying a roasted turkey on a platter," Big Roly would say. "I've heard you can smell that turkey even after she disappears." If they liked that bit of local lore, he continued on along the railroad tracks until they reached the J road, cutting back across the highway bridge, where many of the river angel sightings took place. "Of course, I've never seen it myself," Big Roly always said, "but I know a man who did. He'd gone for a dip, caught himself a cramp, and just when he thought he was going under, it carried him to the shore."

And then, perhaps, he'd glance in the rearview mirror, catch the couple exchanging a look, and one of them would say, "How on earth do stories like that get started?" or something along those lines. In that case, he'd laugh sheepishly and say, "To be truthful, I didn't know the man myself—although my daddy did, and he swears it's true." But if the couple seemed interested, he'd tell them how the river angel had watched over Ambient since the flash flood of 1898. Those settlers who'd survived reported an angel had led their families to safety.

"You can look it up at the library," he'd say; he had heard that this was so. "The museum's probably got some records too. We have a lovely little museum for a town this size," and then he'd chauffeur them back into Ambient, past the library and museum and town square, ending the tour in Cradle Park with a walk across the footbridge, and maybe he'd even hand them a penny to toss the angel for luck, just the way he did with Christina.

"How about right here by the IH?" he asked her now, and he pulled off the highway, followed the plow track around to the back of the building, where they wouldn't be seen. God only knew why anyone bothered to keep the parking lot cleared; only teenagers used it now. On weekends, they'd hollow caves in the walls of the packed plowed snow, then sit inside drinking beer and making out, and if they got cold, they simply built a bonfire in the parking lot. You could see the blackened circle now, surrounded by beer cans, fast-food wrappers, old tires, and bags of trash. Big Roly parked beside it, got out to switch places with Christina. The plow drifts were taller than he was, boxing them in. It made him uneasy. He hustled around to the passenger's side of the Lincoln, eased his three-hundred-pound bulk into the seat.

"Fire her up," he said, and Christina did, not even grinding the starter. Christ, she could barely see over the dash. He kept a Polaroid in the glove compartment for doing property appraisals, and he wanted so badly to take her picture, but she could be sensitive about stuff like that. "Daddy, stop patronizing me," she'd say.

Daddy. She still called him that instead of *Dad*, even in front of her friends.

"Now what?" she said, bouncing in the seat. Her ponytail

stuck out from under her snug Packers cap. She had Big Roly's red hair, but less carroty, more of an auburn color—strangers were always exclaiming over it. She had Big Roly's freckles too, but thank God, not as many. While he was a mass of pinkish-brown pigments, she had only a fine constellation, distinct as chocolate sprinkles across the vanilla bridge of her nose.

"Put your foot on the brake and hold it there." Thank God I drive an automatic, he thought. She had to slide down a little to reach. Sweet Jesus, but the worst she could do was run them into the plow drift, and he had a good shovel and plenty of sand in the trunk. He leaned over, helped her shift into drive. "You won't need any gas," he said. "Take your foot off the brake and let the Lincoln do the rest."

She drove all the way across the parking lot as if she'd been doing it all her life. He turned the Lincoln around so she could take it back the other way, hands at ten and two just like he showed her.

"OK?" he said. "Enough?"

And she nodded, batted his hands away, and put it in park herself.

"Don't tell your mom about this," he said, more for the fun of sharing a secret than out of concern for what Suzette would think. Suzette believed in taking risks. Each morning, she put on her snow boots and walked to work at the fertilizer plant, where she'd been the first female to rise past Floor into Management. "Don't put up with bullshit from anyone," she'd tell Christina, and Christina nodded because she already knew. From the time she was born, she was wise beyond her years. By six months she was speaking, and real words too, not just *ba* for bottle, like Big Roly's sister's kid. There just wasn't any comparing her to other kids her age—hell, she figured as well as he did, better than her teachers at school. Just last Saturday, she'd been with him when he dropped in to see Pops Carpenter about some snow-removal work. Pops was baby-sitting his grandson, Gabriel, and while he haggled with Big Roly over his fee, Christina sat down with the boy, who was in her class at school. By the time Big Roly came to get her, she was helping him do his math homework.

"That was awful nice of you," Big Roly had said as they walked back out to the Lincoln. Everybody knew how Gabriel's dad had abandoned him to his uncle and aunt. Big Roly didn't think too much of the aunt; a battle-ax if there ever was one. No wonder the boy kept running off. People were always finding him, bringing him back home.

Christina shrugged. "I have to help him anyway," she'd said. "Mrs. G. has me tutor kids because I'm so far ahead."

"Really?" Big Roly said. Just out of curiosity, he took all the rents they'd collected that day, stacked them in her lap. "How much have we got here, Scoot?" he said, and she'd tallied them up, just like that—no paper, no pen.

On rent Saturdays, Suzette always slept in. Big Roly rousted Christina out of bed around eight, and the two of them fried a pound of bacon and scrambled a dozen eggs into the grease and ate the whole mess in front of *Bugs Bunny*. Then, when they'd finished their coffee—he fixed Christina's special, with sweetened condensed milk—they headed out. Usually they didn't get back before three: After the Fair Mile Crossroads, there were the duplexes in Ambient to inspect, the weekend houses by the Killsnake Dam to check up on, stops at a couple–three businesses on North County O (the oldest one, the Moonwink Motel, was about to fall to Best Western), and then, back at the Solomon strip, they drove past Big Roly's apartment complexes, checking for vandalism, trash, graffiti. The graffiti was a recent thing, and Big Roly carried a can of beige paint and a roller to wipe everything clean. He was proud to say each of those units had a waiting list, and unlike his units in Ambient, these rented mostly to locals. The old farmers liked the convenience of the strip; young people worked at the fertilizer plant, or at the Badger State Mall just up the road, or at the various outlets and stores and restaurants scattered along the way.

People who weren't moving out of state were moving into town, and Big Roly bought their property when he could. Wealthier folks from the cities actually preferred old to new— they liked nothing better than a broken-down farmhouse to restore. And land that fell around the intersections was better than gravy, good as gold. The McDonald's at the Fair Mile Crossroads, for instance, had a twenty-year lease, and Big Roly had signed several other leases along the strip: one to Wal-Mart, across from the Kmart; one to a Morrison's Cafeteria franchise. Someone else had landed Kentucky Fried Chicken and a Southern restaurant called the Cracker Barrel. Lucy Kimmeldorf and the rest of the City Council could holler till their throats bled, but development was what Free Enterprise was all about. You bit or got bitten, and those toothless little overpriced businesses on Main could move someplace else if they didn't like it. Why shouldn't people enjoy the variety and low, low prices of a Wal-Mart, a walk-in optical center, a Jiffy Lube?

Big Roly himself was an old farmer at heart. He saw more beauty in an inexpensive place to buy necessities, in plenty of free parking, in all things handy and hassle-free, than he'd ever find along a pothole-ridden, bass-ackwards country road. People sometimes asked why he and Suzette still lived near the fertilizer plant when they could afford something by the millpond, or a big country farmhouse with a view of the river. "Convenience!" Big Roly told them, and it was true. Most days you couldn't even smell the plant, and when the wind was wrong—well, you barely noticed it after a while.

"Is this where they took those kids who got kidnapped?" Christina said as they pulled back onto the highway.

"Naw," he said, though it occurred to him it might be. He

wondered how she'd heard about that business. Mel Rooney, the assistant chief of police, had kept it out of the *Ambient Weekly* despite old Stan Pranke's grumblings. Mel understood how a thing like this could hurt community growth, snuff a burgeoning tourist industry. Mel was pro-development, an active member of the Planning and Zoning Commission, a man with a vision that paralleled Big Roly's. It couldn't be much longer now before the old chief retired and Mel—who had been, for all practical purposes, running the police department—finally claimed the title. Already he'd managed to nudge Buddy Lewis, one of his fresh young officers, onto the City Council. Another election or two, and Lucy Kimmeldorf wouldn't have enough weight left to squash a daisy, despite the campaign money downtown business owners kicked her way. "You worried about kidnappers?" he said.

"Nuh-uh."

"That's good," he said. "Cuz there's nothing to worry about." But he did think about those kids, scared half to death, slipping and sliding back to town through the snow.

The first kidnapping—if you could really call it that—occurred just after the summer festival in July; Sammy Carlsen had been playing in a vacant lot when two high school boys forced him into their car, drove him around, and finally dumped him somewhere off County O. The second had been one week ago; this time it was Joy Walvoord, out walking with her sister. Joy said there were high school boys and girls in the car, but she couldn't say how many, and they'd taken her only a couple of blocks before they let her go. Descriptions of the car itself were contradictory, and the single thing both kids were sure of was that the driver had had very short hair.

Frankly, Big Roly thought it was for the best that the kids couldn't ID anybody. It was just a stupid teen prank, the sort of thing that's blown out of proportion once the media get a whiff.

The sort of thing that winds up costing good people business. When Mel asked Big Roly's opinion one night after a Planning and Zoning meeting, Big Roly had told him as much. It wasn't like they hurt those kids—just drove 'em around and scared 'em a bit. High school kids, they got out of hand. Big Roly remembered how it was; who didn't? There was something about a cold winter night, maybe some girl with her hand in your pocket, maybe some liquor to warm you wherever she wouldn't or couldn't and a full-lipped moon in the sky—not that Big Roly had known too many of those nights. He had been the fat freckled kid, the boy whom girls managed not to see unless they needed change for the pop machine. And certainly, he didn't mean it was OK to snatch a grade-school kid off the street. But punishing those high schoolers was the parents' job, not the job of the community, not the job of the police or the courts. God knows, they had enough of government nosing around their lives already.

"If it were me," Big Roly told Mel, "I'd remind the parents of those kids who got nabbed that they should thank their lucky stars it wasn't a *real* kidnapper. Who in this day and age lets an eleven-year-old out to play after dark? No way would me or Suzette let Christina do a thing like that."

Besides, if anybody tried to grab her, Christina knew just what to do. "Don't be shy about it, either," he told her. "Right in the nuts, no questions asked." She hurt a little fella at school, but what was he doing? Lifting up her skirt. Big Roly said, "Mrs. Graf, if every girl was raised like Christina, you women wouldn't be tying up the courts with all this sexual harassment." And then he took Christina out to the McDonald's for a Big Mac and fries and a hot apple pie.

"Daddy," Christina told him, "I like driving."

"Me too," he said, and he reached over and flipped her pretty ponytail. They had just passed by Tom Mader's cross; someone had dug it out of the plow drift and left a fresh wreath of roses, startling as a flock of cardinals against the snow. Christina rubbernecked to look, and he wanted to reach over, cover her eyes. He would have been willing to spend his whole life beside her, shielding her from unpleasant things, if that were a possibility. But it wasn't. Already her brow was furrowed; she was thinking hard about something.

She said, "Where do people go when they die?"

"Heaven," Big Roly said without missing a beat. "Look at the odometer, Scoot. I believe you took us across thirty thousand."

"Where is heaven?"

He changed tactics, shrugged and tried to laugh. "Beats me. You'll have to ask your Sunday school teacher about that." He and Suzette had joined the Lutheran church a few years earlier. When a child asked the kind of hard questions Christina did, it was important to have some handy answers.

"It doesn't matter," Christina said. "I don't believe in it anyway."

"You don't?" Big Roly said.

"Do you?"

Now he was stuck. "Do you remember where the odometer is?" he asked.

"Right here." She pointed. "I don't believe in God, either."

"Well," Big Roly said.

"I believe in angels, though," she said, brightening. "Gabriel Carpenter says he's seen the river angel."

"Imagine that," Big Roly said, relieved. He supposed it was better for a child to believe in angels than nothing at all.

"That's why the other kids hate him," she said. "They pick on him all the time."

"But you never pick on him, do you, Scoot?" he said.

Christina shook her head.

"That's good," he said. "Everybody picked on your daddy when he was a kid, you know."

That got her attention. "How come?"

Big Roly rubbed his big stomach self-consciously, swiped at what was left of his carrot top. "Well," he said. It hadn't taken long for some wise child—he couldn't even remember who—to modify Roland into Roly-Poly and, later on, Big Roly. But it was more than his weight. For some reason, he'd been born with his incisors missing. One of his ears was slightly lower than the other. How many hours had he spent in front of the mirror, trying to tug it into place? His dad had caught him there, told him not to worry. *Make something of yourself, and nobody'll care what you look like.* It was good advice, though it had taken Big Roly another twenty years to realize that. How did the old joke go? The older I get, the smarter my old man gets? These same kids who'd once made his life a misery now came to his office with their hats in their hands. They still called him Big Roly—in Ambient, childhood nicknames stuck—but the way they said those words had changed. He sold their properties at a profit. He held mortgages on their family homes. He collected rent from them once a month, evicted them if they couldn't pay it.

"It's like this," he finally told Christina. "Your daddy's kind of funny-looking, if you think about it. Kind of like Gabriel."

She studied him closely. She did not contradict, the way Suzette would have done. "Oh," she said, and then, "Did you ever see an angel when you were a kid?"

"No, Scoot," he said. "I'm afraid I never did."

"Me neither," she said.

He sure was happy to see they were coming up on the Fair Mile Crossroads. "Maybe you're just not looking hard enough," he said. "Say! You ready to visit Auntie Ruth?"

The old Pump and Go sat in the crux of the J road and County O, catty-corner from the little outdoor mall called Riveredge, which had been one of his first developments. Originally, he'd had his real estate office in the space currently occupied by Ye

Olde Pet Shoppe, but he'd long since moved into downtown Ambient, across from Jeep's, where visibility was better. Here, there was nothing but fields that sprawled behind the buildings in all directions, though a few ranch houses—some of which Big Roly himself had sold—now dotted the horizon, and a new supersize grocery store was under construction. The contractor had fallen behind, and the ground froze before he could pour the foundation. Now the whole project was on hold till spring: steel beams rusting beneath ill-fitting tarps, the crane's open jaws bearded with ice. Hickory trees marked the line between this land and the acreage owned by the Farb family; a homemade sign boasted the Farbs' stud service in a childish scrawl: *Bulls, milch cows with the Guts, Buts and A—— to Do the Job!* The Farbs were still dairying, but on a smaller scale than in the past. Big Roly heard they'd been having success with organic crops and were starting to concentrate on that market. He made it his business to know who was farming what, who was showing a profit, who was having tentative, restless thoughts.

Ruthie's rusted-out Chevy Nova stood in front, along with a couple other cars. Big Roly recognized Maya Paluski's bumper sticker: GOD IS COMING, AND BOY IS SHE PISSED! He'd barely parked the Lincoln before Christina was running for the front door; she slipped inside without waiting for him to catch up. Christina loved Ruthie, had started calling her *auntie* without prompting, even made her little gifts at school. The woman had a sweetness about her, plain and simple; she made you want to sit right down and talk about things you didn't even know were on your mind. True, she was religious as the day was long—and not exactly a rocket scientist, if you wanted to be truthful—but she never made Big Roly feel uncomfortable about where he did or did not stand with God almighty, a topic he never liked to dwell upon. The fact was that he understood the meaning of the universe, and it was simply this: Work hard. Provide for those you love.

He got out of the Lincoln, stretched, walked leisurely up to the door. Except for the gas pumps, he would not have recognized the place. *Whatever you ladies want to do,* he'd told Ruthie when she signed the lease, and she'd taken him at his word. First thing she did was paint the outside green, with yellow flowers all around the door, and the inside—well, when he walked in, there was a half-finished painting of Jesus on the opposite wall, tall as Big Roly and skinny as Christina, his arms outstretched like a glider plane. His face wasn't filled in yet, though he had a full head of hair. His arms and legs just ended, as if someone had hacked them off with a cleaver. Angels swirled around his body like a cloud of gnats, and not regular angels, either. They looked just like ladies you might see on the street in Ambient. Except for the wings poking out of their shirts and dresses.

Some folks laughed at the Circle of Faith, it was true, but no one could deny all the work these women did. They planted flower gardens at the nursing home in summer and ran a Women's Crisis hot line ten hours every week. They'd organized crime watches in downtown Ambient, day care at the fertilizer plant. It was said that tragedy could bring out the best in a person, and in Ruthie's case, that certainly was so. She was always cheerful, always smiling. "The best cure for trouble is helping someone else with theirs," she'd told Big Roly more than once. Over seven years had passed since the day Tom Mader was found dead beside the road; the coroner had counted one hundred broken bones. For weeks afterward, church leaders asked their congregations to pray for the hit-and-run driver, that he or she might have the courage to step forward. But no one ever did. Big Roly figured it had been one of the new people, maybe a tourist, somebody passing through.

"Roland!" Ruthie said, as if the very sight of him had just made her day. The room was covered with piles of clothing, sorted according to size. Stan Pranke's wife, Lorna, and Maya Paluski were busy folding everything into boxes, while Ruthie's daughter, Cherish, ironed a pile of shirts. Cherish Mader was so goddamn beautiful it hurt Big Roly's eyes to look at her. But he stared at her anyway, for just a few months earlier, he could have sworn he'd seen her behind the McDonald's with some tough-looking kids, digging through the dumpster for the warm bags of burgers the kitchen tossed at closing time. They scattered at the sight of his Lincoln, dropping foaming cans of Pabst. Big Roly notified Mel Rooney; still, the manager complained he'd arrive in the morning to find the parking lot littered with wrappers. Once, he'd padlocked the dumpster, but the lock got shot clean off. It had crossed Big Roly's mind that he might be forced to pay for a security guard, someone who'd be visible in the evenings and on weekends. It made him angry just to think about that extra expense.

"Hello, Mr. Schmitt," Cherish said politely. She met his gaze without flinching. Perhaps it had been another girl he'd seen. The parking lot had been dark. And Cherish Mader—it just didn't figure. No one had a negative word to say about the girl. When she wasn't at church on Sundays, she was right here at the Faith house, helping her mother out.

"Morning, Cherish," Big Roly said. "Ruthie. Ladies. Any of you seen my daughter under one of these piles?"

"She's in back, helping herself to a doughnut," Ruthie said. "You're welcome to do the same. The Salvation Army closes at noon, and we're rushing to get these things over there."

"Lorna made those doughnuts from scratch," Maya said with admiration. She wore paint-spattered bib overalls, like a man, and if you asked why she'd never married, she'd tell you women needed men like fish needed bicycles. It was the sort of thing Suzette found amusing.

"My mother's recipe," Lorna said, pleased. *She* wore a nice blue pantsuit, a sparkly pin in the lapel. "Cinnamon and sugar."

"That so?" Big Roly said, hiking up his belt. He tried not to eat sweets in public, because of his size. It embarrassed him to be caught smacking his lips over some dainty confection. "Nonsense," Suzette always said. She, too, tended toward the heavier side of the spectrum, but if she wanted to walk over to the Dairy Queen for a banana split, that's what she did. Sometimes Big Roly worried about Christina: Right now she was slender as a willow, but perhaps their fatty genes were ticking inside her like a bomb. Ruefully, he looked down at his belly. By tilting forward slightly, he could see the tips of his boots. Perhaps he'd lost a few pounds. He could taste that doughnut, the buttery slush moving over and under his tongue.

" 'Fraid I'll have to pass," he said.

Christina marched in from the back room, her mouth full of doughnut. "They're still warm," she said blissfully, sputtering crumbs.

"Say thank you," Big Roly said.

"Thank you." Powdered sugar drifted down the front of her jacket. "Why don't you eat that outside?" Maya said, in a voice that made Big Roly remember she taught school. "We've spent the past two weeks washing these things."

"OK," Christina said. "I'm going to look for angels."

"Isn't she sweet," Ruthie said.

"Keep back from the highway," Big Roly said. "And don't go too far into the field."

Cherish told Christina, "There's a fort back under the hickory trees. Me and a friend used to play there when we were kids."

"Cool," Christina said, and she headed out the door.

"I remember that fort," Ruthie said. "You and Lisa Marie spent hours out there." Cherish didn't answer; Big Roly watched her flip the shirt she was ironing with a light, practiced movement of her hands. Christ, that girl was a knockout! Long black hair falling halfway down her back. High cheekbones. Full red mouth. She was the spitting image of her grandmother Gwendolyn, whose looks had gotten her in trouble way back when Big Roly was barely old enough to understand the whispered talk. Now he was thinking it *was* Cherish he'd seen behind the McDonald's. And yet how could that be? He remembered how Tom used to show Cherish off in that rusty little Bobcat, mail lights flashing. He'd bring her along on his Saturday route; if you came out onto the doorstep, she'd run right up with your mail. People shook their heads a little at a man who'd give his daughter a name like Cherish, but that was Tom; it was just how he was. He loved that girl, loved her as much as Big Roly loved—

—dread lapped the edges of his heart. But nothing was going to happen to him, or Suzette. Nothing was going to happen to Christina.

"I do believe I'll try one of those doughnuts," he said.

By the time he returned from the back room, still licking powdered sugar and cinnamon from his lips, Cherish was holding the door for the women, who were busy loading the taped-up boxes into Lorna's minivan. Big Roly helped, trying not to huff. Across the street, beneath the Riveredge marquee, a man sifted through the trash people had thrown from their cars. His face was copper-colored from wind, anonymous as a penny, but the whites of his eyes were curiously bright when he looked up to watch Big Roly watching him. Big Roly glanced out into the field, but Christina was circling one of the hickory trees, whacking it with a stick.

Lorna's van was full, so they moved on to Maya's Escort. Still, there were three big boxes left, and as Maya and Lorna pulled away, Big Roly found himself volunteering to drop them off.

"I'll just throw 'em in my trunk," he said. "I pass almost right by there on my way to Ambient." As he spoke, he glanced back at the marquee. Now the man was leaning against the pole the marquee was mounted on; it shook a little whenever he shifted his weight. Big Roly thought again about the possibility of a security guard—not that he'd use that title. *Greeter*, maybe. *Welcomer*. Some nice retired person in a bow tie and a trim uniform, who'd say hello and help with packages and discourage loitering. This wasn't the first time he'd seen drifters at this intersection, begging change from shoppers, aiming thumbs toward the I-90/ 94 split.

"That'll save me the trip," Cherish said, more to her mother than Big Roly. "I need to work on a paper for school."

Ruthie said, "We don't want to inconvenience Mr. Schmitt."

And though, in fact, it wasn't exactly on his way, he said, "It's no inconvenience."

"So I'm done, then?" Cherish said. "I can go?" Big Roly looked at her. Her face was the same smooth beautiful mask. But there was something in her voice that reminded him of a dog whining at the door to get out. That high, straining note.

"But, honey, you promised to work on the mural."

"I know, but I have a paper," Cherish said. "History."

Ruthie sighed. "OK. Just be back to pick me up at two."

"Keep the car—I'll walk," Cherish said, and she started across the parking lot, zipping her coat.

"I don't like you walking by the highway," Ruthie said. "Cherish? Take the car."

Cherish was walking backward. She took a pair of mittens from her coat pocket, jammed her hands into them like boxing gloves. "But Lisa Marie is picking me up."

"What are you going to do with Lisa Marie?"

"I told you," Cherish said. "We're working on this paper, OK?" She spun around and kept right on walking. Ruthie sighed, a quiet, helpless sound, and Big Roly was embarrassed for her.

"Teenagers," he said foolishly. What did he know about it? But Ruthie nodded.

"It's a hard age," she said. "That's what everybody tells me. And she misses her father so. More than she used to, it seems to me. Though she won't talk to me about it."

Big Roly didn't know what to say.

"She was so good about everything after he died. When people offered condolences, she'd say, *My daddy is living with God.* A child's faith is truly something to witness."

"That it is," Big Roly said awkwardly.

"Well," Ruthie said. "I suppose I should fetch you that rent."

She led him into the small back room, where her desk was wedged between the refrigerator and the wall. There was a hot plate, and a microwave too; a space heater stood beside the bathroom door. All these things had been donated, and Big Roly felt a small bubble of guilt when she pulled the cash box out of the top drawer and began counting out fives and singles. True, he was renting this place at a fraction of what he could get for it, but that was a result of the verbal agreement she'd given him two years earlier. She'd taken out a second mortgage on her land— one hundred acres running alongside the Onion River—and when Big Roly heard about it, it didn't take much to put two and two together. She had Tom's pension from the post office, sure, and a small income from renting out her fields, but Cherish was probably looking at college, and taxes had just gone up and were set to go up again. Ruthie made a few dollars from her sheep; in addition to selling the meat, she sheared them, carded the wool, and spun it into rough, beautiful yarn she used to make sweaters and scarves and blankets she sold in the craft tent at the summer festival. She tended a huge vegetable garden; made and sold wine from each fall crop of grapes; kept a roadside stand in the summer, stocked with apple butter, spiced pears or tomatoes, homemade cheese from her nanny goats, fresh eggs from her Rhode Island reds, ground-cherry pies. Ten dollars here, five dollars there—clearly, Ruthie's financial condition was troubled.

So Big Roly stopped by one day, sat down on the couch in Ruthie's living room, and drank the tangy rose hip tea she served him. The old dog Mule sprawled at his feet, groaning with dreams; the cats blinked sleepily along the windowsills; the good thick odor of baking bread wafted in from the kitchen; but as she talked, Big Roly took in the cracked plaster over the fireplace mantel, the patched front window, the sound of the utility room toilet running nonstop, and the faint musty odor he knew meant a problem with the septic tank. He observed the paintings Cherish had done over the years—inspirational scenes, mostly, with a couple–three sunny landscapes—and noted that all were unframed, stuck to the walls with pushpins. If Ruthie was forced to sell—and he understood she did not intend to—but. If she was *forced*, she would come to him, let him work out a civilized offer. Keep everything simple. Quiet. In exchange, she could have the gas station for her ladies' meetings for fifty dollars a month. It was just an agreement between old friends, he assured her, nothing anyone else needed to know about. Especially not the city, he'd thought to himself. Buddy Lewis had reported the council wanted to purchase land for a second public park; if the Mader farmstead went on the open market, eminent domain gave them first dibs. So Big Roly stuck out his hand to shake on the agreement, and then Ruthie said, perfectly friendly, "You'll never get this land."

And, perfectly friendly, he said back, "What makes you so certain?"

"Because I'm going to pray for a miracle," she said, and the way that she said it, he believed it might be true. Part of him hoped it *would* be true—he had no desire for Ruthie Mader to experience any more unhappiness. He even felt a small flutter of joy when, last year, she'd won that Bingo pot. But he could afford his joy, his generosity. She was only delaying the inevitable. And gracious God—that river view, barely a mile beyond the city!

That gentle swell where her house and outbuilding stood, high enough to be out of the floodplain! Those fields sloping gradually down to the water, cleared and sown with sweet peas—unbuildable floodlands, of course, but scenic as all hell. Big Roly had already spoken to an architect. The condos would be tasteful, authentic to the "river town theme" the City Council itself had told the Planning and Zoning Commission to encourage.

When Ruthie turned and held out the money, Big Roly took it, and the little bubble of guilt went *ping* and disappeared. "You still praying for that miracle?" he said, quite sincerely, and she said, "Absolutely." Big Roly could not imagine believing, with such certainty, that God or anybody else was out there listening to your prayers.

"What else are you ladies praying for these days?"

"A little of this, a little of that," Ruthie said. It was what she always answered. Big Roly had heard that the women discussed deeply personal things. It was said that they had visions, even talked with the dead. Every now and then, they'd hold an evening meeting, and when they got to praying and singing, you could hear them halfway to the highway bridge and back.

"I guess I better be going," he said. "Me and Christina got a long day ahead of us."

Ruth nodded at the window. "Look at her," she said. Out in the field, Christina stood beneath the trees, staring up into the dead black branches. How small she was against the backdrop of all that white, beneath the wide blue cradle of the sky! Yet in six years, she'd be driving for real. In eight years, she'd be gone. Somehow eight years didn't seem as long a time to Big Roly as it once would have.

"When Cherish was that age," Ruthie said, "we'd walk to the cemetery every Sunday after Mass. We'd take turns telling Tom everything that had happened during the week, and so I heard what Cherish was doing at school, and with her friends, and around the house—in a way, I knew her better than if Tom had been alive.''

"She sure is a pretty girl," Big Roly said, hoping this was the right thing to say. "Prettiest Festival Queen we ever had."

"That's when she started seeing this new boy, Randy," Ruthie said. "I don't think he's good for her. She hardly talks to me anymore."

"Aw, Ruthie," Roly said helplessly. He wasn't any good at conversations like these. He thought of telling her he'd seen Cherish behind the McDonald's, then dismissed the thought. The worst thing you could do in a situation like this was get involved. And besides, maybe it hadn't been her. It couldn't have been. "A pretty girl like that, she'll have another boyfriend soon. You wanna get the door while I carry these boxes out?"

Outside, he dropped the boxes into the trunk. The man wasn't under the marquee anymore; Big Roly glanced up and down the highway, but he was gone. Vanished. Big Roly hit the horn, waved Christina toward him, patted his pockets for his gloves. In spite of the sunshine, it was damn cold. So much, he thought, for all that global warming hoopla.

"Hurry up, Scootie!" he called, waving again, and he was about to get into the Lincoln to wait for her there, out of the wind, when he was struck, again, by how small she looked, how insignificant. Vulnerable. Like a field mouse or a rabbit. And with that thought, his gaze swept the sky, looking for the hawk. A terrible fear rose in his throat. "Come on!" he shouted, and he began walking toward the edge of the parking lot where the snowmobile path led out into the field. But this was ridiculous. She was absolutely safe. No predator would plummet from the sky and snatch her away. No drunken teenagers or drifting men would carry her off in broad daylight. No lightning could strike in the middle of winter. He surprised himself by breaking into a wild, clumsy run. She reached the edge of the parking lot just as he did, and he wrapped her in his arms, amazed by the sudden, solid safety of her body, living and real and whole.

"You must be half froze," he said into her hair, trying to disguise his emotion.

"I think I saw an angel!" Christina said. "I think I maybe saw one in the trees!"

"I think I'm maybe seeing one right now," Big Roly said, and he kissed her hard on the forehead, smothering her giggles. The field looked no different than it always did. In the distance, at the slumbering construction site, the jaws of the crane swung slightly in the wind. There was nothing in the sky, nothing coming down the road. The wind felt warmer too. It was a lovely, clear March day.

Ridiculous, Big Roly thought.

To the Editor:

My wife and I came up from Chicago last weekend in order to relax in a peaceful and scenic environment. Saturday afternoon, we walked around the downtown and fed the ducks in the park, feeling as though we'd stepped into a Norman Rockwell painting. Our accommodations at the Moonwink Motel, while far from luxurious, were adequate, and we settled in for what we thought would be a good night's rest. Imagine our surprise when we heard squealing tires and profanity just outside our window. Apparently, the parking lot is a gathering spot for drunken youths. When we called the front desk to complain, these youths revved their engines and drove away, only to return an hour later, radios blasting. You wouldn't want to print what they said to me when I went outside to reason with them. Does Ambient not have a police department? Does its Mayor not care what kind of impression Ambient makes to those who would patronize its businesses? We will not be back, and we will let others know of our experience here.

Sincerely,

Dr. & Mrs. Robert J. Barrington
Lake Forest, IL

—From the Ambient Weekly
April 1991

s i x

Cherish Mader sat at her bedroom desk, physics textbook
open, waiting for her mother to leave. It was Saturday night, one
week before Easter, and Ruthie had an eight o'clock meeting at
the Faith house. But at a quarter till, she knocked on Cherish's
door. Cherish braced herself and said, "Come in."

It was always the same thing. Ruthie would sit on Cherish's
bed and chatter on about nothing until Cherish wanted to scream.
Then she'd ask if anything had been on Cherish's mind. "You
seem so quiet lately," she'd say. "You're always up in your
room."

And Cherish would say, "Homework. You know."

And that would be the end of it.

But tonight Ruthie said, "I know you're busy, but you've been
promising to finish the Faith house mural since the beginning of
the year. Maybe tomorrow?"

"Maybe," Cherish said. "I'll see how much schoolwork I get
done tonight." She truly hated that mural; it had been Maya Paluski's idea in the first place. Of course, Maya stuck Cherish with
Jesus and reserved the angels for herself. There just wasn't much

you could do with Jesus—people had certain expectations. So Cherish's Jesus was turning out pretty much like all the others she'd seen. He had good muscle tone. His skin was bare and shiny, as if he'd been shaved and dipped in oil. His loincloth was draped just so, with nothing bulging underneath it. His face and hands and feet were still blank spaces: Cherish kept saying she needed more time. How was she supposed to know what Jesus' face looked like? And the wounds in his hands and feet—gross. They'd have to be life-size. Big as dimes.

"Physics," Ruthie said, glancing at the open textbook, and she shook her head. "Sounds difficult."

"It's OK," Cherish said.

And Ruthie said, "There's something else. Sweetheart? Lisa Marie's mother called. She says that last Saturday night Lisa Marie went to Milwaukee without permission. With her boyfriend."

"She did?" Cherish said.

"She says you and Randy were with them."

"Lisa Marie said that?" Cherish tried to keep her voice steady.

"No," Ruthie said. "But Mrs. Kirsch seems to think it's a possibility."

"I was here last Saturday," Cherish said. "Studying. I told you good night, remember?"

"I know," Ruthie said. "But I promised I'd speak to you." She paused. "Lisa Marie came home quite upset. Something about Randy. Drinking too much, that kind of thing."

"He's not like that around me," Cherish said. "Maybe with other people, though. I'll ask him about it."

They looked at each other.

"Well," Ruthie said. "I'll see Mrs. Kirsch at the meeting tonight, and I'll tell her I spoke with you."

"OK," Cherish said, but when Ruthie reached the doorway, she said, "Mom? You would have heard me take the car. Or if someone had picked me up, you would have heard them in the driveway.''

"I know," Ruthie said. "Don't worry about it. I just want you to remember . . ." She paused again. "If anything ever should come up, I'm always here for you. You can talk to me. About anything."

"I know," Cherish said. "Have a good meeting."

Cherish watched from the window until the sorrowful red eyes of her mother's taillights disappeared down the driveway. Then she shut her physics book with a slam and tried to decide what to do. It didn't sound like Lisa Marie had ratted them out, not exactly, but still. She'd have to call Randy. Something had to be done. She rolled a fat doobie, sucked the bitter smoke deep into her lungs, holding it, holding it, concentrating on the rows of dolls that lined her bedroom walls. Barbies and Mrs. Beasleys. Raggedy Anns and Cabbage Patch Kids. Betsy Wetsys and Love Me Tenders and even Snow White with all seven of her dwarfs, still in their original boxes. Her mother had been giving her dolls ever since she could remember. It didn't seem to matter that she was seventeen, that she'd stopped liking dolls a long time ago. The smaller dolls stood erect on tiny stands, steel rods stiffening their plastic spines. Others lolled in bassinets and cradles, rode in miniature strollers, slept, sucked thumbs, fingered real human hair. Some wore hats and elaborate dresses and intricate leather shoes. Some could cry or crawl or eat, but most of them simply stared straight ahead, smiling their manicured smiles: empty, symmetrical, perfect.

Cherish exhaled. Sweet smoke circled her head. When she was a little girl, people often said she looked just like a doll, and she'd think of her dolls' cool plastic cheeks, the unnatural paleness of their skin. She'd stare at her face in the bathroom mirror; it seemed normal enough to her. She wondered what it was that people saw when they looked at her, and they always seemed to be looking at her, exchanging remarks in hushed voices, whispering into the backs of their hands. She'd never forget the day her mother caught her in front of the mirror—it must have been just after Dad died. Vanity was sinful, Ruthie had explained. Cherish's beauty, like all things, was a gift from God, a tool to be put to good use for His honor and glory, did Cherish understand? Cherish hadn't known what to say. Before that moment, she'd never realized she was beautiful.

She smoked the rest of the joint down to its dusty tip. The pot had been a gift from Randy; he'd tucked it into the plastic-lined makeup bag she kept in her locker at school. Nobody dared slip Randy Hale anything less than grade A. Randy wasn't someone you messed with. He was captain of the wrestling team, an all-state middleweight champion. Once, when somebody parked him in at school, he and Paul Zuggenhagen picked up the back end of that person's car and dropped it, picked it up again and dropped it, until they had bounced it to the edge of the lot and wedged it between two trees. Cherish thought it was the funniest thing she'd ever seen. That was Lisa Marie's biggest problem. She had no sense of humor. She took everything too seriously. Cherish tore a piece of paper out of her notebook, scrawled: *Went to bed. Hope the meeting went well.* She taped the note to the outside of her bedroom door, set the door lock from the inside, and pulled it shut behind her; she'd pick the lock with a bobby pin when she got home. Downstairs, she phoned Randy, told him to fetch Paul and meet her at Lisa Marie's.

"Give me time to talk to her first," she said. "Promise?"

Dad's old dog, Mule, was lying under the kitchen table; he whined and thumped his tail. Cherish hung up, reached down, and smoothed back his ears. She found a flashlight in the drawer. Then she bundled up in her winter coat and boots. Out of habit, she checked the burners and the coffeepot to make sure everything was off. It was time to find out what, exactly, was going on. Almost a week had passed since Lisa Marie had been saved at the Blessed Victory Church of Christ Alive! Lisa Marie had been saved before, but this time Cherish was worried it might stick. She'd heard that Lisa Marie had actually taken a vow of chastity. She'd heard that Lisa Marie had stopped drinking and smoking. She'd broken up with Paul Zuggenhagen too, though Cherish suspected this was something she'd been wanting to do long before the night they'd gone to Milwaukee and things had kind of gotten out of hand.

What had happened was this: The four of them had gone to a sports bar called the Alley Cat, where Randy had heard that no one was ever carded and Paul had heard the Brewers came to drink. They'd crushed into a back booth, ordered hot wings and double shots of tequila. "Time for some body shots," Randy said, and Cherish leaned back, unbuttoned her shirt, let him lick a line of salt from the tops of her breasts.

Paul turned to Lisa Marie, but she crossed her arms firmly over her chest. "No way," she said. "Somebody's going to see."

"Tough luck," Randy said, thumping Paul on the shoulder. "But hey—if you're nice, maybe Cherry'll share." He gave Cherish a shove in Paul's direction, and the rest of the salt tumbled down her shirt.

"Fuck you," Cherish said, but she was laughing. She could feel how both Paul and Randy were looking at her throat, at the warm tops of her breasts. She did not look at Lisa Marie as she accidentally-on-purpose let another button of her shirt fall open.

"All right, I'll do it, I'll do it," Lisa Marie said. "But just on my arm, OK? You guys are going to get us thrown out."

"On her *arm*," Randy said.

"C'mon," Paul said. "Live a little."

"On my wrist, then," Lisa Marie said miserably.

"On her *wrist*," Randy hooted. "Paul, how can you stand it? This girl is a nympho. I want her for myself."

Paul blushed, glared at Lisa Marie. "I wish you'd relax once in a while," he said. But Randy wasn't finished with her yet. As soon as Paul had licked her wrist clean, Randy pinned her hand to the table and put his tongue to the wet trail where Paul's had been. Lisa Marie screamed, Paul yelped, "Jesus!" and that was when the manager asked to see ID.

They should have just laughed the whole thing off. They should have driven around for a while, found another bar. Or they should have ended up at Randy's house, the way they often did. His mom and stepdad went to bed early; they had to get up at four to make the commute to their jobs in Milwaukee. But Lisa Marie was angry, angrier than Cherish had ever known her to be. "Take me home," she said, not even bothering to wait until they'd left the Alley Cat. "I've had enough of this juvenile bullshit. Every weekend it's the same damn story, and I'm sick of it, sick to death of it."

"Don't hold back," Randy said. "Feel free to express your feelings," and right there where everyone in the Alley Cat could see, Lisa Marie punched him in the solar plexus, hard enough to make him gasp and take a step back.

"Take me home," Lisa Marie yelled again, and all the people watching applauded and cheered. Still, Randy recovered himself, held the door for her like a gentleman. "After you," he said, but clearly he was pissed. Who wouldn't have been? Paul was angry too. Lisa Marie had embarrassed them, all of them, right there in front of a roomful of strangers. Cherish couldn't help but agree when Randy mouthed *bitch* as Lisa Marie stormed past.

Cherish let herself out of the house. In the distance, a train was passing; its bold light swept over the darkness, scorched the icy surface of the river. It was two miles to Lisa Marie's house in Ambient, and she usually could make it there in half an hour. She might even beat her mother back home; evening meetings often went well past midnight. They were held only when the

Circle was praying for something particularly urgent, but Cherish knew better than to ask what tonight's concern was. Not that she cared. Not anymore. Since she'd started seeing Randy, she hadn't had much interest in her mother's religious activities. Religious activities of any kind, for that matter. Her mother, of course, had no idea. She still thought Cherish was the same little girl who'd loved her doll collection, who'd begged to wear flowery dresses that matched her mother's, who'd confided every thought, every secret. Ruthie often told people that she and Cherish were more like sisters than mother and daughter. Ruthie couldn't wait for Cherish to turn eighteen so she could join the Circle of Faith.

Back when Faith meetings still were held in the living room, Cherish had sometimes squeezed behind the couch to eavesdrop. Mostly the women just talked about somebody's job or illness, but sometimes they'd talk about people Cherish knew. Every now and then, they talked about Cherish's father, and when that happened Cherish held particularly still. Once, Ruthie told the group she'd had a revelation: Trouble was God's way of getting people's attention. "When life is fine, we ignore Him," she said. "It's when we're in pain that we reach out. I've come to realize that even tragedy has its purpose." The others agreed that this made sense, but Cherish thought, *Just because it makes sense doesn't mean it's true.* How did you know you weren't simply seeing what you *wanted* to see? Like what had happened at Dad's funeral, when Cherish saw the coffin move very slightly, as if Dad had only been sleeping and now he was trying to sit up. Ruthie explained, in her most patient voice, that Cherish's brain was giving her eyes happy pictures to see so that she wouldn't be sad, and that was called imagination, and imagination was a good thing, but you had to know the difference between imagination and truth. Cherish tried to listen to what her mother was saying, but all she could think of was how it would be when they opened the coffin and Dad jumped out and said, *What on earth is going on here?* "Ask them to open it," she pleaded, "just in case," and Ruthie finally said, in a totally different voice, "Some of him isn't even in there; they're still hunting pieces by the road, do you understand!"

Lucy Kimmeldorf had taken Cherish's hand and led her outside, past all those people—more than five hundred, the *Ambient Weekly* would say—who'd come to pay their respects. Later, at the burial, Ruthie hadn't cried a single tear, and the mothers of Cherish's school friends all told Cherish how brave Ruthie was, and soon they were saying the same thing about Cherish, for whenever they asked how she was doing, she answered the way Ruthie told her to: *It's selfish to be sad when Dad's so happy in heaven.*

The fact was that after her father died, lots of things stopped making sense to Cherish. Familiar things became unfamiliar. The house seemed smaller, the fields larger, the sky as pale as a bowl of weak soup. Yet she acted as if things were the way they'd always been, and her mother did the same. Year after year, they woke up in the morning and went to bed at night, attended Mass, did farmwork, housework, charity work. They visited the cemetery Sunday afternoons, and when they happened to pass the small white cross on County O, they each made the sign of the cross as they drove by.

Cherish was seven years older than she'd been the last time her father had seen her. Sometimes she wondered if he'd even recognize her. Sometimes she wondered if she'd recognize him. Now, cutting across the frozen field toward County O, she pulled up the hood of her coat. With her scarf concealing everything but her eyes, she was completely, deliciously anonymous. No one who happened to see her would recognize last summer's Festival Queen, the beautiful doll everyone admired: active in charity work and school fund-raisers, upbeat and cheerful, confident, outgoing. The brave girl whose father had died a terrible, pointless death. Ruthie Mader's daughter.

Ruthie never suspected that Cherish was sneaking out this way, night after night, walking to town. Often, Cherish only had to make it through the field to where Randy would be waiting in his Mustang, the thud of the bass from his stereo like a living, beating heart. Sometimes, after sex, he'd push his face between her breasts, breathe deeply, whisper, "Precious." *Precious.* As Cherish turned north onto County C, following the plow drifts along the shoulder, she imagined Randy speaking her name. Randy lighting a joint, releasing the smoke into her mouth. Randy moving wet between her thighs. Her breathing sounded hollow inside her hood, as if she were walking under water. The wind gusted at her chest. When you were with Randy, anything might happen. Anything was possible.

That night, driving home from Milwaukee, Randy started mimicking Lisa Marie, talking about how everything was *juvenile bullshit*, how *every damn weekend was the same damn thing*. By the time they reached the Solomon strip, Paul and Cherish were laughing too. He took the D road over to Ambient, but instead of turning south onto Main, where Lisa Marie lived, he continued on to the River Road. The whole time, Lisa Marie stared out the window. She refused to look at any of them, to speak.

"A girl needs a little excitement once in a while," Randy said, making his voice high and silly.

"A girl needs variety," Paul added from the backseat, "not just the same old juvenile bullshit."

Randy laughed so hard that the car swerved across the yellow line, and Cherish had to grab the wheel to steady it. She felt sorry for Lisa Marie, but at the same time, she didn't. The truth was that none of them really liked Lisa Marie that much anymore. She was always getting her feelings hurt, leaving parties early, complaining about Paul and Randy. She worried that things were getting too wild, that her parents were going to find out.

"We're sorry, Lisa Marie," Randy said. "Really. Let us make it up to you." He turned into one of the residential neighborhoods north of Cradle Park and drove up and down the streets, slowly, as if he were looking for something. "I know!" he said, snapping his fingers dramatically. "We'll get you a present. Something special. Something that will make this a night to remember."

"What about one of those fat ladies?" Paul said. They were passing a small brick bungalow. A plywood woman was bent over beside the mailbox, as if she were planting flowers in the snow, her fanny aimed at the road. The headlights bleached her panties a brilliant, blinding white. "Come on, Lisa Marie. Lighten up. You want us to get you one of those?"

Cherish said, "Yeah, let's collect a whole bunch. We can stick them in front of the railroad museum."

Randy pulled over beside the mailbox, looked back at Lisa Marie. "Do you accept our apology?"

"Just say yes," Paul pleaded. "Seriously. We were just kidding around."

The whole thing could have ended there. But Lisa Marie said nothing.

"Guess not," Randy said. "Lisa Marie is holding out for something better. A lady of taste, our Lisa Marie."

"Aw, cut it out," Paul said. He sounded tired of the game. Cherish was too, and she said, "Let's just take her home." But Randy ignored them both. "Our Lisa Marie won't settle for any old reproduction. Our Lisa Marie demands the real thing."

Paul got very quiet then. "What do you mean?" he said.

Randy pulled away and continued down the street. Behind each living room window, the blue square of a TV screen poured its odd, insistent light into the darkness. Sleds and hunchbacked snowmen were scattered over the lawns. They passed a woman out for a walk, enjoying the quietness of the evening. It was early still. Barely nine o'clock.

"I think you know what I mean," Randy said.

"Wait a minute," Paul said, "You said last time was *it;* you promised."

"What are you talking about?" Cherish said.

"You're going to get us arrested, man."

"Our Lisa Marie is worth the risk, don't you think?" Randy said, and he rounded the corner, where two little girls were standing beneath a streetlight. The oldest was eleven or so, and she wore a woolly stocking cap with a tassel on the end. Randy threw the car in park, and like something in a dream, he slid from behind the wheel, leaped the curb, and had one steel arm around her before she or the younger girl understood what was happening. Paul jumped out then and held the door, calling, "Hurry, hurry," as Randy half carried, half dragged the girl the last few feet, her stocking cap pulled down over her eyes. "Quiet and no one gets hurt," he said, and she tumbled in against Lisa Marie. Paul squished in beside her, Randy got behind the wheel again, doors slammed and locked, and off they went—it was as simple as that. The younger girl watched them go, stock-still, as if she thought she might have imagined the whole thing.

"Are you crazy?" Cherish said. She couldn't believe they'd just kidnapped somebody. "What are we going to do with her?"

The girl had her arms wrapped around herself; she breathed loudly through her mouth. The ridiculous tassel bounced against one shoulder.

"That's up to Lisa Marie," Randy said.

Lisa Marie was crying. "Let her go," she said.

Randy said, "What? You don't like your present? After all the trouble we went through? I thought you wanted some excite-

ment, sweetheart. I thought you wanted a night to remember."
But after another block or two, he pulled over, let the little girl
out. She fled between two houses; Lisa Marie jumped out and
ran down the street.

"Lisa Marie!" Paul called after her, but Randy pulled him back
inside. A porch light flickered on. "Don't worry," Randy said,
peeling away. "She'll get over it."

But Lisa Marie hadn't gotten over it. Instead she'd gone to her
mother, just as Cherish had worried she might do. She'd been
avoiding Paul and Randy and even Cherish ever since. And when
she opened the door and saw Cherish standing on the steps, she
looked anything but pleased.

"Hey," Cherish said. "I was worried about you. What's going on?"

"Nothing," Lisa Marie said. She was wearing sweatpants and a
stained sweatshirt. Her hair looked unwashed, her permanent
frizzy.

"Nice hair," Cherish said. "Aren't you going to ask me in?"

"OK," Lisa Marie said doubtfully, but she led Cherish down
the hall to the kitchen, where she opened the oven door. A frozen
cheese pizza bubbled on the top rack, releasing its greasy smells.
"This'll be ready in five minutes," she said.

"Great," Cherish said. "Afterward, maybe we can take a walk
down to Cradle Park, see who's there."

"It's freezing out," Lisa Marie said, setting out paper plates.
"I'm staying in."

"Or we could find a ride out to International Harvester."
There was usually a party going on at IH, and if your feet
started going numb, you simply built a fire out of the cardboard
boxes, paper, and furniture that people dumped there. Cherish
hoped that Lisa Marie would suggest they call Randy and Paul
to drive them. Then she could tell her that, well, actually they
were already on their way. Things would get back to normal.

She could stop worrying about what Lisa Marie might tell her mother next.

But Lisa Marie shook her head. "I'm done with all that," she said. "I know it sounds hokey, but I've been washed by the blood of the lamb. If you want to hang out with me, you're going to have to respect that." She laid out two forks, two knives, a couple of potholders. "My mom left a couple of movies," she said. "We can watch them, if you want."

"Movies," Cherish said. "Oh, boy."

"We used to watch movies together all the time," Lisa Marie said. "We used to do our homework together. We used to help our moms with stuff at the Faith house. We used to date boys who didn't get us thrown out of every place we went."

"And we used to complain about how boring it all was," Cherish said.

"Well, maybe it was boring then," Lisa Marie said. "But it's different, now that I've found God."

Cherish stared at Lisa Marie. It was like talking to a complete and total stranger. Before Lisa Marie got saved, they might have risked hitching out to the Hodag, flirted with some old married guy until he shared his pitcher. They might have met up with Randy and Paul to set off firecrackers in the millpond, or else to get blasted in the parking lot of the Moonwink Motel, or else to play mailbox baseball along the River Road. Sometimes they'd race the freight train across the tracks just past the highway bridge; sometimes they combed the fast-food dumpsters after closing, gorging on bags of cheeseburgers and lukewarm apple pies. Sometimes there'd be parties at the homes of kids whose parents were away. But now God sat between them, the same way he sat between Cherish and her mother: an immense, warty toad, bloated with importance.

"There's this story," Lisa Marie finally said, "about this little boy who always takes five minutes to ride his bike to church before school. Every day, he kneels down at the back of the church and says, *Hello, God, this is*—" Lisa Marie stopped. "Wait, I can't remember his name."

"Timmy," Cherish said. "I know this one."

"*Hello, God, this is Timmy.*" Lisa Marie didn't seem to care if Cherish knew the story or not. "That's all Timmy ever says, and he does this for, I don't know, years. Then one day, as he's biking away, he gets hit by a car. And as people gather around his lifeless body, they hear a voice, and it says—"

Cherish broke in, making her voice deep and solemn. "Hello, Timmy, this is God."

She waited for Lisa Marie to laugh, but Lisa Marie said, "I'm serious, OK? The point is that if you take time for God, He'll take time for you."

Cherish gave Lisa Marie a flat, disbelieving stare. "Or maybe if you take time for God, He'll shove you under a car."

"That's not what it means, and you know it," Lisa Marie said.

The pizza, which had smelled so good just moments before, now smelled like the slab of bubbling fat that it was. Cherish said, "I can't believe anyone would be stupid enough to believe a story like that."

"It's a *story*," Lisa Marie said. "It's not supposed to be, like, literal or anything." She finished setting the table, then began slapping dirty dishes from the sink into the dishwasher. Cherish couldn't remember the first time she'd heard the Little Timmy story, but as a child she'd loved it, begged her mother to tell it over and over. She'd sit in her mother's lap, her forehead tucked into the notch of Ruthie's neck and shoulder, feeling the soothing vibrations of her mother's voice. Then, she could not have imagined a time when she wouldn't believe that story, any more than she could have imagined a time she wouldn't be close to her mother. Mornings, she'd linger in bed just to hear the happy music of Ruthie making breakfast in her breezy kitchen, the bacon's sizzle and spat, the sound of the back door opening as Ruthie let the cats in and the whining dogs out. Next came the sound of toast being made, the slap of the jelly jar on the table. The crack of eggs stolen from the quarreling hens. The splash of milk from the nanny goats, thick with butterfat, stored in wide-mouthed jars.

Eventually, she'd get up and wash her face, coming down the stairs with her hair parted neatly and tucked behind her ears, her face still wet and smelling of Ivory and already lifted to receive her mother's kiss. Outside, the dogs barked and scuffled to get in. The cats leaped onto the counters, got shooed down again, tangled underfoot. Toast popped up, eggs shimmied in the pan. Suddenly Dad was there to make wet fart noises against the top of Cherish's head. "Daddy!" she groaned, but he was already letting the dogs back in, and the dogs were nosing the cats' rear ends and chasing them round and round, and her mother was filling Dad's plate, then Cherish's, then her own. After breakfast, there were beds to be made, and Ruthie and Cherish made them together, Cherish playing parachute with the sheets. There were dishes to be washed, dust bunnies to be corralled with the hand-made broom, more dust to be wiped from the windowsills. And then it was time for chores, the dogs dashing ahead of them to the barn, doubling back to greet them as if there were no greater happiness than their company. Inside, the nanny goats were already waiting, and as soon as Ruthie shoved the heavy door aside, they'd clamor up onto the milking platform, bleating, blinking their strange gold eyes. Winters, the air was thick with dust and the stinging smell of urine, the odor so intense Cherish had to climb into the sheep pen and pull down her snow pants to pee. There was such pleasure in that. The sheep crowding close and closer, sniffing wetly at the air. The hens clucking tenderly from their roosts. Even now, as Lisa Marie twisted in front of the mirror, Cherish could feel the first warm, brown egg taking shape in her hand. It was enough to bring tears to her eyes, except that Cherish never cried anymore, couldn't have, now, if she'd wanted to. *It's selfish to be sad when Dad's so happy in heaven.* The egg shattered, the yellow yolk popped, the sharp shell stung Cherish's palm. She and Lisa Marie had been best friends ever since second grade. She wanted to apologize for what had happened. Wanted to, but couldn't.

The timer went off like an accusation.

"You want me to get that?" Cherish said, and Lisa Marie said, "I got it," which meant she'd decided she wasn't going to stay mad. They ate pizza and drank Diet Dr Pepper as if everything were just fine between them, talking about what they were going to do after graduation. Lisa Marie planned to continue working at the Wal-Mart, at least for now; she'd been promised a promotion, and her employee stock was doing well. Cherish had been accepted at both UW–Eau Claire and Stevens Point, and Maya Paluski had Ruthie convinced that Cherish should major in art education. But the thought of teaching art to grade schoolers made Cherish want to slit her wrists. The truth was, she didn't even care for drawing and painting anymore. Secretly, she'd decided she wasn't going to college. People were always saying she should be a model; maybe she'd go to New York City, the same way her grandmother had done. Or maybe she'd marry Randy—it was something they'd discussed, though always in a teasing kind of way. "Did you know Randy got another scholarship?" she said. "Some big wrestling university in Texas."

At the mention of Randy's name, Lisa Marie got up and folded her plate into the trash can under the sink.

"Would you lighten up?" Cherish said. "It's not like we hurt that girl. It was just a joke."

Lisa Marie came back with a dishcloth. "The movies are in the living room," she said, and she began wiping off the table, even though Cherish wasn't finished. "There's three of them. You choose."

Cherish took her pizza with her, selected a movie without looking at the title, and shoved it into the VCR. By the time Lisa Marie joined her on the couch, the credits were over, and she could see that this was going to be one of those heartwarming movies about a family that sticks together to overcome its problems.

"You want popcorn?" Lisa Marie said.

"Gee, that would be awesome! And maybe we can put on our pajamas and pierce each other's ears!"

"Fine," Lisa Marie said, and she turned up the volume. "Nobody's forcing you to be here. *You're* the one who showed up at *my* door, remember?"

"I was worried about you," Cherish said. "I *am* worried about you. I'm really sorry about what happened. And so is Randy."

"I don't know what you see in that guy."

"He's fun," Cherish said.

"Fun for you," Lisa Marie said. "Look. I'm tired of pretending I'm having a good time with you guys when I'm not. You're the one who has the good time. You're the one they're both attracted to." She sighed. "The only reason you're here is because you're afraid I'm going to tell someone what happened. Well, I'm not."

Cherish said. "My mom got a call from your mom."

Lisa Marie gnawed on a fingernail. "I didn't tell her anything about you. Only stuff about me. It's part of what you do when you get saved."

They watched the movie for a while. One of the sisters was crying now. The others tried to comfort her, which only made everything worse.

"I suppose I shouldn't tell you this," Lisa Marie said.

"That means you're going to tell me, right?"

Lisa Marie picked at a spot on her sweatshirt. "You probably know about it already."

"What?"

"You probably know the reason why the Circle of Faith is meeting tonight."

Cherish shook her head.

"I heard my mom on the phone with Mrs. Pranke. Unless there's, like, a miracle or something, your mom is selling your farm to that Big Roly guy."

Cherish almost laughed. "No way," she said. "Mom would never do that." Big Roly Schmitt was an asshole. He would come by the Faith house to collect his rent, then eat all the cookies or butter horns or doughnuts that Mrs. Pranke brought to share. Cherish thought he'd seen her trespassing behind the McDonald's once, but if he had, he wasn't saying anything about it.

"She doesn't have a choice," Lisa Marie said. "She's totally in debt. She's planning to move to Solomon after you graduate, use the money from the farm for your college tuition. Not that *you* care."

Cherish didn't say anything.

"Me, if that were my mother, if that were the house I'd grown up in, I'd be down on my knees asking for God's help, but I guess you're above all that."

"Shut up," Cherish said.

For the first time that evening, Lisa Marie looked happy. "Maybe God's trying to teach you a lesson," she said. "People bring hardship on themselves, you know?"

Cherish walked to the front window, looked out at the cold, quiet night. The farm had belonged to her father's parents; her father had grown up there, married there, lived out his whole life. Perhaps that was why the house and barn and the surrounding fields remembered her father far better than Cherish ever could. Sometimes she still heard him outside the kitchen window, playing fetch with the dogs. She smelled his Saturday-night breath whenever she poked her fingers into the pickled-egg jar in the pantry. He took shape in the hall closet, where his winter coat still hung, his smell trapped in the sleeves, and in the welcoming posture of his favorite chair, which, even now, remained in its spot by the window. She still stepped past his rubber barn shoes whenever she went into the milk house, and sometimes, in the mudroom, she'd stare at the bottom of the hamper and, for a split second, see his balled-up athletic socks, bulldog-faced, stiff with dried sweat. Or she'd trace an imaginary necklace of whiskers, delicate as lace, around the bathroom sink. Or, falling asleep, she'd hear him whispering to her mother as they came up the stairs together, and then would come the sunny, silly sound a man makes when it's late and he's tired and he starts to giggle foolishly.

But now even that was being taken from her. And if it happened, when it happened, her mother would quote the Bible, saying they should give thanks in all circumstances, for whatever came to pass was His will. Cherish tried to picture Ruthie in an apartment in Solomon. She tried to imagine how it would be to wake up in the morning without the sounds of the animals, to fall asleep without being rocked in the cradle of the fields. Outside, it was snowing lightly. It was already April, yet it seemed to Cherish that this winter would never end.

"You're really upset about this, aren't you?" Lisa Marie said. "I'm glad to see *something* still matters to you."

And Cherish understood that the two of them would never be friends again, that they hadn't been friends for a long, long time. In fact, they hated each other. The only thing holding them together had been habit. And like any habit, once you'd stepped away enough to look at it objectively, you had to wonder why you'd ever been drawn to it in the first place.

Lisa Marie stood up. She said, "I wouldn't have told you if I'd known you'd be this upset."

"I'm not upset," Cherish said. But she wanted to throw Lisa Marie to the floor, pull her ugly, frizzy hair out by the fistful.

The doorbell rang. Lisa Marie didn't move.

"Aren't you going to get that?" Cherish said.

"I'm not expecting anybody."

"Maybe you are."

"What do you mean?"

Cherish gave her a thin, cold smile. "Maybe I happened to mention to Randy and Paul that I would be here."

"Cherish!"

The doorbell rang again.

"You know they won't give up till you answer it," Cherish said, and with that, Randy and Paul walked into the house just like they used to, just as if nothing had ever happened. "Hi, honey, we're home!" they yelled in unison, crashing down the hallway, through the kitchen, and into the living room, all clomping boots and swinging shoulders and bulky letter jackets.

"Please, come in," Lisa Marie said, sarcastically.

Paul sat down on the couch. "Hey, Lisa Marie, how goes it?"

"The only word you need to remember is *go*," she said, but Randy had already ducked back into the kitchen; they could hear him rummaging through the refrigerator.

"I've missed you," Paul said. "Really. Here, I brought you something." He pulled several bags of Easter candy out of his jacket—bite-size chocolate bunnies, marshmallow chicks, coconut eggs.

"You didn't steal those," Lisa Marie said.

"I paid, don't worry about it," Paul said, looking hurt. "Go on, you can have some."

Randy came back into the room with his mouth full of pizza. He threw an arm about Cherish. "What are we doing tonight?"

"Watching a movie," Lisa Marie said.

"Speak for yourself," Cherish said.

"I've got money for a six-pack," Paul said. "If we can find someone with ID."

But Cherish shook her head, glared at Lisa Marie defiantly. She said, "Let's visit the blind house instead."

"The blind house," Randy said, and he pulled away to stare at her with frank admiration. "Are we up for it?"

"Risky," Paul said, but his tone said he'd consider it.

"Count me out," Lisa Marie said. "I'm not doing any stealing."

"What's wrong with stealing?" Randy said.

"I'm serious," Lisa Marie said. "I'm done with all that."

"Yeah," Cherish said. "She'd rather blab to her mommy."

"I told you," Lisa Marie said. "I didn't tell her anything."

"Not yet anyway," Randy said.

"I swear," Lisa Marie said, and her voice rose nervously. "I won't tell anybody anything, OK?"

"We believe you," Randy said. He was walking around the living room. He paused in front of the window, wiped his pizza fingers on the curtains. There were bookshelves on either side, and he plucked out a leather-bound volume, dropped it on the floor.

"What are you doing?" Lisa Marie said, and she looked at Cherish pleadingly. "Make him stop."

Cherish shrugged. "Maybe God's trying to teach you a lesson."

"Because if you do tell anybody . . ." Randy continued. He picked up a framed picture of Lisa Marie and her mother, hefted it, considering. "We'll all just say it was your idea. Get it?" He dropped the picture. An intricate spiderweb spread over their faces. He picked up a crystal paperweight.

"Please," Lisa Marie said. "Just leave me alone."

Paul said, "You could still come with us. It's not too late to change your mind."

"Yes, it is," Cherish said, and she took the paperweight away from Randy. "She's history. But, Leese, don't forget what you told me."

"What was that?" Randy said.

Cherish smiled. She put her face close to Lisa Marie's. "People bring hardship on themselves."

The snow was falling harder as they fishtailed out of the driveway and shot onto County D, the shortcut to the strip. The perfect fullness of the moon flooded the fields with white, and when Randy's hand cupped the back of her head, Cherish leaned into it like a kiss. She tried to feel bad about Lisa Marie but couldn't, not really. *Maybe God's trying to teach you a lesson.* It was something Ruthie might have said. It was something that, once, Cherish might have believed. But that was like saying to someone who was sick: *God must be punishing you for something.* Or saying to someone who'd just gotten well: *God must be rewarding you.* Things happened or they didn't happen, and God had nothing to do with it. If Dad had arrived at the Neumillers' mailbox one minute later, he'd be alive today. If Cherish had gone with him that day, maybe she'd be dead.

"What's up with Lisa Marie?" Paul said.

"She got saved," Cherish said. "You didn't hear?"

"Saved?" Paul said.

"She's a certified warrior for Christ," Randy said.

Paul didn't smile. "*I've* been saved," he said.

"Yeah, you're a real saint," Cherish said. "Saint Zuggenhagen."

"No, really," Paul said. "I mean, I know I'm not perfect. But I believe that Christ is my savior, don't you?"

They drove along in silence.

Randy said, "No."

Paul said, "But you believe in God, don't you?"

Pink Floyd was playing on the radio; Randy turned it down. "I believe in something. I'm not sure I'd call it God."

"What would you call it, then?" Paul said.

"Lighten up," Cherish interrupted. "If I wanted to listen to this, I'd have stayed with Lisa Marie."

"Well, *you* believe in God, don't you?" Randy said. "What with your mother and all."

"I don't believe in anything." She'd said it just to shock them, but the moment the words left her mouth, she realized they were true. And she felt as if she'd suddenly forgotten the name of the town where she'd lived her whole life. She felt the way she'd felt as a child, saying her name over and over until it lost all meaning. Panicking. Scrambling to find her way back to what was familiar. Cherish.

"Nothing at all?" Paul said.

"That's right," Cherish said.

"So what do you think happens when you die?"

"You die," she said. She swallowed hard. "You rot."

"That's harsh," Randy said.

"You don't mean it," Paul said. "Because if you did, then what would you think about your father? I mean, you believe he's more than worm bait, right? You believe he's in heaven or something."

Cherish thought of her father's grave. She thought of his absent body. She thought of how it was harder and harder to remember him, how lately what she remembered always seemed to be borrowed from a photograph. She thought about how she no longer remembered feelings so much as recalled what she had felt: She'd loved him, admired him, missed him. Valiant, empty words. And it was as if the farm were already sold, the animals auctioned, the house and barn bulldozed, the fields subdivided and developed. Soon not only her father but everything he'd ever worked for would be gone.

"Shut up about her father," Randy said. "Hey, Cherry, you ready for a drink?"

The blind house wasn't really a house; it was a trailer in a park called Shady Acres, which sat behind the Solomon strip, less than a mile from the fertilizer plant. And the couple who lived there weren't blind; they were just old and slept very soundly. Most nights, they were in bed by eight, and they left both their back door and their well-stocked liquor cabinet unlocked, facts leaked by a teenage grandchild. A great cross blossomed in the center of their lawn; it was painted red, white, and blue, and a cloth flag hanging from the lamppost beside it read SALUTE THE FLAG AND KNEEL BEFORE THE CROSS. Though the couple did not go to any local church, they never missed the tent revival that traveled north from Indiana and set up along the banks of the Onion River for a week each August. People spoke in tongues and played tambourines. Cherish had gone with the Circle of Faith when she was young, and it embarrassed her now to remember how she'd clapped and sang too, caught up in the music and the miracles: the crippled man who got up and walked, the woman who felt the cancer leave her lungs forever, the orphans in Africa who would be saved by donations people made as they approached the altar. Faith too was a habit, something you could step away from. But once you did, what path did you follow? How did you choose your steps?

Paul waited in the car while Cherish and Randy walked leisurely down the sidewalk, holding hands, as if they were on their way to visit a friend. Not much had changed since the last time they'd been there, the only time, over six months before. The smell of the plant still hung in the air. The patriotic cross still guarded the front lawn. There was a paper Easter bunny in the window, and the bald tree in the front yard was decorated with plastic Easter eggs.

Randy tried the door. The windows were dark, but once they were inside, a night-light beside the kitchen sink made everything easy to see. He cracked the refrigerator, helped himself to a jar of olives. "Here," he whispered, digging his long fingers into the brine, and then he held one out, firm and dripping. Cherish ate it off his fingers; salt flooded her mouth. She ate another, another, saving the pimentos, and when Randy bent to kiss her, she fed them back with her tongue. They chose two bottles of Jack Daniel's from the cupboard; still neither one was ready to leave. Wordless, hungry, they clasped hands again and moved deeper into the house.

The air smelled musty, tinged with wintergreen. In the living room, they could already hear the couple's snores, and Cherish followed the sound down the hallway to the tiny bedroom where they slept. Here, the wintergreen odor was laced with alcohol and urine. Both the man and the woman slept on their backs, their bodies not touching, mouths open to reveal their toothless gums. Perhaps the woman had once been beautiful, the way that Cherish was beautiful. Perhaps she had even been a Festival Queen. At the foot of the bed, a pool of darkness expanded, contracted, sighed. It was a cat, black and fat and affectionate, rolling over to let Cherish rub its stomach, its seedlike nipples.

The old couple snored. They sounded like Mule, groaning happily on the living room rug. Mule didn't seem to miss Dad anymore, though for almost a year he'd whined at any closed door, barked at nothing, vomited food. Cherish had been just as fickle. Sometimes days would pass without her thinking of her father even once. The cat's purr rose from a bubble to a boil, and Randy opened the first bottle of whiskey, uncapped it, drank, and the sound of his throat working made Cherish want to drop to her knees and slide down his jeans, to cover his body with her own as the old couple slept, oblivious, innocent. No doubt they believed, the way Ruthie believed, that something would be waiting for them on the other side of death: the reward of immortality, a reason for all they'd suffered. Cherish wanted to believe that too. But Randy put his lips to her ear, spoke the very words she was thinking. "These people," he said, "are insignificant. They could die right now and it wouldn't make any difference."

Like Dad, Cherish finished the thought. And then, *Like me*. She opened the second bottle, choked down that bitterness, forcing her very marrow to digest it. The cat rolled, arched its back, frenzied with desire.

They'd barely made it halfway up the sidewalk when the Mustang thundered out of the darkness, dazzling them with light. "You took long enough," Paul said, and he hopped out to let Randy behind the wheel. "What did you do, have a quickie?"

"Jealous?" Cherish said, and she took another long drink from her bottle. He reached for it, but she shook her head. "This one's mine," she said.

"The lady is thirsty," Randy said, tossing Paul his bottle.

They drove from the Solomon strip to the Fair Mile Crossroads, passing the cross where her father's life had ended. They slid through the stop sign, passed the Faith house—the curtains were drawn, the parking lot was full—continued west over the highway bridge till they hit the River Road. Spun a few doughnuts in the shoe factory parking lot before heading north, past Cradle Park, to the Millpond Road at the dam. And then it was east to County O and back down toward the Solomon strip, the Fair Mile Crossroads, the highway bridge. This was known as the loop, and Cherish figured she'd driven it a thousand times. You felt as if you were getting somewhere, making good time. You forgot that it was an illusion. Just like life itself. You were born and you lived and you learned things and worked hard and loved, but when you died, you were right back where you'd started. So what was the point? You could let your brain give your eyes happy pictures to see: heaven, angels, Jesus rising from the dead to save the world, just like the Faith house mural. Or you could face facts, cut loose, be crazy. Have a good time—why not?

Above the fields, the moon hung so high and crisp and clear that Cherish wanted to take it upon her tongue like a great forbidden Host. She could see every detail of its exacting landscape, those desolate mountains and craters where no one and nothing had ever lived and, yet, people longed to go. "Easy, girl," Randy said, but she sucked on the bottle anyway. She was drunk, drunker than she'd ever been, and still it was not enough. She missed her father—that's what it was. She ached for him, grieved the way her mother had always forbidden her to do. For she knew she'd never see him again, no matter what anyone believed, no matter how much she longed to.

"Cherry's *wasted*," Randy said, laughing, and Paul said, "Hey, I think she's had too much."

Their voices came from far away, like the voices of ghosts.

"I'm fine," Cherish tried to say, but her tongue was a cold slab of meat in her mouth. It didn't matter. Her eyes had grown strangely powerful. She looked out the window and saw into houses where children slept, where grown men and women made love. She saw her mother at the Faith house, face damp, eyes closed, swaying in silent prayer. She saw her father's bones, floating inside the anonymous earth. She saw the blind couple, their open, empty mouths. When she saw the figure walking along the J road toward the bridge, she was surprised that Randy and Paul could see it too.

"Jeez," Randy said, and he slowed to a crawl. They were twenty feet behind the boy; he twisted to look at them, shielding his face against their bright headlights.

"Would you look at the size of that kid!" Paul said.

"Two-for-one special," Randy said. "Should we take him for a ride?"

"What's *with* you?" Paul said, and Randy said, "Relax, will you? There's no one out here to see."

"Tell him we won't hurt him," Paul said. "Don't freak him out like that last kid, OK?"

Cherish struggled to sit up straight. She thought she'd seen the boy before, but she couldn't remember where.

"What do you think, Cherry?" Randy said. "You want him?"

"Man, she's too hammered to know what she wants," Paul said, but Cherish found her voice.

"Lisa Marie got a present," she said, and she closed her eyes as if she were making a wish. "I want a present too." And when she opened her eyes again, Paul and Randy were running down the highway toward the bridge—she could just see Paul's red jacket—and she got out of the car to run after them, the bottle tucked under her arm like a purse. But somehow the bottle slipped, shattered. She was lying on her stomach, on the highway's snowy shoulder, gritty pieces of glass sparkling under her eyes. Her mouth flooded, hot and wet, and she felt herself fading, her hands and feet and finally her face; in her mind's eye, she looked like the mural she'd never finish now. She thought of Jesus, dying on his cross, believing that his suffering could somehow make a difference. His poor bleeding head and side. His broken hands and feet. His thirst. And for the first time in her life, she truly loved Christ—loved him for his failure. For his last anguished cry: *Why have you forsaken me?* At the moment of his death, he must have understood—life was precious, not because it would endure, but because it would not.

And then she began to struggle for breath. Fighting as hard as she could. Fighting for a second chance. She flipped herself over, rolled to her knees. Blood on her hands. Salt in her mouth. The cold air tore at her throat. She stumbled onto the highway, glass falling from her, a trail of stars. Someone was running toward her, coming closer, closer still. And she found that a part of her still hoped it was her father, come back from some otherworldly place to save her. The sky behind him shouted with moonlight.

If only she'd closed her eyes just then. If only she'd been satisfied. But, doubting, she raised her head once more and saw that it was Paul.

"Jesus!" Paul was screaming. "He's gone, the kid's just fucking gone!"

"Gone," Cherish tried to say, but the ground rose up and struck her down.

To the Editor:

Wake up, Ambient! Dare to care! On March 26, the Ambient Planning and Zoning Commission met to discuss plans to rezone the River Road Apple Orchard for development of approximately 35 homes on 5-acre lots. At present, this is a working orchard and is zoned for agricultural use. I, for one, will not sit back and let the GREED OF MONEY *destroy the peace of country living so many of us take for granted. Another subdivision on the River Road will only mean more traffic, the need for road service and sanitation, not to mention the effect on groundwater levels, school enrollments, loss of habitat for wildlife,* NEED I SAY MORE!!! *No doubt this would mean another increase in our taxes too. Put a stop to urban sprawl. May we have enough sense to protect what God has blessed us with here in the Ambient area.*

 Mrs. Virginia "Fronnie" Steinholtz

—*From the* Ambient Weekly
 April 1991

seven

Snow was falling as Stan Pranke pulled up in front of Jeep's Tavern. He'd just stepped inside when the lights flickered, sputtered out, then flashed back on even before the first chorus of *oohs* could be completed. Beneath the laughter that followed was a sound that might have been thunder. Lightning a week before Easter? Stan fingered the lucky rabbit's foot Lorna had hooked to his key ring years ago. More likely it had been a car backfiring somewhere along Main. Or a freight train rumbling through on its way to the lumberyards up north, the vibrations magnified by the cold, bouncing off the flat brick faces of the downtown buildings. Or an old man's imagination.

He heard Lorna's voice like she was sitting right there beside him. *You're not an old man, Stan.*

It sure had sounded like thunder, though. Stan sat down at the bar, caught the eye of the bartender, Fred Carpenter, old Pops Carpenter's son. Stranger things had happened. There'd been three days in November when the temperature soared to seventy. And then all that rain and flooding along the Mississippi last spring. It was a sign of the times, Lorna said, that even the weather didn't know how to behave. He listened, cocked his heavy head first to the right and then to the left, but he didn't hear anything else.

Fred brought his shot of whiskey, placed it dead center on a cocktail napkin, along with a chocolate peanut cluster—owner Jeep Curry's trademark.

"Did you hear that?" Stan asked Fred.

"Hear what, Chief?" Fred said. He'd been tending bar at Jeep's for the past fifteen years, and he could mix up any drink you'd ever heard of without looking at the recipe. He'd even invented a couple of his own: the Bobbsey Twins; the Geraldine Ferraro. The Geraldine Ferraro wasn't half bad, though Stan preferred his shot—just one, which he'd nurse for hours. *That thing's growin' teeth, Chief*, people would say, thumping his shoulder on their way out.

"I thought I heard something, I don't know," Stan said, and he took his first golden sip, held it until the soothing warmth spread over the walls of his cheeks. "Never mind."

Technically, he was on duty, but Mel Rooney knew where to reach him. Mel was only assistant chief, but over the course of the past few months—how had it happened?—he'd assumed nearly all of Stan's responsibilities. At first, Stan hadn't minded: Mel never forgot things, never misplaced things, never messed up on the little details that, lately, seemed to flee Stan's head "like rats from a sinking ship," he'd joke, even though it was starting to worry him. Lorna tried to help, phoned him at work to remind him of things, but she hadn't been in any great shape herself since the hysterectomy. Her pretty gray hair was different now, wiry, almost brittle. Mornings, there was as much of it on her pillow as Stan found on his. He sighed, dipped his tongue into his whiskey. Soon they'd be just another pink-skulled old couple, doddering down the sidewalk, clutching arthritic hands.

But Mel was a young man, still in his forties, capable and energetic, and—as Stan often had to remind himself—not a bad guy at heart. He was just ambitious, that was all, and these days you couldn't fault a fellow for that. Mel had a degree in criminal justice from the University of Illinois. He'd worked first as a beat cop and later as a detective for police departments around the Midwest. But in 1988, he'd gotten a divorce and moved back home to Ambient. Soon after, everybody—especially Mel—was talking about how he'd be the next chief of police once Stan Pranke finally retired. The trouble was, Stan wasn't *ready* to retire. After all, he was only seventy-two; the last chief, Karl Vogelstern, wore the badge till he was eighty. And Mel might understand things like computers and statistics, but Stan Pranke understood *people*. He could sense what they were feeling, anticipate what they'd say or do. And, recently, he'd acquired the ability to hear their thoughts as well. Not in actual words, of course, though he sensed that might be coming, the way, so he'd been told, a man who'd lost his sight would develop better hearing. For now, it was like a humming, like the sound of the bees he kept in ten frame hives behind the shed.

Take, for example, handsome Don DeGroot, sitting at the bar to his left. Don was always an emotional sort, but tonight there was something downright high-pitched about the man, sort of like a hive on an overcast day, which let Stan know old Don was itching to sting. To Stan's right sat Glen Glenbeulah, somber as a drone; when Glen didn't even nod or say hello, Stan understood it was only because he felt he'd be obliged to begin talking and, with seven kids at home and a day job at the plant, Glen was a man who savored silence like honey. Nights like tonight, the sound of everybody's thoughts all together was like the close warm rumble of a healthy swarm: There was Bill Graf, who ran the funeral home; Danny Hope, who'd come home from Texas to open a chiropractic care center; Joe and Lucy Kimmeldorf; Margo Johnson—freshly divorced—with her best friend, Bess

Luftig; Bob Johns; the back booth full of Kiwanis members (Jeep always waited on them himself); the twin pool tables with their ongoing games. The cloud of good-natured insults, the periodic *crack* of a good break. The sound of the jukebox. The way people called, *Hey there, Chief!* The grand busy humming of the hive.

It was enough to bring foolish tears to Stan's eyes. But wasn't it right for an old man to enjoy some sentimental feeling, having lived his life, a good life, mostly, among the same people in the same place? *You're not an old man, Stan,* he heard Lorna say, but the truth was—and he could take it—he was even more outdated than the beloved T-bird he kept covered in the shed and drove every year in the Fourth of July parade, Lorna by his side, the latest Festival Queen perched on the seat back, tossing candy to the crowd. The only thing that hadn't changed during the past forty years was his bees, and he loved them for that: their consistency, their doggedness, their collective sense of purpose. Workers didn't aspire to be queens; drones never tried to be workers. Bees took care of their own, requiring no more than the nearby clover fields, a fresh supply of water. During the hot summer months, when they threatened to swarm, Stan ruptured the queen cells with his pocket knife; each spring, he added a little dry sugar, united the weaker colonies. He handled them with only a face veil and a couple–three puffs from his rusty smoker.

For the past fifty years, he'd been approaching police work the same way he approached his bees, trusting there was something inherently good and reasonable in human nature, believing that, left alone, people would order themselves in a way which would ultimately benefit them all. Goodness in some folks could be hard to see, but most had it in them like a small hard seed—all it needed was a little splash of water, a little bit of bullshit now and then. Whenever possible, he tried to let folks work things out among themselves, without the law's interference, without jail time or fines. Then Mel Rooney came along, and Mel's approach was—well, different.

Mel catered to the whims of the wealthier folks, the tourists and weekenders and millpond people, and they were certainly a nervous bunch, quick to scare, quicker to sue, always threatening to pack up and leave if things weren't exactly to their liking. So if a man had a bit too much to drink at Jeep's and laid himself down in Cradle Park to contemplate the stars, likely as not he'd be rushed, sirens wailing, to the drunk tank in Ambient. Men thumbing their way to the VA hospital in Madison, drifters passing through to the I-90/94 split—these people were given stern warnings and swift rides to the city limits. Worse still, as a member of the Planning and Zoning Commission, Mel had campaigned hard for laws that set strict property maintenance guidelines within city limits. Comfortable porches filled with old furniture, functional yards lined with cars and appliances (who knew when someone might need cheap parts?), weedy lots and overgrown thickets—any of these was enough to send one of Ambient's finest knocking at your door. And if you had a dog, Christ almighty, it better be on a leash twenty-five hours a day.

Stan picked up his whiskey, swirled it around, teased himself with it, then put it down untouched. At first, he'd argued with Mel, tried to make him see the light of reason. It was human, he explained, to overindulge now and then, to lose track of the family dog once in a while, to accumulate things you couldn't bear to throw away. Rules like Mel's would only increase existing resentment between the haves and have-nots, which translated into vandalism around the millpond area: Every weekend, another family lost a mailbox or found detergent in their swimming pool, a car or boat was keyed, a newly landscaped yard uprooted. The thing to do, Stan explained, was get people mixing with each other. If you'd had a ride in that nice fast boat, or had been invited swimming in that fancy backyard pool, you might learn to look at those things in a different way. Similarly, if you'd sipped iced tea outside on that broken-backed couch with that barking dog wagging its tail at your feet, you might be more inclined to accept that there's different strokes for different folks.

But the fact was that the law supported Mel's way of thinking, and the millpond people, weekenders and summer folks both, supported Mel. They came to Ambient to experience country living—fresh air, quiet streets, maybe a little bit of fishing—and they brought their checkbooks with them. By God, they didn't drive all that way to encounter town drunks and radio-blasting teens and mongrels that chased them, unneutered balls bouncing happily, if they tried jogging down a scenic country road. They didn't want to see ramshackle houses, rusty cars; they didn't want their pretty daughters seduced by local boys' rough talk. The latest thing they'd done was restrict public access to the millpond itself. A public swimming area remained by the Killsnake Dam, but the parking lot accommodated less than a dozen cars, and all the little streets around the millpond itself were posted No Parking. The fine was one hundred dollars, and Mel enforced it like one of God's commandments. He himself had bought one of the lots, built a fancy house with his new wife's money.

"These people are our bread and butter," he said. "I'm not going to let the wildlife scare them off."

It was true that the millpond people brought in money, but to Stan's way of thinking, they also brought drugs and bad tempers, clogged the roads with traffic, and caused taxes to go up and up. Their homes attracted burglars as well as vandals, and the alarms they installed to protect themselves were constantly triggered by wind or whim. On a record weeknight last August, police responded to thirteen calls—all of them false alarms. That same week, three people were arrested for possession of narcotics, two men for domestic violence, another man for attempted rape. Once, Stan would have recognized the name of each person involved, but these days everyone was a stranger. The world was getting more and more complex. Perhaps Mel was right and it was time for Stan to retire, to move over and out of the way. And yet Stan thought of Karl Vogelstern. He thought of his own mother, who'd hand-milked her last few remaining cows, mucked their stalls, and kept up with her quarter-acre garden until the day she died, at eighty-six. It seemed to him that folks were different than they used to be—not as tough, more inclined to take it easy, less inclined to help a neighbor or put in the extra hour it took to get a job done right. They were lonelier too. They didn't rely on each other. They talked about *stress*. They didn't have fun the way people used to.

An idea that had occurred to him recently—kind of a compromise between retirement and work—was how nice it would be for him and Lorna to buy one of those mobile homes and travel around the country for a while. See a few things. Enjoy themselves. Sure, he'd have to get rid of his bees. And the T-bird. (He took another itsy sip of whiskey.) And Lorna was awfully attached to the house—each morning she drank her coffee looking out over the river—plus she had all those friends in the Circle of Faith. But the house was just too big for them, now the kids were gone, and they could have it sold in two weeks for more money than they'd ever dreamed of. Outside money. Maybe Mel was right. Maybe it was pointless to go against the times. Stan searched through his pockets for his Pepto-Bismol tablets, slid one from its plastic sheaf, and tucked it in his mouth. Crunching, he looked up to see Fred Carpenter, the telephone held in front of him like a platter of cocktail wienies.

"It's Mel," Fred said, placing it on the bar. "Sounds important." Stan figured it must be. Mel had never once called Stan about anything. At the police station, Stan would turn to do something and discover it had already been done. He'd pick up the phone to make a call and find out it had been made days earlier. Stan sometimes got the feeling that Mel would have been just as happy to see him spend all his duty time at Jeep's and never come into the station at all. He put the receiver to one ear and stuffed his finger in the other.

"We've got a problem." Mel's voice was uncharacteristically nervous. In the background, Stan could hear the slamming of car doors, the fading wail of a siren. "How fast can you assemble a search party?"

"Got 'em," Stan said, glancing around the bar. Instinctively, he reached into his pocket, grabbed his rabbit's foot. "Where do you need 'em?"

"At the highway bridge. Some high school kids were fooling around, and a younger boy fell in the river."

"Jesus," Stan said—

—and then his heart skipped a beat, the same way it had on that foggy Friday night, two years ago, when there'd been a six-car pileup on the Solomon strip—four injuries, one fatality. And the time the Tauscheck boy had been playing with his daddy's pistol. And the time Tom Mader was killed on County O— Christ, that had been a tough one. Stan himself had been the one who'd notified Ruth. And it had been after Tom's funeral that Ambient really started to change. Whoever had knocked Tom off the road was living right under everybody's nose, waving hello and going to church and shopping for groceries at the Piggly Wiggly. You couldn't believe in appearances the way you maybe once did. You couldn't trust anyone completely. People pulled apart from each other; the new people sensed that, pulled away too. And then Mel came on board with his goddamn regulations. . . .

"How long has the kid been in the water?" Stan said.

"Near as we can tell, since a little after nine."

It was almost ten o'clock.

"You're just telling me now?" Stan bellowed, and Mel said,

"Now, Stan, I would have called earlier, but I didn't want to bother you over nothing."

"Nothing?" Christ, oh, Christ. "What's the kid's name, do we have ID?"

"Not yet. The high school kids, they just—you know—picked him up. They wanted to tease him a little," Mel said, and now Stan began to understand why he sounded so peculiar.

"The same group who grabbed Sammy Carlsen and the Walvoord girl?" Stan said. "The ones you said we shouldn't bother the papers about? Christ, Mel, this is more than a prank! If you'd taken it seriously from the start—"

"Look," Mel said, his voice abruptly low and mean. "You wanna talk about the papers, then let's talk about what the papers are going to say when they hear the chief of police was sitting cozy at his favorite watering hole while all this was going on. Now get your people together, sober if that's possible, with flashlights if they got 'em. Take the River Road—we've coned off the J road from the bridge to County C. We'll walk both sides of the river as soon as the chopper gets in from Madison."

Stan slammed down the phone so hard it slid off the counter, crashed to the floor. The warble of conversation, the thoughtful humming that had cocooned it, cut off like water from a tap. Jeep, who was joking with the pool players, spun around, and even mild Fred spilled the drink he was carrying. Within the silence, the jukebox went on playing.

"Listen up," he said, conscious of the way his voice was shaking. "Unidentified boy fell off the highway bridge. I need volunteers to search the banks, and before you say yes, think how much you've had to drink, and then think about how warm you're dressed. It's a cold night out there."

Every man in the bar plus half the women volunteered. The women these days, they wanted to be involved in everything, and they sure got mad if you left them out. So Stan picked Margo

Johnson and Bess Luftig along with eight men, assigning Danny Hope and Bill Graf as drivers. His own squad car was parked smack in front, technically in a loading zone, the same spot where old Pops Carpenter left his tractor whenever he went inside for a toot. There was little Stan liked better than to see that old John Deere chug-chugging up Main on a Friday night, the impatient line of cars headed for the millpond choked up behind it—Illinois plate after Illinois plate, doctors and lawyers and corporates helplessly blowing their horns. When Mel brought it up at a staff meeting earlier in the month, Stan had said, "People want country living? Well, here it is." The other officers chuckled at that, but Mel didn't even smile.

"His property is in violation, that tractor isn't licensed for the road, and his kid costs taxpayers money each time he runs off."

"It's his *grand*kid," Stan explained. "The boy's being raised by Pops' son and daughter-in-law."

"Well, clearly they're not keeping up with him. Contact child protection, let them handle it."

"Oh, no, no," Stan said quickly. "Look, Mel, I'll go talk to them, see what I can do. Pops' wife, God rest her, was Lorna's second cousin—"

"If there's neglect, you notify the state," Mel interrupted. "You file appropriate charges. I mean it, Stan. Take care of it. Next item?"

Now Stan turned on the siren and swung around the rotary, Bill and Danny behind him with the rest of the volunteers, and they all headed south toward the highway bridge. The full moon floated in absolute darkness, illuminating the long, crooked spine of the river, heightening the hulking shapes of the new houses perched along the River Road, which ran parallel with the highway on the other side of the water. Snow rushed at the headlights, shaping swift pictures Stan could almost understand; he was still hoping that by the time they arrived, the kid would be

found, already on his way to the hospital. No doubt he'd be air-
lifted to Madison. These days, doctors at the universities could
do the most amazing things. Stan had seen on TV where they'd
revived a man who'd been underwater two hours. Could it have
been two hours? Well, anyway, the water had been cold, and cold
water acted like a preservative. Ice water could even—

—Stan's heart skipped again. It was a strange feeling, those
skipped heartbeats. It was a taste of what was coming—the silent,
empty hive. He'd lost a whole colony once; he'd never figured
out exactly why. But there was nothing worse than that silence,
the dried-up husks of the bodies in the outer chambers, the
bloated gray corpses trapped within the soured honeycomb. Now,
as he wove past the orange warning cones, he steeled himself
against whatever he was about to see.

He parked on the bridge, with his headlights shining downstream; Bill and Danny did the same. Stan tapped on their windows, told them to wait while he appraised the situation. Then
he approached the tight cluster of men—*officers*, he corrected
himself—who were standing beside the guardrail. Five in all:
Leroy Kulm, Pete Stahl, Buddy Lewis, Bart Todd, and the lady
officer Mel had insisted they hire—Jean? June? Stan could never
remember. He fingered his lucky rabbit's foot. The set of their
shoulders told him that they too expected the worst, and their
expressions—hardened, silent, watchful—reminded Stan of his
military years. Unlike Mel, he'd served his country with pride;
he'd been twice decorated in the Second World War. Thirty years
later, Mel had stayed home to burn flags and brassieres and God
knows what else, yet now he was in his squad car, calling the
shots as if it were his right to do so. In the old days, Stan thought
with satisfaction, Mel would have been arrested. Mel would have
occupied one of the very cells he loved to brag about at civic
meetings.

"Evening," Stan said. "Who wants to fill me in?"

Disrespectfulness and doubt clouded their thoughts like static; still, he was able to piece together the gist of what they were thinking. He was incompetent, out of touch. He was . . . it took a moment for the word to take shape; then it appeared, sudden as a knife. Lazy. *Lazy?* But he was always busy! He worked so hard that when he got home, he'd fall asleep smack in the middle of a conversation! Lazy. He stared at his officers, trying not to take it personally. After all, who knew what all Mel was saying behind his back? A wasp in the hive, Stan thought. But he knew what happened to wasps. The bees eventually wised up and destroyed them.

Leroy Kulm finally cleared his throat and brought Stan up to date. Three teens had been involved. The girl had been taken to Our Lady of Mercy Hospital, suffering from alcohol poisoning and lacerations from a broken bottle. The boys were at the police station, and their story was that they hadn't meant to hurt the kid, they'd just pulled over to talk to him, maybe offer him a ride (here Leroy rolled his eyes), but the kid started running and the boys jumped out and chased him down the J road, and when they caught up with him on the highway bridge, he panicked, slipped over the edge, or maybe he jumped—the kids weren't sure; they couldn't remember: Everything happened so fast and they'd been drinking. One boy stayed to search the riverbank, while the other ran back to the car, where he found the girl passed out on the road, half covered in blood, and he said he didn't know how she got that way but he just threw her in the back seat and drove to the McDonald's for help. The only thing any of the searchers had found so far was a Snoopy flashlight, on Ruthie Mader's land, about a quarter of a mile downstream.

"Those boys were drunk as skunks," Buddy Lewis said. It was no secret that Mel had worked hard to put him on the City Council. "I got a buzz just talkin' to 'em. They say they got the liquor 'from some guy somewhere.' "

"Don't know his name, of course," Leroy said. "Don't know the missing kid's name, either."

"So who are these boys?" Stan said, trying to keep the anger out of his voice, picturing hoodlums, young toughs, wannabe gang-bangers.

"Paul Zuggenhagen and Randy Hale," Leroy said. The officers shook their heads at those names, and Pete Stahl said, "Christ, that Hale kid can wrestle. I saw him last year at state finals."

"Zuggenhagen's old man works at First Wisconsin," Buddy said. "They moved here in '85. Good people."

"All three kids have clean records," said the lady officer. Jill? Jane? *What* was her name?

"I just can't believe it," Stan said.

"Well, it gets worse," Leroy said. "The girl is Cherish Mader."

"Aw, no," Stan said.

Leroy made a regretful sound with his tongue. "They pumped her stomach, stitched her up. She ain't gonna look like no Festival Queen after this, from what they say at Mercy."

"Zuggenhagen says the kid never hit the water. Says he was there and then he wasn't. Poof," Buddy said.

"Alien abduction, maybe," the lady officer said.

The group guffawed unhappily. In the distance, a freight train blew its whistle; Stan tracked its bright approach, felt the rattle of the passing cars against the cold soles of his feet. He wadded up a piece of paper from his notepad, tossed it over the edge of the bridge to check the current. Not much. The moon stared down at them all, wide-eyed and infinitely patient.

"Watch out Mel don't write you a ticket for that," Leroy said, deadpan, and with that, Mel got out of his squad car, approached the group at his no-nonsense pace.

"Got probable ID," he said. "Bethany Carpenter phoned in minutes ago. Says she got back from town, went next door to collect her kid from her father-in-law, but—surprise—no kid."

"Gabriel," Stan said. "The boy's name is Gabriel."

"Well, *Gabriel* matches the description the Hale kid gave us," Mel said. "Jesus." He tossed something at Stan; by some miracle, Stan caught it. It was the Snoopy flashlight, in a plastic bag. In the distance, cars were collecting on County C, flashers winking like fireflies, and several people had started cutting across the field toward the river. It occurred to Stan that announcing the incident at Jeep's was a little like broadcasting it over WTMJ. "All right, everybody," Mel said. "The aunt is on her way over. Stan's gonna wait for her, see if she can ID Snoopy. And if she can, *this* time Stan's gonna charge her with neglect and reckless endangerment of a child and anything else that's appropriate—you get me, Stan? I don't care how far you and somebody's poor dead wife go back. That kid was left unsupervised. The rest of you, grab a couple of volunteers apiece and we'll all fan out along the river. Ten paces apart, half the group on either side. Chopper will be here to light us up any minute."

"I don't appreciate you telling me my job," Stan said stiffly.

"If you'd called child protection like I'd told you, none of this would have happened."

"Now wait a minute here," Stan said, shaking the Snoopy flashlight angrily. "If you hadn't hushed things up to keep your business buddies happy—" But at the sound of the approaching helicopter, Mel turned away from Stan to wave the volunteers from their cars. A floodlight encircled them all, and as Stan watched from the guardrail, the officers and volunteers picked their way down either side of the icy embankment, black flecks against a brilliant white backdrop. The chopper pulled back, lifted high, higher still, then began to follow their slow progress downstream. As the individual lights of the searchers became visible, forming a widening horizon like ripples moving outward from a tossed stone, Stan realized he'd been left behind. He thought about going after them. He even walked to the edge of the guard-rail and considered the rough trail cutting down the embankment. But somebody had to wait on Bethany, and the fact was that Stan's toes were already aching from the cold, despite his lined boots. The footing along the river was treacherous, uncertain. His bum hip hurt just to think about it. He said Mel's name aloud and spat, twice, the way his granddaddy used to do. Then he put the Snoopy flashlight in his pocket and went back to the squad car. As he held his hands up to the heat vents, he eyed the cell phone, fighting an immense longing to talk to Lorna. But Lorna had had some to-do at the Circle of Faith; most likely, she wasn't even home yet. There was nothing to do but sit tight. Wait for Bethany. Wait for the boy to be found.

The boy. Stan felt around in his pockets until he found his Pepto-Bismol tablets. He slipped three into his mouth, ground them to a creamy paste. The last time he'd seen Gabriel Carpenter was at the old farmhouse a few weeks earlier, a warrant from Mel folded up in his pocket. "By the book," Mel had reminded Stan. But Gabriel had run off only—what?—five or six times, maybe. And he wasn't exactly running off. He was out looking for the river angel; he'd tell anybody who asked. He'd gotten it into his head that the angel could make his daddy come back. It was no use explaining to Mel that this was just a phase, that eventually the boy would adjust and settle down. He'd be far worse off in a foster home, where he'd feel even more abandoned, where he'd miss his daddy even more.

Of course, Stan hadn't needed the warrant. He'd knocked on the door of the new double-wide, discovered that no one was home. But next door at the farmhouse, Pops welcomed him in with a handshake that just went on and on. "Gabey?" he bellowed. "He's probably in the kitchen." And there he was, eating a bowl of frosted flakes, wearing a Green Bay Packers cap that

Stan was used to seeing on Pops' head. Stan held out his hand for Gabriel to shake, but Gabriel didn't respond. Stan was the one Mel always sent to take him home when he ran off.

"Is he in trouble again?" Pops said, and he winked. "Or is it me this time?" He was nearly as old as Stan, yet he looked limber as a wire.

"Not yet," Stan said. "But we need to have a chat."

"Uh-oh," Pops said, and he led them to the living room, seated himself in an orange beanbag chair that made Stan's back ache just to look at it. Three cats were curled up in a cozy tangle on the floor; Gabriel came in and flopped down beside them. Stan claimed the couch.

"When's the last time you were in town?" he asked.

Pops thought about it. "Oh, I'd say about a week ago."

"How'd you get there?"

Pops showed all of his this-way-thataway teeth. "Now, Chief, you know the state ate my license. How else am I going to get around?"

Clumps of fur drifted through the air. Stan glanced up and wished he hadn't when he saw all the cobwebs hanging from the ceiling. The whole house was a disaster. Still, Pops was doing better than anyone might have expected. After his young wife died, he went into a kind of depression that had lasted for years; Fred and Shawn had pretty much raised themselves. Over time, he'd come back to himself, and now he even worked a bit— serving drinks at Jeep's when things got busy, picking up trash along the highway for the city, doing bush-hogging and snow removal for Big Roly Schmitt. And Stan could see Pops loved the boy. He could hear it in his thoughts, which were thick with devotion, like a golden retriever's. He also knew that Bethany Carpenter, brusque though she could be, wasn't the type to neglect a child. This was something Stan could handle himself. So he told Pops, in his best cop voice, that some changes were required. From now on, if he needed something in town, he should let Fred give him a lift or, better still, fetch it for him. He could use the time at home to drag some of the stuff along the highway closer to the house, or maybe even behind it, so it couldn't be seen from the road. And above all, he and Bethany and Fred all had to keep a closer eye on Gabriel.

"From now on, we're gonna charge a fifty-dollar vagrancy fine each time the department picks him up," Stan said.

He was lying, of course; there was no such fine. Well, at least not yet. But it was something both Pops and Fred could understand—unlike the threat of child protection, which was too abstract to be effective.

"Fifty bucks!" Pops said. "Christ, for that I should just let you keep him."

"You wouldn't really do that," Gabriel said. He'd draped one of the sleeping cats over the back of his neck like a scarf.

"That's because there won't be a next time—right, Gabriel?" Stan took a shiny toy badge out of his pocket. Cost him two bucks at the Wal-Mart, but what the hell. "Tell you what. If you promise me you'll stay close to home, I'll make you a special deputy."

"Can I arrest people?" Gabriel said. He wasn't so bad-looking when he smiled. Give him a few more years, Stan thought, shave about fifty pounds off of him, and he might turn out OK. Come to think of it, Shawn had been kind of a butterball himself.

"Sure, why not?" Stan said, and he beckoned the boy over so he could pin the badge on his T-shirt. After Gabriel had run off, still wearing the cat, to look in the bathroom mirror, Stan asked Pops, "Don't he have friends at school he can play with?"

"Naw. They all give him hell—his cousins included. He says his only friend is Jesus."

Stan had to laugh at that. "My wife would sure approve."

That had been—what?—two weeks ago? The tractor had been

seen on the road only once since. Two refrigerators, a bathtub, and most of the bashed-in TVs had disappeared from the road-side. And Gabriel stopped wandering off—or so it had seemed. Until now.

Someone was driving too fast up the J road, swerving past Mel's orange warning cones and onto the bridge. Stan clambered out of his car just as Bethany and Pops emerged from theirs. The old man seemed confused. He stared out over the river, which was black and cold as the universe itself. "Gabriel?" he called.

"What happened?" Bethany hurried toward Stan.

"We're not sure yet," Stan said. "Some high school kids saw him fall off the bridge, but we don't know the exact circumstances."

"Off the bridge!" Bethany said.

"Gabriel?" the old man shouted, and Bethany whirled on him and said, "What on earth was he doing at the bridge? If you'd kept an eye on him like you promised—"

"He told me he was going back to your place," Pops said, pulling at the zipper of his coat. "He said he had homework."

"Didn't I tell you to keep him with you?"

"Why was that?" Stan said, placing a steadying hand on her shoulder.

"He and my Robert John don't get along. I figured it was better to split them up until I got back home."

"And where were you?"

"Working!" Bethany said, and she shrugged off his hand. "Where else would I be? A lady at the millpond calls up, says her in-laws are coming in the morning and she'll pay me one hundred dollars to get her house in shape—" She broke off, stared out at the distant hazy lights of the search party. "Those high school kids, they didn't hurt him?"

"We just don't know right now," Stan said, as gently as he

could. "They were the ones who called the police. It appears they tried their best to find him."

"Maybe it ain't even him," she said. "Maybe they made a mistake." But when Stan took the Snoopy flashlight out of his pocket, she covered her face with her hands. Pops closed his eyes and began to swear, a long string of cusses that made no sense whatsoever, and Stan swore right along with him. He could not charge either of these people with neglect. They were doing the best they could. Let Mel file his goddamn charges if he wanted. Stan would tender his resignation as soon as he got home. He and Lorna would sell the house and buy that RV and drive it all the way to Alaska. Somewhere with lots of trees and fresh, clean air. Somewhere with a little town like Ambient used to be: friendly people, safe streets, nobody bothering to lock their doors. What was the world coming to that a thing like this could happen? And as if he was thinking the same thing, Pops said, "He was just looking for the angel. He wasn't bothering nobody. All he was doing was looking for that angel."

And Stan said what he'd said to Ruthie Mader, and Roy Tauscheck, and family members of the one who'd died that foggy night at the strip. "He's out of our hands and into the Lord's. Go home, get some rest. We'll search all night if we have to, and we'll call the minute we know something more."

After they'd gone, Stan radioed Mel to let him know he'd sent the Carpenters home. Then he told him he could kiss his wrinkled ass and drove to his own house, where Lorna was waiting for him, a cup of warm milk in her hand. The police had come to the meetinghouse. Anna Grey Graf had driven Ruthie to the hospital, where Cherish was in stable condition. "What in God's name happened out there, Stan?" Lorna said.

"I don't know," Stan said. He took the warm milk she gave him, sat down at the kitchen desk. "Pull up a chair and write something for me?" he said, and then he handed her a pen, a yellow tablet of lined paper. He rested his chin on his hands and wept as she took down his resignation.

He learned what had happened on the morning news, just like everyone else. It had been dawn before Ruthie Mader finally came home from Our Lady of Mercy to feed and water her sheep. Her old dog was oddly anxious; he led the way to the barn. Inside, despite the dim light, she could see everything with remarkable clarity—the hens in the rafters, the golden-eyed goats, the sheep huddled in a close circle as if guarding one of their lambs. A snow-white pigeon rose from the straw, and it was then that she realized it was not a bird at all, but the source of the light that filled the air, a light so beautiful it took her breath. She watched it rise up to the apex of the barn, disappear into a tiny slice of sunlight. The boy was lying in the sheep pen, hands folded on his chest. She placed her finger to his neck. She could not say how much time passed before she walked over to the house and dialed 911.

"His body was warm when I touched it," she said. "There was a smell like flowers. When I saw him there, I thought he was just sleeping."

Prayer of the Blessed Virgin (never known to fail): O *most beautiful flower of Mt. Carmel, fruitful vine, splendor of Heaven. Blessed Mother of the Son of God, Immaculate Virgin, assist me in my necessity.* O *Star of the Sea, help me and show me here you are my Mother.* O *Holy Mary, Mother of God, Queen of Heaven and Earth, I humbly beseech you from the bottom of my heart to succor me in my necessity (make request). There are none that can withstand your power.* O *Mary, conceived without sin, pray for us who have recourse to thee (three times). Holy Mary, I place this prayer for your hands (three times). All you have to do is say this prayer for three consecutive days and then you must publish and it will be granted to you if you believe. Grateful thanks.*

    G.Z.

  —*From the* Ambient Weekly
    April 1991

eight

His body was *warm when I touched it. There was a smell like* *flowers.*

It had been very early Sunday morning when Ruthie Mader dialed 911. By the middle of the week, nearly everyone within a hundred-mile radius of Ambient could have chanted those words by heart. The news shows played her breathless call; her words were quoted and requoted in the papers, repeated again on radio talk shows, around supper tables, at country bars over icy pitchers of beer. Old Bill Graf, flanked by his son, made a statement to WTMJ from the county morgue. The Carpenter child's body, he said, was the most beautiful thing he'd ever seen, and he was proud to handle the funeral and subsequent cremation at no charge whatsoever to the family. Bill junior and his wife made a statement as well; the wife had been the child's fifth-grade teacher. "He'd bow his head down in the classroom to pray," she said. "He was truly a special child." Another woman had seen the boy walking along the highway bridge only a few weeks earlier; when she'd pulled over to offer him a ride, she'd seen a strange pale light around his face and hands. The child's father

175

could not be located for comment, but the grandfather confirmed that the boy had been *deeply religious.* "I believe Mrs. Mader's story," Pops Carpenter said, scrubbing tears from his eyes. "I take comfort from the thought of it." An address flashed up on the screen: Donations were being accepted on behalf of family and friends, who were hoping to place a monument on the spot where the boy had been found. Half a dozen papers had already called the Saint Fridolin's rectory for a comment on the rumor of a shrine.

"Each year in the United States alone, hundreds of supernatural occurrences are reported to the Church," Father George Oberling said. "I don't mean to suggest people deliberately *misrepresent* what they see so much as *misunderstand.*" He'd tried to be as diplomatic as possible.

Now he turned off his TV and wearily rubbed his temples. It was Saturday night, exactly one week since the poor boy's death. The rectory phone had been ringing around the clock with calls from people whose lights had flickered (Wisconsin Electric blamed a power surge) and others who had heard a sound "like thunder" (Father George himself had heard nothing) and others still who had seen a flash of light, and all of them wanted to know if Father had heard of the old river angel stories, and did he believe in things like that, and how did he think the boy got across the field without leaving tracks, and was it true there wasn't a bump or bruise anywhere on his body? In fact, Our Lady of Mercy had confirmed that the boy had died of exposure. In fact, Mel Rooney had assured him that the lack of external physical evidence could be blamed on human error rather than celestial favors: Stan Pranke had assembled his search party at Jeep's. Within an hour, Mel was fighting off dozens of spontaneous volunteers, many of whom parked on the County C and then cut through the fields toward the river, trampling the fresh snow into slush. One good thing, however small, had come out of the whole fiasco. Stan Pranke, God bless him, had finally resigned.

The funeral, delayed by the autopsy, was set for Monday at eleven, and at the request of a Catholic aunt, Father George had agreed to officiate. He could only hope that afterward, all the talk about *how* the boy arrived at the barn undetected would fade enough to allow the community to focus on *what* had actually happened. The *true* implications of this tragedy. Clearly the Carpenter boy had fallen through the cracks of the system, abandoned to the care of people who hadn't the skills to look after him. But worse was the thought of a child's death at the hands of other children. It wasn't happening only in big cities like Milwaukee or Chicago anymore. The real question was, what did parents plan to do about it? Hide their heads in the sand? Or else get their houses in order before this kind of violence took root? He'd heard that the Mader girl wouldn't face charges; she was badly disfigured, still recovering from her injuries, and had no memory of what had happened on the bridge. The boys themselves—well-known high school athletes, one a banker's son—already had good lawyers. No doubt they'd walk away with slaps on their wrists, maybe some community service. They still insisted they'd never touched the child, that he'd jumped from the bridge of his own volition; recently, one had started to claim that *he* had seen a flash of light. And why had he neglected to mention this initially? "I thought nobody would believe me," Paul Zuggenhagen told the *Ambient Weekly*.

Father George shook his head. Eventually, people were going to have to recognize the angel for what it was: an embodiment of guilt and sorrow and shame. A whole lot of wishful thinking. But when he showed up for eight o'clock Mass the next morning, he discovered Saint Fridolin's packed to the rafters, as if it were Christmas Day. After recovering from his astonishment, he proceeded with the service, but when he returned for the ten o'clock

Mass and found not only the pews but the aisles clogged with worshipers, he stepped down from the podium and addressed the congregation directly. Didn't they see what was happening—that the very *real* tragedy of a child's death was already starting to pale beside rumors of the so-called supernatural? Didn't they understand that God was not a magician producing rabbits from a hat, that faith was so much more than smoke and lights and special effects? The Eucharist—the transubstantiation of bread to body, wine to blood—was a *true* miracle, sanctioned by the Church, yet every day, Catholics around the world ate the Host as nonchalantly as a potato chip. But let someone revive an old folktale— he paused to strain the grim note of frustration from his voice— and they'd come to a service they hadn't attended since Christmastime.

"Don't be distracted by the fabulous," Father George said. "Go home and pray for the soul of Gabriel Carpenter. Pray that those young people responsible will make their peace with God and change their ways. And pray that, as a community, we will learn to instill our children with strong moral values through our own adult examples of sobriety, respect, and devotion to our faith."

Still, the rectory phone continued to ring, parishioners bearing new bits of information like gifts. Did Father know a church bus had arrived from the Dells? Had Father been past the highway bridge, where people were leaving bouquets of flowers and taking photographs?

"It's nothing to worry about," Father George told the archbishop at the end of the day. "I know the woman involved, and I doubt many people are taking her too seriously." But when he turned on the nightly news at ten, he was greeted by a shot of Ruthie's courtyard. That afternoon, over one hundred people had made an impromptu pilgrimage from the bridge to the barn, where the police were concluding their investigation. The animals had all been transported to a neighbor's barn; trouble began when two local officers stated there was still an impression in the straw where the boy's body had lain. Lots of people desired to see that impression for themselves, and when they started ducking under the tape police had wound around the barn walls and prying off the boards that had been nailed over the windows, Mel Rooney took his bullhorn and announced that everyone would have to step back. But no one obeyed, and there were more people showing up all the time, avoiding the barricade at the end of Ruthie's long driveway by parking on the highway and walking through the fields, or else driving in through the old apple orchard, and all of them wanted answers. "This is *our* community," one man shouted at the camera. "We *live* here! We have the right to know what's going on!" Abruptly everyone pressed forward, sweeping Mel's line of officers with them into the barn, and the clip ended with the whole crowd singing "Amazing Grace."

Why me? Father George groaned. *Why my parish?* He tried to look on the bright side—there were worse adversaries than the river angel. At least he wasn't stuck at Saint John's up in Antigo, where the Virgin kept appearing to a local housewife and delivering messages regarding "the purity of the white race." Or at Immaculate Conception in Dickeyville, where numerous parishioners had reported seeing the ghost of a one-armed man in the church confessional. (A new confessional finally had to be built.) But the sad fact was that although his situation could have been worse, it also could have been better, and he wondered if God would ever see fit to allow him to return to New England. He'd arrived at Saint Fridolin's in 1980, and within a year he'd requested reassignment so many times that the diocese still joked about it. Over the past eleven years, he had learned to call Ambient home, and he'd even developed a certain affection for his flock of pale, slow-moving Midwesterners. But he would never learn to accept the mind-numbing flatness of the land, the long, indifferent winters, the aching boredom of small-town ways: the old hurts, the petty grievances, the strange lack of worldly curiosity, born of isolation, which made the mind fertile ground for wild imaginings and poisonous seeds of the sort sown by Ruthie Mader. He hadn't seen her anywhere in the crowd, but he had no doubt she'd been there, fanning the flames along with the other members of the Circle of Faith.

This wouldn't be the first time he'd battled Ruthie over an angel. The last one had sprung from the mind of Lily Schobruller. Lily had always believed there was an angel watching over her family; it seemed harmless enough on the surface, as such things usually did. But when Lily's daughter, Emily, started high school, the angel reported that Emily was having sex with boys, sometimes more than one at a time. Father George spent an interminable afternoon with the whole troubled family in his rectory parlor, trying not to wince as Lily and her husband, Dan, accused their daughter of unspeakable things. Father George knew when he was in over his head; afterward, he spent an hour on the phone, investigating psychiatric care. But a neighbor was one of Ruthie's followers, and she took Lily and Emily along to a meeting at the Fair Mile Crossroads. The next thing Father George knew, they were all back in his parlor, eager to let him know that the angel was, in fact, Lily and Dan's first child, a stillborn little girl whom Lily and Dan had never told Emily about. Now this child was jealous of her living sister, making up vicious lies.

How very interesting, Father George said. And how will you keep her from lying in the future?

No problem. Faith members had simply joined hands and told the little girl they recognized and loved her. Emily reported that later that same night, her sister had come to her in a dream and apologized for what she'd done. In the morning, a ring that she'd lost weeks earlier was sitting on her nightstand.

A peace offering, Lily said eagerly, happily, and what was Father George to say? He shook Dan's hand and patted Emily's shoulder and suggested it still might be a good idea for Lily to get a complete neurological and psychiatric workup at the hospital, just in case. But of course, Lily never did. Sometimes Father George had the strange sense that he was fighting Ruthie Mader for his parish, particularly when it came to his female parishioners. If a woman was dying, Ruthie beat him to her bedside with votive candles and soothing words. If a woman was unhappy, chances were she'd call Ruthie's Women's Crisis Hot Line before she'd even consider making an appointment at the rectory. At Our Lady of Mercy, Ruthie made weekly rounds just like a priest, and though she didn't go so far as to administer blessed oils, he had seen her massage a dying patient's hands and feet and temples with rose water.

It was hard to believe that before Tom Mader's death, Ruthie had been a parish cornerstone. When Father George first arrived at Saint Fridolin, she'd been secretary-treasurer of Christian Mothers, an elected member of the parish council. Now she apparently found no contradiction in practicing both Catholicism and what, as far as Father George was concerned, bordered on the occult. Faith meetings were shrouded in secrecy, yet he had heard accounts of healing-prayer circles, supernatural occurrences, spiritual "gifts" that ranged from visions and prophecies to communion with the dead—it was enough to make his thinning hair stand on end. No wonder newspapers throughout the Midwest were jumping on the story: the *Sentinel*, the *Sun-Times*, the *Tribune*. The media loved this kind of thing. What did they care if the citizens of Ambient came off looking like hysterics and eccentrics, likely as not to report the appearance of a UFO the following week? More than once, Father George had considered driving out to the J road to shine the light of reason on the crowd of curious onlookers—especially if they happened to be his own parishioners. But the mere presence of a priest could be interpreted as a kind of validation.

The best way to handle a situation like this was not to pay it any attention. Thirty-five years ago, when he was still a seminarian in New York, there'd been an old priest named Father Gluck, blind and bent nearly double with arthritis, who had done parish work for over fifty years. All the acolytes confided in him, sought out his advice, took turns walking with him in the garden, where he'd pat the faces of the flowers he loved but could no longer smell or see. One warm spring day just before Father George's ordination, Father Gluck gave him this piece of advice: "From time to time," he said, "a woman from your parish will come to you—and it *will* be a woman—and she'll say, 'Oh, Father, I have seen our blessed Mother,' or 'Father, Our Lord has appeared to me.' When that happens, son, do not dismiss her, and do not disbelieve her. Simply say, 'My dear lady, the next time this apparition appears, please give it my warmest regards.' "

Father George had had reason to remember Father Gluck's advice more than once during his tenure as pastor of Saint Fridolin's. During his first year, he'd counseled old Mauva Schikedantz, who thought she saw Christ in her fireplace, pacing the flames in a long white robe. Father George suggested that the next time it happened she say an Our Father and add another log, but on Good Friday, she'd reached out her hand, wanting to touch His side as the apostle Thomas had done. These days, she seemed happy enough at the nursing home in Solomon; when he brought Communion, she ferried the Host to her mouth unassisted, clamped between her thumb and a melted nub of finger. The home, like Our Lady of Mercy, attracted a fair number of visions—Jesus, Mary, dead spouses, all the usual culprits—but Father George was less inclined toward professional skepticism when the ill or infirm were involved. After all, some things simply could not be explained. That was the beauty and power of God.

He himself had nearly died of a childhood bout with pneumonia; one night, he'd drifted away to a place of warmth and light, returning free of fever and with the first inklings of a vocation.

But anything could be taken to extremes. Far too many of his parishioners came home from Mass and, without a second thought, checked their horoscopes in the Sunday paper. Some spent good money on star charts, or tarot cards, or crystals to wear around their necks. Some latched onto health food and New Age thinking, talked about synchronicity and reincarnation, invented their own mongrel system of beliefs, in which Jesus was a kindly big brother, God was the Wizard of Oz, and there was certainly no such thing as sin, as long as you didn't hurt anybody. *Smorgasbord Catholics*, Father George called them, people who picked what they wanted instead of eating the whole, nutritious meal.

"Maybe you didn't like brussels sprouts as a child," he'd told his congregation only one month earlier. "But as a parent, you know they're chock-full of vitamins. Maybe you don't like abstinence," he said, and here he paused significantly, looking at the young people. "Or fidelity." He stared at the middle-aged couples. "Or the idea that there's a very real hell in which sinners shall abide for all eternity." He raised his head to address them all. "Or any of the other things about being a good Catholic which, at times, you may find hard to swallow. But the Church is like a parent. And if you place your trust in her teachings, you'll have no desire to supplement her wholesome diet with cheap fast food: charms, crystals"—he paused again—"angels, and the like."

He'd been proud of that particular sermon—he could tell by certain flushed faces that he'd driven the point home. Yet Ruthie Mader and the Catholic members of her following lined up for Communion, identical gold crosses shining at their throats as if to ward off the evil eye. Father George's hand shook as he slipped the Host into Ruthie's waiting mouth. He had tried his best to be understanding—after all, Tom's death had been a terrible shock. But nearly eight years had passed. Enough was enough. He couldn't treat Ruthie like Mauva Schikedantz, who hadn't known what she was doing when she put her hand to the flame. After the Lily Schobruller incident, he'd called on Ruthie personally to suggest, as gently as he could, that her energy and time would be better spent on the parish instead of an independent prayer group. He praised her for the work she had done in the past. He warned her that praying with people of other faiths could lead to an erosion of her own faith.

"You know I've been a Catholic all my life," Ruthie told him. "Nothing can weaken my devotion to the Church. But after Tom died, I realized that sometimes it takes other women to understand what a woman is going through—not only in times of grief but in everyday life."

"But why all the secrecy?"

"We have open meetings the first Saturday of every month."

"But they're never open to men. What are we supposed to think?"

Her brow furrowed; she took a long time to reply. "I guess," she said quietly, "the same thing many of *us* wonder about the priesthood."

Father George turned off the TV and read for a while. Then he climbed the stairs to his private quarters, where he put on his long johns and knelt beside his bed. *Guide me in this matter*, he prayed. *Make me a good shepherd as I follow in the steps of our Lord Jesus Christ.* He'd speak with the archbishop again tomorrow after the funeral; it might be that an investigation was in order after all, if only to put the whole thing to rest. Then he crawled beneath the covers and shook until the warmth of his body took the chill from the sheets. He imagined how the boy had felt, plunging into the icy waters of the Onion River, and for the first time since he'd heard the news, he was moved to genuine sorrow. Truly, he understood the desire to believe that the boy's last moments on earth were filled with grace, that he had not suffered, that an angel had embraced him like a good mother and carried him across the frozen fields. But old Father Gluck had taught him to observe how the mind completes that which is left unfinished, in the same way the eye reconstructs its blind spot, filling in the gaps to create an acceptable whole. The greatest act of faith was learning to live with the incomplete picture, to endure the injustice, ugliness, evil that welled from the void like blood from a wound.

Still, as he drifted off to sleep, Father George remembered the light he'd seen as a child, how the warmth sliced through the agony of fever, opening the channels of his burning lungs. He remembered Father Gluck's own face transformed with genuine pleasure at what he could neither smell nor see. The scent of the flower. The color of its petals. The tender way he cupped each blossom, briefly, between his trembling palms.

To the Editor:

I am writing to express my outrage that the teenagers involved in the kidnapping of Joy Walvoord and Sammy Carlsen and finally, on April 3, the murder of Gabriel Carpenter are still walking the streets, free as you and me. I did not know the Carpenter child, but I understand he was devout in his faith and truly a fine young person. I extend my deepest sympathy to the Carpenter family and I want to say that those who are making a circus of his death with talk of angels and other hysteria should be as ashamed as the parents of the teens who did this to him. I do know Sammy Carlsen, who is my neighbor's son, and also Joy Walvoord, who is the daughter of a co-worker. I can assure you that these are two wonderful kids who deserve to walk from one end of the block to the other without being terrorized. What Chief Mel Rooney calls a "prank gone awry" (see last week's Weekly*) I—and every sensible citizen— call a heinous crime. What is the world coming to that we can let such atrocities pass with only a slap on the wrist for the offenders? How can we imagine our city is a safer place for our children as a result of this leniency? I am* DISGUSTED, *and I'm not the only one.*

Name Withheld

—*From the* Ambient Weekly
May 1991

nine

Paul Zuggenhagen lay with his head beneath his pillow and the damp, dark covers locked over him. He could hear his younger brothers running up and down the hall, getting ready for school. He squished his fingers into his ears, but sound leaked in through his fingertips, and then his dad was pounding on the door. "You're going to get your butt to school if I have to kick it there, you understand?" Regular attendance was one of the terms of Paul's suspended sentence. Passing grades were another. And within three months of graduation, he'd be expected to show evidence of full-time employment or enrollment at an ac-credited university. Dad felt employment was the route to go; he'd been talking with an old college buddy who owned three auto dealerships in Indianapolis. "Best to give yourself a fresh start," Dad said, and Paul nodded, pretending he hadn't figured out that Dad was sending him away. Dad was senior vice-president of the Ambient branch of First Wisconsin, and even now he worried about how all this would affect his job. "Com-munity relations is the number-one priority in banking," Dad liked to say. "You boys reflect on me, don't you forget that."

"Paul?" It was his mother now, her voice soft and pleading, and he got out of bed and said, "I'm up." It was too late to take a shower—not that it mattered. Everybody stared at him regardless of what he looked like, remembering how he'd stood before the DA and told his story, just the way Mr. Powell had made him rehearse, only leaving out the part about the flash of light. "We were running after him, but we didn't touch him physically," he said. Then his mind went blank and he forgot what he was supposed to say next. "It was a joke—it was just supposed to be a joke," he said, and then, right there, in front of the court and the community cable cameras and everyone, he'd broken down and started to cry. Mr. Powell said it had worked in his favor. Later, his brothers giggled when they showed it on TV. Mom hushed them and laid her hand on Paul's arm and told him they were just too young to understand what was going on. She was the only one who touched him anymore. Today she'd fixed his oatmeal with brown sugar sprinkled into a heart. On his way out the door, she hugged him, just the way she always had, just as if it had been someone else on the bridge the night Gabriel Carpenter died.

The snow had melted, except for a few thin gray patches along the roads. The trees were budding; daffodils and tulips poked up from the soft spring soil. At school, the other kids avoided him, and most of the teachers didn't call on him. There'd been a petition—some of the parents had started it— saying that he should be permanently expelled along with Randy, but Mom and Dad went to the superintendent and Paul was allowed to finish his last term. He felt as if he'd materialized in another country, somewhere he'd never been before and yet knew intimately. Everything was the same and not the same. His court-appointed psychologist said that was pretty normal, and then he asked Paul what he had dreamed about during the past week. Paul always made something up about snakes and tunnels and trains. The truth was that he had never been able to remember his dreams.

At lunchtime, he sat by himself in the far corner of the cafeteria, eating his fried chicken and Tater Tots and chocolate pudding without really tasting anything. A group of girls walked by, Lisa Marie Kirsch among them. None of them said hi. Each wore the little gold angel pendant you could get for free if you visited the shrine. All over town, you could see those same little angels hanging from rearview mirrors; businesses posted angels in their windows and, beside them, the words *I believe*. Paul hadn't seen the shrine yet, though he very much wanted to. Kids said you could make any wish you wanted. They left things underneath the white stone angel that Cherish's mom had bought with money from hundreds of donations: rings and candles and barrettes from girls' hair, flowers and photographs. Paul wanted to leave something too. He didn't know what; he hadn't decided yet. But Dad said that if Paul showed up at Ruthie Mader's barn, it would be like pouring gasoline on a fire, and why in God's name would Paul want to do that? He said maybe Paul should use his head once in a while. He said maybe Paul would have been better off at a military school, where people could do his thinking for him.

Randy had been sent to a military school to finish his senior year. It was in West Virginia. He'd mailed Paul a picture of himself, posing in a crisp uniform in front of the American flag, and Paul could tell his face was set so he wouldn't flinch when the flash went off. He said he liked the academy OK and that he'd enlisted in the navy for next year. He hoped to wrestle for the navy team. *Maybe we can hang out next time I come home*, he wrote, but Paul didn't think he meant it. A few days after the sentencing, Paul had sneaked over to Randy's house, waited by the back door till the coast was clear, then followed him down the stairs to his paneled bedroom in the basement.

"If that little fucker only hadn't jumped," Randy said, and he punched the sandbag that hung from the ceiling. "It's his own damn fault. He'd be fine if he hadn't jumped." Paul sat at the desk, wishing he hadn't come. The room was too warm, and it smelled of sweat and pot and Randy's rage. "But Cherry's the one who takes the cake," Randy said, and he threw himself on the bed. "Ol' Cherry pretending she was too drunk to remember anything. All she had to say was that we didn't touch the kid."

"You really think she remembers?" Paul said.

"Where have you been for the past two years? She can drink like a soldier. She just didn't want to get herself involved."

"Well, it worked out anyway," Paul said.

"Worked out, yeah," Randy said. "Three hundred hours picking trash by the highway and whatever other shit they decide we have to do this summer. The rest of my senior year at a fucking military—"

He broke off then and started to laugh. "But I got to hand it to you," he said. "That story you told the papers. A flash of light! I nearly wet my pants when I read about that."

"You didn't see *anything?*" Paul said faintly.

"You mean like an angel?" Randy said, and he wasn't laughing anymore. "Get a grip on yourself. You know what happened. The kid freaked. We never laid a hand on him. We didn't do anything wrong."

They hadn't seen each other after that, but Paul still saw Cherish nearly every day, passing by him like a ghost in the halls. He tried to catch her eye, but she never lifted her gaze from the floor, and the few times he'd approached her, she'd scuttled off in the opposite direction. She didn't seem to hang around with Lisa Marie anymore. She hadn't found another boyfriend. Like him, she kept to herself. Girls whispered about her—after all, she'd nearly died. The doctors said she was lucky. He'd heard she was working at the public library after school, saving for tuition. He wondered if what Randy had said was true—that she really hadn't been all that drunk. That she remembered everything. He wondered if she'd seen the flash of light. He wondered if, each time she crossed the highway bridge, she searched the water, the sky, the fields, the way he did, looking for clues, trying to understand what had really happened.

The lunch buzzer rang, and Paul picked up his tray, carried it to the cafeteria window. As he separated his silverware and glassware and paper products, Cherish reached her tray onto the conveyor belt, then walked away before he could say anything, as if she hadn't even noticed him there. You could see the scars on her face from the whiskey bottle, red creases like lipstick around her mouth and under one eye. One side of her chin was still swollen. He envied her. At least she had concrete evidence, proof of what she'd done. To him the whole night seemed like something made up, like a lie he'd told and now had to live by. During class, when he should have been paying attention, he went over it again: how Randy had leaped from the car, how he'd followed, how the boy had taken off running like a deer. The ache in his lungs from the cold, still air. The whiskey spin in his head. The bridge and the long shine of the guardrail. Randy had run past the boy, cutting him off; the boy spun around, and Paul had lunged, missed, and then—

What he remembered for certain was Randy's face afterward, the wide-eyed, open-mouthed expression, like somebody mimicking shock. *Where the fuck did he go?* There was nothing in the water. There was no one on the road. There was the strange feeling that they'd dreamed the whole thing, even after he'd run back to the car and found Cherish in the road.

After school, he walked home slowly, his back tensed for the mudball, the soupy clot of leftover slush. A busload of kids passed by, and one of them spit a gluey-gray lunger that missed him by an inch. Robins waddled over the lawns, fat as toddlers. Spring clouds nudged each other across the sky. He had fifteen minutes to make it to his supervised service assignment; the tracking bracelet he wore around his ankle could be checked by his case-worker at any time. And yet when he passed the library, he stared at the front door as if he might be able to catch a glimpse of Cherish through the small, square window. What could it hurt to ask her? It would only take a minute. If he was late, he could blame the beautiful day. He could say he'd just stopped by Cradle Park to watch the ducks paddling under the footbridge, toss a penny into the water for luck.

The library was quiet and clean. Other than an older woman sitting behind the checkout desk, there didn't seem to be anybody inside. He wanted to ask if Cherish was working, but he was afraid the woman might recognize him, say something mean, which people often did. They said he should at least have gotten involuntary manslaughter, if not worse; they said what goes around is sure to come around, and maybe he thought he'd gotten away with something, but God would make him pay. They said what they would do to him if he were their son, if Gabriel Carpenter had been their son, if they had five minutes with him in the alley behind Jeep's and they could guarantee there'd be no angel to save him. The day after the *Ambient Weekly* ran a photograph of old Pops Carpenter, weeping in the barn where the body was found, someone had scrawled *Murderer* in permanent marker across Paul's locker. He worried that it had been Pete Carpenter, who was only a freshman, but big for his age, and was rumored to carry a switchblade in his pocket.

It didn't seem to matter to anyone that Paul was sorry. It didn't seem to matter that he'd written long letters of apology to the Carpenter family, as well as the families of Joy Walvoord and Sammy Carlsen. It didn't matter that he'd have to pay back the cost of their private counseling, which was part of the settlement Dad had made to keep things out of civil court. It didn't matter that, when he'd first heard the Circle of Faith was collecting money for a monument, he'd taken his checkbook and written Cherish's mom a check for three hundred and twelve dollars and fifty-three cents, which was everything he'd saved. "Are you crazy?" Dad said when he found out, but Mom said, "Bob, his heart's in the right place; he's trying to do what he can."

"A donation to a reputable charity is one thing," Dad said, "but these people are fanatics. God knows what they'll do with that money."

Cherish's mom had sent a kind note back; it had made Paul feel better for a while. *Time and time again*, she wrote, *I've seen how goodness comes out of tragedy. I know you must grieve over everything that's happened. Be good to yourself and remember that you were—and are—a part of God's plan.*

The woman at the checkout desk was looking at him. He ducked down the nonfiction aisle and nearly collided with Cherish, who was reshelving books from a cart. She started to back the cart out of the way, but then she looked up and saw him. He smiled, but she didn't smile back. "What do you want?" she whispered.

"How are you?" he whispered back stupidly.

She started reshelving books. "I'm working," she said. "I can't talk now."

"When can you talk?"

She evened out a row of books, dusted their tops with a feather duster.

"I was just wondering if you remember anything else about that night." He fought to keep his voice from trembling. "Like, some kind of light from a train going by? Or maybe a truck passed while we were—"

"I don't remember anything," Cherish said. "How many times do I have to tell people that?" She picked up an armload of books. He stared at the scars around her mouth, which were every bit as real as the books she was shelving, one by one. He'd lunged for the boy, he was certain of that, and suddenly the world had shattered with light. And then Randy's face with its shocked clown mask. No one in the water. No one on the road.

He was going to be late. But as he turned to leave, Cherish touched the back of his coat, and for that gift he wanted to embrace her, to put his nose into her neck and weep. Something in his eyes must have told her that, because she quickly stepped away. "All I remember was you running toward me," she said. "Just like I told the police. I wasn't at the bridge with you. I didn't see a flash of light. I didn't hear thunder. I don't know what happened out there, OK?"

The boy. The light. Randy's face, and the dark, still water. He was crying, right there in the library, crying like a little sissy girl.

"I don't know, either," Paul said.

To the Editor:

I want to make public an inspirational experience. I visited the River Angel Shrine on June 1 with my nine-year-old son who suffers from severe asthma and allergies. Despite weekly shots, his breathing is labored throughout the summer months, and he must carry his inhaler wherever he goes. When we got to the shrine, I wrote a short note asking the angel to help with my son's condition. My mother was with us and she kidded me about it, but I pinned it to the wall anyway and we left a small donation. That night, as my husband and I were going to bed, he said, "Listen," and both of us realized we couldn't hear Ricky's breathing. Of course, we both thought something was wrong and we raced down the hall only to find him sleeping peacefully. His breathing was perfectly clear. Neither my husband nor I can explain what happened, but our son hasn't used his inhaler since, and his doctor is ready to try reducing his shots. At a time when we open the newspapers daily to read stories of violence and negativity, I thought people might want to know of our experience with the shrine. We have grown closer as a family as a result. Others might remain skeptics, but—

We Believe!

Pauline Strathe

—From the Ambient Weekly
June 1991

ten

All day it had rained, the sort of warm, prattling rain that urges the hand to reach for a third cup of coffee, the gaze to linger on a second slice of pie. At ten past four, Lucy Kimmeldorf had just shooed the last customer out and flipped the COME ON IN! sign over to SORRY WE MISSED YOU!, when she heard the sharp rap of a woman's knuckles on the glass. Men didn't use their knuckles; they tended to thump with a fist, which made a deeper sound, more like a roughly cleared throat. In either case, the key was simply not to look up. SORRY WE MISSED YOU! meant just that, and so Lucy continued moving from table to table, loading the little cloverleafs of ketchup, mustard, pickle relish, and vinegar onto the tray she balanced neatly on her good shoulder. There were twenty-one tables in all, and by the time she'd cleared each one, stored the condiments in the fridge out back, and mopped the counters with the same damp rag she'd used on the tables, she figured it was safe to sneak a peek.

Janey Fields had her nose pushed to the glass. When she saw that Lucy had seen her, she rapped again, until Lucy could feel the hard surface against her own red knuckles. Gosh darn it. She unlocked the door, opened it an inch, braced it that way with the toe of her crutch. "I'm closed," she said, politely but firmly. It was, after all, a Sunday afternoon. Her busboy had called in sick, her waitress had begged off early, and Joe was still home with bronchitis. She'd be finishing up late enough as it was.

Janey's expression did not change. Her deep-set eyes were shining with infinite patience. The last time she'd come to the café after hours, she'd been collecting money for the white stone angel that now marked the spot where Gabriel Carpenter had been found. Lucy had forked over five dollars, not realizing Joe had already given twenty to another Faith member just that morning. Twenty bucks! But that was Joe, a good man, a kind soul, the sort of person who believed in a God who sent angels to rescue the weak, the innocent, the deserving. Lucy herself wasn't so sure—it seemed to her that God mostly favored powerful men like Himself, not to mention their sons. Take Paul Zuggenhagen and Randy Hale, for example. Both had had Chicago lawyers. Neither would serve a single day behind bars for what they'd done.

"If you want a whole cake," she told Janey reluctantly, "I suppose I could box one for you."

"I don't want anything to eat. I just want a minute of your time."

It was just as Lucy had suspected. Once, Janey had put her hand on Lucy's twisted shoulder and told her God could straighten her spine like a ribbon—that was the expression she'd used—if only Lucy would believe He could do so. "That poor girl," Joe had said afterward. "Anyone can see that she has a troubled mind." But things were going better for Janey now— she'd found work at the Badger State Mall and gotten engaged to Danny Hope. The two were planning an August wedding. Lucy saw no reason to humor her. "Sorry," she said, and she bumped the door closed, locked it, and lowered the shade.

That was the thing she most disliked about pious types like Janey. Regardless of professed philosophy, regardless of liberal or conservative leanings, they fixed their eye on anyone or anything showing signs of irregularity, variety, difference. Mystery was intolerable. Things had to happen for a reason. One couldn't view Lucy's childhood bout with polio as simply that—it must mean something, it must stand for something, and Lucy herself must be treated as a symbol. How often people like Janey took it upon themselves to assume disability weighed on *her* mind the way it apparently weighed on *theirs*. Sometimes, in the restaurant, strangers would say things like "You must be very brave," or "You must be a courageous person," as she served their meals, her right hand busy with her crutch, her left steadying the tray on her shoulder. No one who truly knew Lucy Kimmeldorf would have thought to say such a patronizing thing. If she was remarkable, it was because she'd had the gumption to start a business of her own in 1962, a time when a married woman, a mother, rarely did such a thing. It was because she'd gone back to school for a business degree when she was forty-five. It was because she'd run for City Council at fifty and won—the first woman to be elected. The only woman, still, out of five council members.

She closed out the register, enjoying the racket of the adding machine, the clean white coil of paper. Another good day. Regardless of what she might think of the shrine personally, everybody on Main Street was enjoying effects that some were calling, well, miraculous. The river angel story had put Ambient, Wisconsin, on the map, and after ten years of painful, wasting decline, the downtown was holding its own. People—only the papers called them *pilgrims*—came to Ambient from places no one could have imagined. They were mostly curiosity seekers, the sort who would drive fifty miles out of their way to see, say, a plane crash site, or the birthplace of a movie star. After visiting the shrine,

they usually continued on to someplace else, cars and trucks and
Winnebagos loaded with kids, coolers, bicycles, dogs. But they
spent the day in town, poking around the shops, picnicking in
Cradle Park. Some visited the Crane Foundation, where wounded
birds were nursed back to health, or the Kauths' llama farm,
which advertised daily tours, or the railroad museum on Main.
Others fished, or rented canoes, or explored the antique shops,
not knowing they were little more than rummage sales that people kept going year round.

Local merchants like Lucy finally had an edge over the chains
at the Solomon strip: What these pilgrims wanted was a glimpse
of local color, a slow walk through a quaint river town, a quiet
afternoon with family that ended with an old-fashioned meal at
a ma-and-pa restaurant exactly like Kimmeldorf's Café. Early in
May, Lucy had whipped up a new recipe called Angel Pie,
which came with a tiny plastic angel on the top. It was big with
kids—lots of meringue and sugary sprinkle on what was, basi-
cally, banana custard. Next door, Cheddarheads was selling angel
T-shirts that said I BELIEVE! on the front and CHEDDARHEADS
GIFTS—AMBIENT, WISCONSIN on the back. The River Stop sold
the same angel charms that the Circle of Faith gave away free,
plus angel key chains and music boxes and bottles of river water,
angel candleholders and Christmas tree ornaments, angel picture
frames and angel wind chimes and even bumper stickers that
boasted THIS CAR PROTECTED BY THE RIVER ANGEL. Stan and
Lorna Pranke, after briefly putting their house up for sale,
changed their minds and opened a novelty shop called Angels
Everywhere in their two front rooms. Now they sold angel
watches and ties and underwear, angel birdbaths and stepping-
stones, angels to mount on your dashboard or desk, even little
guardian angel charms that could be attached to a cherished
pet's collar. Not to be outdone, Ambient Blooms advertised a
special arrangement called A Band of Angels, and Jeep Curry

had invented a new drink, Angel Tonic (Guaranteed to Make a Believer out of *You*!).

Even Big Roly Schmitt had an angel in his window; Lucy had asked him, pleasantly enough, if it wasn't the angel of death. During those rare moments when Lucy believed in a deity, she hoped a special hell had been reserved for Big Roly, who had single-handedly laid the groundwork for the big chains like Wal-Mart and McDonald's to move in. Of course, there'd been other developers involved, but Big Roly wasn't some newcomer out to make a few bucks off strangers. Big Roly had been in Lucy's own graduating class at Ambient High. Who would have guessed that fat, shy, funny-looking little boy would grow up to be such a bastard? All fall he'd been looking for loopholes in a city ordinance that restricted buildings to two stories; at the last council meeting, he'd won a petition to build three-story single-family residences. Such a structure was completely out of character with the rest of Ambient—it would make existing homes look dowdy, impact on property values, drive taxes up and the little ranch home owners out. Lucy had leaned over and said to Jeep Curry, without bothering to cover her mike, that Big Roly was no better than a cannibal, picking his teeth with Ambient's bones. The quote made the *Tri-City Weekly*; Marv Weissbrot, the publisher, chaired the Ambient Preservation Committee. The caption beneath Big Roly's jowly picture read: "Schmitt Denies Cannibalism."

Lucy locked the register, checked the burners, and stepped outside into the drizzle. Exhaust from the bridge traffic sweetened the air, and she felt the dampness settle in her hip. She locked the door and headed toward her car, but after a block she paused to rest, pretending to look into the darkened window of what had once been Fohr's Furniture. Sometimes she still experienced an odd weakness in her left leg, and this seemed to be getting a little bit worse each year.

"You OK?" Joe would say anxiously as she struggled to get up out of a chair, and she'd say, "Nothing's wrong with me that one of those Carnival Cruises wouldn't cure." Surely some tiredness, some aches and pains in her back and shoulders, were normal enough. After all, she was fifty-six years old; she worked fifty-hour weeks in a body that had carried, then raised, three boys to manhood. She glanced at her reflection in the display window and discovered Janey Fields' ghostly outline standing right beside her.

"I really need to talk with you," Janey said.

Lucy jumped like a cat. Her crutch skidded out from under her; she barely managed to keep from falling. "Do you always sneak up on people like that?" She turned down the alley toward the municipal parking lot, but Janey followed, just a few steps behind, and Lucy could feel how she was looking at her leg, the brace that gripped it just below the knee, the way her shoulder bobbed as she walked. *Dear God*, she thought, *she's going to tell me Jesus wants to heal me, and I'm going to beat her to death with this crutch*. There were two vehicles left in the parking lot; Lucy's was the world-weary Econoline. She got in, shut the door, vigorously turned the key.

The engine wouldn't catch.

She tried again, then again. The click-click that resulted sounded like dropped change. Janey stood at the edge of the alley, watching. To her credit, she didn't look smug when Lucy got out of the van.

"This is me right here," Janey said, pointing to the other vehicle, a shiny new Buick. Her dad had been a doctor—none of the Fields kids had ever lacked for anything. "I can give you a ride."

"Thanks, I'll just call Joe." But she hated to do it. He'd been sick off and on since spring: colds, flu, now this stubborn bout of bronchitis. Ironic, considering all the vitamins he'd been taking, the special supplements and powders he bought at the health food store at the mall. Beeswax. Shark cartilage. Ginseng. She suspected he'd carry a charm against the evil eye if he knew where to find one. This morning, once again, she'd left him flushed and feverish in front of the TV.

"Don't you find," Janey said, "that sometimes things happen for a reason? Like, maybe you're meant to listen to me, whether you want to or not?"

And at that moment, the sniveling sky opened up and released an all-out downpouring rain. What could Lucy do except follow Janey to her car? "You wanted a minute, you got it," she said, and then, steeling herself to hear about Christ's infinite love, she checked her watch. "Go."

"Big Roly Schmitt's buying Ruthie Mader's farm, and I'll tell you what—he's planning condominiums bigger than the Taj Mahal." Janey spit it all out in one breath, like a child.

Lucy stared. "What on earth are you talking about?"

"She's double mortgaged and she owes back taxes and now Cherish has turned herself around and plans to go to college and Ruthie doesn't even have a savings account—she just doesn't know what else to do. He says he'll pay her moving expenses and handle everything for her, even give her a break on one of his apartments in Solomon."

No wonder Big Roly had been so concerned about rezoning. Lucy could imagine those condos already, three-story brick monstrosities with circular driveways, towering glass windows glaring at the town like demonic eyes. And all that river frontage built up with boat docks, fenced off and privatized. And all those people wanting their conveniences. And the Fair Mile Crossroads just down the road. Within two years, it would be another Solomon strip, the fields sown with golden arches and giant doughnuts, video stores and liquor stores, grocery stores and banks.

"Has she signed anything?"

"Not yet," Janey said. "You're on the City Council, and I know Ruthie would never ask herself, but I just thought maybe you could do something . . ."

"Well . . ." Lucy was already thinking in that direction.

"Maya Paluski says the city can control anything within a mile of its limits."

"A mile and a half. It's called eminent domain. The council can legally block development if it will adversely affect the city. That's certainly one possibility."

"It isn't, though, not really," Janey said. "Because if Big Roly doesn't buy it, the bank will foreclose."

"Then why deal with a big developer like Schmitt? Get an honest broker to find some city couple who want a twenty-acre parcel for a single-family home. Ruthie could pay down her debts, keep the land around the house and . . . barn." She could not bring herself to say *shrine*.

"The house sits on the high ground. Big Roly says anybody wanting to build closer to the river wouldn't get a mortgage because it's in the floodplain."

He was probably right.

Janey said, "I can't accept it's God's will for Ruthie to lose that farm—not now, after everything that's happened. One lady from Prairie du Chien, they thought she had this tumor in her brain? And when she got back home from the shrine, the doctor couldn't find any trace—"

"I'll see what I can do," Lucy said quickly.

"Just don't tell Ruthie I told you, OK?" She clutched at the gold cross all the Faith members wore. "We're not supposed to repeat anything we talk about at the Faith house." She looked at Lucy with such anguish that Lucy wanted to smooth back her hair, the way she would have done with an overwrought child. And yet Janey was a grown woman. An engagement ring sparkled on her finger, and not for the first time. She'd had female trou-

bles, or so the story went, until the day she'd rescued Gabriel
Carpenter from a group of taunting boys. Lucy herself had rescued Gabriel once, but he'd seemed like an ordinary kid to her,
grubby the way her own sons had been grubby, alternately
friendly and shy. He said he'd been saved, but so did half the
kids in Ambient. The only thing remarkable about him had been
his appetite. And now, of course, the fact that he was gone. It
was likely that no one would ever know what had really happened
on the highway bridge, how he'd reached the barn despite the
cold. It was one of those things. A mystery. Perhaps, if one
needed an explanation, the river angel story was as good as any.

"You did the right thing," Lucy assured her. "Now I'd sure
appreciate that ride home before Joe starts to worry."

"Let's try your van one more time," Janey said. "Maybe it was
flooded."

"I didn't smell gas."

"Give me your key," Janey said, and Lucy followed her back
across the parking lot. Janey turned the ignition key, then de-
pressed the accelerator, held it to the floor. "Don't wear down
my starter," Lucy said anxiously, but even as she spoke, the van
roared to life.

"Burns off the gas," Janey said. "I guess I could have showed
you that trick a little sooner." She grinned so sheepishly that Lucy
had to smile back.

It was well after six by the time she pulled into her driveway.
Sunday nights, she and Joe watched *60 Minutes* together, pretending they weren't remembering a time when the kids would
be sprawled on the floor between them, wriggling like eels in their
striped pajamas. Now Mike was in southern Illinois; Charles was
in Indiana; Preston was in New York City. If there was one thing
that Lucy could not forgive the Big Rolys of the world for, it was
this: Her children had had no choice but to move away. What
else could they do? Lucy had a brand-new baby granddaughter

she still hadn't seen; she'd met Charles's wife only twice. Perhaps it was this sense of isolation that was weighing on Joe lately. Nights, she smelled his worry like a film of perspiration, salty and strong; in the morning, the odor lingered in the bedsheets, clung to his clothing, his favorite chair. He double-checked doors and windows to make sure they were locked. More than once, on their way to work in the morning, they'd had to turn around because Joe was convinced a burner was on. He'd point at a freckle on his arm, a mole on his chest—had it always looked this way? Was she certain? He watched her as she moved around the café, and if she happened to slip a bit, his caught breath whistled between his teeth.

"That leg bothering you?" he'd say. "You sure you're all right?"

"I'm fine, Joe," she'd say, even though the honest truth was that she was, well, tired. Perhaps they should just sell the restaurant, move down to Florida like so many of their friends seemed to be doing. Perhaps she should leave Big Roly in peace—after all, who could be certain that Ruthie wouldn't be better off in Solomon? Let the shrine and all its hysteria die down, let people get on with their lives. Let the Circle of Faith return to its clothing drives and fund-raisers, its oh-so-secret meetings at the Crossroads. But what would happen to the downtown without the lure of the shrine? What would make Ambient stand out from every other little town on the Onion River, jostling for exposure in the state's tourist brochures, desperate for outside money?

There were those who said the shrine was deeply moving. Stan Pranke visited it nearly every morning, often stopping by the café afterward to hand out Angels Everywhere business cards. He was only one of many who claimed to have felt the presence of the angel at the shrine from time to time. Others had been granted special favors: an easy labor, a message from a lost loved one, recovery from an illness. Smokers left cigarettes wrapped in dollar bills; those who kicked the habit took out personal ads in the *Ambient Weekly*, crediting the shrine and leaving instructions for others who wanted to quit. Letters to the editor from out-of-town guests praised its rustic beauty. Of course, there were plenty who claimed it was the tackiest thing they'd ever seen—a mile of white Christmas lights wrapped around a barn that still stank of sheep, a three-foot white stone angel beneath a rough white wooden cross. Still, a Church investigation was in progress. Church buses representing various denominations groaned into town on weekends, coughing black clouds of exhaust. A sociologist from some Florida university was interviewing everyone who had seen or heard or experienced something unusual on the night of Gabriel's fall. A New England woman writing a book on angels had taken a room at the newly remodeled Moonwink–Best Western, and she could be seen in the railroad museum, squinting at old letters and newspaper clippings.

Lucy let herself into the house, hung up her jacket and purse. Joe had made a split-pea soup, and she ladled some into a bowl, cut herself a slice of bread to go with it, all the while thinking, thinking. What if the council *could* establish the city's interest in the shrine's preservation? The farm would be kept from development, yes; still, that wouldn't solve the problem of Ruthie's debt. Selling off acreage was clearly the solution, but a specialized buyer would be required, someone who wanted that river frontage for fishing, for boating—

—for a new city park! Lucy closed the bread drawer with a gleeful slam, imagining the look on Big Roly's face as the city snatched that land out from under him. It would take some fancy footwork, sure, but they'd been having the same discussions regarding recreational space since she'd first been elected. Cradle Park was jammed all summer long, and there were no bike trails or walking paths, no public boat ramp anywhere along the river aside from the one by the Killsnake Dam—where there were less than a dozen parking spots, thanks to the millpond crowd. Everyone wanted another park. Of course, no one, least of all the taxpayers, wanted to foot the bill. But in order to save the house and barn, Ruthie might be convinced to set a price the city couldn't afford to refuse. And as for the rest of the land—it would almost be like she still owned it. The only significant development would be along the water, and that would be—what?—a boat ramp, picnic tables, rest rooms, some parking. Swings for the kiddies. Maybe sand for a beach.

"Lucy, that you?" Joe called from the living room, and she hollered back, as she always did, "It better be." He was on the couch, watching Ed Bradley, the bedroom comforter pulled up to his chin. Wadded-up tissues littered the coffee table, and the air smelled of cherry cough syrup. "I was starting to worry," he said as Lucy sat down beside him with her soup.

"You always worry," she said. "Guess what?"

"Narrow the topic."

"Big Roly Schmitt."

Joe groaned. "What now?"

"He's made Ruthie Mader an offer on her property."

"The shrine? What would he do, charge admission?"

"Better still," Lucy said. "Build monster condos on top of it."

Joe shook his head. "She would never sell that property."

"She's in debt, Joe. She may not have a choice."

He looked at her. "You're kidding, right?"

"Nope."

"I would hope," he said, his voice shaking a little, "that the city will do what it can to protect the shrine from development."

It surprised her to see that he was upset; *she* was the one who despised Big Roly. "I'm looking into it, Joe," she said. "Soon as I finish this soup, in fact." But when she stood up, her foot landed shy of where she wanted it, catching the leg of the coffee table.

She crashed back down into the sofa cushions. The soup bowl rolled across the carpet.

"Lucy!"

"I just tripped, Joe, for Pete's sake."

"You don't think that leg's getting worse?"

"Maybe you'd get better if you quit worrying over every little damn thing."

"You're not a little damn thing. You're a big damn thing."

Lucy didn't smile.

"I'm sorry," Joe said, and he rested his hot, hot forehead against her cheek. "I just wish I could lay my hands on you and make everything right."

There was something about that that Lucy didn't like. *God will straighten your spine like a ribbon.* The earnest pity in Janey's face.

"Make yourself right, Joe," Lucy said. *"You're* the one who's sick." And she got up without mishap and walked briskly to the kitchen to phone Jeep Curry for his opinion, and then Leland Kramer, the city planner.

The next morning, first thing, Leland stopped by the restaurant. The survey looked promising; he wanted to take a personal look. "Let me talk to Ruthie first," Lucy said. "In the meantime, keep this under your hat."

"Gee, Lucy, I was planning to drop in on Big Roly as soon as I left here." He laughed wickedly. "This sure'll get him huffing and puffing, won't it?"

"I do hope so," Lucy said.

Joe was still out sick, so late that afternoon she turned the restaurant over to her wait staff and headed toward Ruthie's by way of the River Road, which was prettier than County C. After days of rain, the sun had warmed the temperature to a breezy seventy. The corn and wheat and soybeans were up; the River Road Apple Orchard was in full bloom, humming with bees. Perhaps the good weather would give her some pep. Perhaps she and

Joe would get out a little more, drive to Madison for a nice dinner, see a movie at the mall. At the J road, she headed east, crossing over the highway bridge. A white memorial cross had been erected there, along with a small wooden sign in the shape of an arrow, which said SHRINE. There were plastic wreaths, small American flags; even—good heavens!—a picture of the Pope, sealed inside a plastic bag. *Different strokes*, Lucy reminded herself, but the older she got, the less patience she had with this kind of thing. Joe was just the opposite. He'd started going to Mass again; nights he couldn't sleep, he prayed the Rosary. He'd even mentioned once or twice that they ought to take a ride out to the shrine, see what the fuss was about. Lucy just laughed and said that with all the talk around the café, she felt as if she'd already seen it.

"Aren't you the least bit curious?" Joe had said. "It's not every day somebody sees an angel."

"Jeez, Joe, not you too!"

"All I'm saying is there are things in the world that can't be explained. Things beyond our five senses."

"That's why we each have a sixth sense," Lucy said. "*Common* sense. And in case you haven't noticed, Ruthie Mader doesn't seem to have too much of that one. I swear, every time she comes into the café, she's back two hours later, looking for her purse."

Lucy hadn't been out to the Mader farm since last fall, when she and Joe had picked out Halloween pumpkins at Ruthie's unattended crop stand. You selected whatever you wanted from the piles of pumpkins and gourds, the various squashes laid out in rows, jars of preserves and strings of dried fruit. Then you paid on the honor system. There wasn't even a lock on the cash box. Joe had thought it was sweet and old-fashioned.

"More like ridiculous," Lucy said.

Now the crop stand looked as if someone had backed into it, and she was shocked by how run-down the whole place looked in general. The concrete birdbath in the apple orchard had tipped, cracked in two, and the tall pole that once held a purple-martin house was stretched out on its side. Scraps of aluminum foil, paper napkins, fast-food wrappers, and soda cans littered the courtyard, which was fenced in by a string of bright-yellow plastic flags; a new-looking wooden sign hammered to the side of the shed read PLEASE PARK ON GRAVEL SURFACES ONLY. No one was parked anywhere right now, but clearly people had been parking wherever they pleased: beneath the apple trees, carving ruts that exposed the tender roots; on what was left of the sloping front lawn; even beside the barn itself, gouging the wood with their bumpers. A second, more weathered-looking sign beneath the first read RIVER ANGEL SHRINE, with an arrow beneath it pointing to the barn. A third sign, mounted beside the sidewalk leading up to the house, read PRIVATE RESIDENCE. NO PUBLIC RESTROOMS. A yellow angel was painted on each of the signs, and all the O's had tiny halos—Lucy recognized Maya Paluski's artistic hand.

She parked, fished her crutch from the back seat. The sun was crawling to the edge of the horizon, pulling the day's warmth along with it. Swallows and nighthawks wheeled above the barn; a yellow star blinked over the door. Ruthie emerged from beneath it, carrying a garbage bag in one hand.

"Hello?" Lucy called.

Ruthie squinted, didn't answer. Behind her, the fields sloped black and wet until they reached the diamond sparkle of the river. Lucy took a step forward and saw the precise moment Ruthie recognized her—not by her face. By her crutch.

"Lucy! I'm sorry, I just get so many visitors—"

"So it seems," Lucy said, gesturing at the signs. "I can't believe what they've done to the place."

"We set out trash cans just last week, and look—they've already disappeared. It's amazing what people will take as souvenirs. They've picked all my flowers by the house." Lucy could see the bald iris bed, the blind peonies and tiger lilies. "There's a rumor they're good for the sick."

"And the price is right, besides."

Ruthie laughed. "I suppose that's part of it," she said. "So. You've finally come to see the shrine."

"Actually . . ." Lucy said—but then she paused. It wouldn't do to offend Ruthie now. "Well, yes. But I came to see you too."

"We'll go in together, then," Ruthie said. "I need to finish cleaning up."

At first, it was exactly what Lucy had expected. Nailed to the door was a basket filled with tiny gold angel pendants; the sturdy wooden box just below was marked DONATIONS. Lucy noted that, this time, the cash was protected by a padlock. But stepping inside the barn was like entering another world. Christmas lights outlined the beams, creating a box of light into which she felt her way blindly, unable to see the dark floor. On the wall behind the white stone angel, a rough cross opened its arms in a way that made Lucy think of a woman down on one knee to embrace a child. Half-burned votive candles were lined up at the statue's base, a dozen flames flickering sleepily on a flat sheet of aluminum, which was enclosed by a rough brick firewall. As Ruthie bent to replace the burned-out candles, Lucy noticed—with relief—a fire extinguisher mounted in a case. The walls were covered with signatures, and some people had even carved their initials into the wood. Others had pinned up photographs, mementos, cigarettes wrapped in dollar bills. Lucy plucked one down, unrolled the dollar, and read the note inside: *Please help my dad quit smoking, it is killing him, I promise twenty dollars if he quit.* There were two sets of shelves built into the walls, and these were filled with dried Band of Angels bouquets, plastic flowers, wildflowers in cloudy jars of water, dolls and toys and lockets of hair tied with ribbon, letters, small china statues. A child's mitten. A man's dapper hat. A glass paperweight filled with snow.

"So many things," Lucy said, and she sat in a folding chair: There were several scattered along the walls, along with an old couch and parlor chair. Someone had left a wrist brace; someone else had left a cane. A woman's pretty scarf was draped from a low beam. It was peaceful here, she had to admit, with the swallows preparing for nightfall, the bubbling coo of pigeons in the silo, the breath of the wind on the walls. And then, the sound of voices—

—it was a family: two little girls, a father and mother. The mother led a small white dog on a leash. The dog started to bark at the shadows cast by the candles, a shrill, high-pitched barking that set Lucy's teeth on edge.

"Lookit the angel!" the older girl said.

"Stand back from the candles, honey," the man said.

"Shh!" The woman scooped up the dog and rocked it like a child.

"We're from Dodgeville," the man said in a loud, tourist voice. "Are you the lady who saw the angel?"

Ruthie nodded.

"Well, we believe you anyway," the woman said. "I saw an angel myself when I was, I don't know, eight or nine?" She sat down in one of the folding chairs, still holding the dog in her arms.

"You said you were six, the last time you told it," the man said, grinning. "She changes the story every time."

The woman ignored him. "Every morning, I had to lead our cows out to pasture, and then I'd fetch them back at the end of the day. The path wound through a stand of trees, and Lord, was I ever scared of that place! A woman was supposed to have hung herself there, but my mother said that was only a story."

"And you girls think *you* have it tough." The man poked the younger one lightly in the belly. The girls giggled and leaned against their mother, who kept on talking. The little dog had closed its eyes.

"One afternoon, it started to snow, and by four-thirty it was dark as night. I just started to cry at the thought of going out there alone. But my mother said that if I was that scared, I should ask God to send my guardian angel to walk with me. And wouldn't you know, when I got to the stand of trees, a little girl was waiting for me. She was about my age, and she was wearing some kind of fur coat, and when she saw me, she smiled and started walking. She never spoke, just looked back now and then to make sure I was keeping up OK. She walked with me every evening after that, until spring came and the days were long again. I never saw her after that."

It was the sort of story Joe loved. Joe. That scarf caught Lucy's eye again. It was red, with a pattern of elephants marching trunk to tail, just like one she had at home. She got up and tugged it down from the beam, and as she turned it over in her hands, she saw the oil crease where she'd accidentally slammed it into the car door. Still, it took her a moment before she understood.

She wound the scarf around her neck and hurried out of the barn. The sun was setting over the river. Bats flashed through the air, dived at the yellow star above the barn door like hard-thrown stones.

God will straighten your spine like a ribbon.

She walked up to the porch, sat down on the step. From the time they'd started dating, Joe had insisted she was beautiful to him, that she was exactly what he wanted. On their wedding night, she'd been shy until he'd finally pulled the sheet away, revealed her naked and shivering and trying to cover herself with her hands. "You're one of a kind, that's all," he'd said, and at last she'd unfolded her arms. During the thirty-three years they'd been married, he'd always claimed to love her exactly as she was. But now she knew the truth. He saw her as something broken, something that needed to be fixed. He saw her the way any stranger would, walking into the café. Everything they'd shared, everything she'd accomplished, hadn't made any difference. And at that moment, Lucy knew that a particular tenderness between them had been lost for good. She might forgive him, over time, but she'd never be able to forget.

When Ruthie came out of the barn, Lucy stayed motionless in the twilight, wishing she could just slip away. But Ruthie carried the trash bag across the courtyard, headed straight up the sidewalk toward the house. "Oh—there you are," she said. "I'm sorry, I just got so completely caught up in that woman's story. It's amazing how often people are moved to share experiences like that."

"And you believe them." Lucy found she didn't have the energy to form a question.

"I believe that even the most ordinary people regularly experience extraordinary things." Ruthie tossed the bag up onto the porch and sat beside Lucy on the step. "It's just that these experiences are no longer valued, or trusted. So we hide them. We keep them to ourselves."

"Maybe it's better that way," Lucy said. "Sometimes we're mistaken about things, and when that happens, we wind up misleading others. Hurting others."

"All we can do is be true to what we believe," Ruthie said. "At least, that's what my daughter tells me."

"How is Cherish?" Lucy said, changing the subject. She thought of the frightened child she'd led from her father's funeral so long ago.

Ruthie sighed. "All those times she was sneaking out to cause mischief, I thought she was home studying. But now that she's really studying all the time, I wish she'd go out with friends."

"I hear she's working at the library."

"She's going to Eau Claire this fall. She wants to major in

English. *English.* I always thought it would be art." Ruthie looked hard at Lucy. "You've been to school," she said. "College, I mean. Did it change you? All the ideas you read in books?"

"Sure," Lucy said. "That's why you read them. To open your mind."

Ruthie sighed. "Cherish won't go to church anymore. She says she's an atheist—can you imagine?"

"I suppose I am too. Agnostic anyway. Not like Joe." She fingered her scarf, tried to sound casual. "Does he come here a lot?"

"I haven't seen him recently."

"That's because he has bronchitis. No doubt from sitting in a drafty old barn." She'd meant it to come off as a joke, but her voice was so bitter that it was hard to recognize as her own. The family emerged from the barn. There was the clear, clean sound of coins against the bottom of the donation box.

"Look. I have to be straight with you—I didn't come to see the shrine. I'm here because there's a rumor you're selling out to Big Roly Schmitt."

"How did you find out about this?" Ruthie said, and then she put her head in her hands. "No, don't tell me," she said through her fingers. "At this point, it doesn't matter, I guess."

"Have you signed anything?"

Ruthie shook her head, and suddenly Lucy felt ashamed. It wasn't Ruthie's fault about Joe.

"Tell me something," Lucy said. "Do you really want him to have this property?"

"I'll tell you exactly what I want," Ruthie said. "I want to pay off my debts and send my daughter to school. I want to live in this house and maintain the shrine for as long as people feel the need to see it. Tom and I worked hard for this farm, so hard—" Her voice broke. She reached inside the neck of her sweater, fingered the cross at her throat as if the answers to everything were contained inside it. "I've done all that I can do."

"Then let me tell you what *I* want," Lucy said. "I want to keep this town alive. As a *town*—not a suburb or a strip mall. With a Main Street people can walk to. With the sort of character that makes our kids want to stay after they're grown and our parents remain once they retire. A place where people feel safe because it has a center, a soul, and we've lost that somehow. We've lost each other. We need to find ourselves back again." She thought of Joe, his vitamins and prayers. His fear. "I'll be straight with you—I don't believe in the shrine the way it seems my husband does. But I believe in what it means for the city. I want to protect it if I can."

"What can you do?" Ruthie said wearily.

"Did you know the city is looking to purchase riverfront land for a public park?"

Ruthie stared at her. "No," she said. "I don't keep up with the papers much."

"It's not in the papers—yet," Lucy said. "Here's what I was thinking. I'd like to have the city planner come out and take a look. If the parcel looks good, we can make a proposal to the general council. But I have to tell you, it's a long shot. The council might not go for it—not everybody thinks as I do. Or they could kick it to a referendum, in which case the voters could kill it. And I should tell you the city probably won't pay you what Schmitt can."

"I don't care about profit," Ruthie said. "This is the miracle I've prayed for."

"There's no such thing as miracles," Lucy said. "There's good luck and bad luck, and we're going to need plenty of the first kind to make this happen."

"No doubt Cherish would agree with your vision of things," Ruthie said. "But you and I—we'll have to agree to disagree if we're going to work together." She took Lucy's hand like a sister. "Now tell me," she said. "What do you need from me? What can I do to help?"

It was dark by the time Lucy got back home. Joe opened the door as she pulled in the driveway, waited for her as she came up the walk. "I finally called the restaurant," he said, "and they said you'd left hours ago. I was *this* close to calling Mel Rooney—" But before he could say anything more, she unwound the scarf from her neck, balled it up, and hurled it at him like a bomb. Then she stormed down the hall to their room, slammed the door so hard it bounced back open, slammed it again. The minute Joe appeared, she shouted, "What the hell did you think you were doing, Joe? I'm not good enough for you the way that I am?"

Joe opened his mouth, closed it. "I don't see what you're mad about," he finally said. "I thought that this might help. It can't hurt anyway."

She threw her crutch across the room, balanced herself against the bedpost. "This is the package I come in. You don't like it, you shouldn't have married it. You don't want it anymore, divorce it."

"Lucy."

"You said it didn't matter to you!"

"They say it helps people quit smoking. They say somebody's cancer went away. What's wrong with having a little faith?"

She stared at him as if he were someone she'd never seen before.

"You said it didn't matter, Joe," she said. "All these years."

"You're blowing this out of proportion. You know how I feel about you."

"And how's that, Joe?"

She could see him choosing his words as if both their lives depended on it. The room seemed to hold its breath. The faces of their children and grandchildren watched them from the dresser, from the top of the TV, from the wall above the bed.

To the Editor:

I am writing on behalf of my husband and myself to ask again if anyone knows the whereabouts of Fred's brother, Shawn James Carpenter, that you please call me or you could always leave a note at Jeep's, you do not have to sign your name either. The detective we hired last April has found nothing except that maybe he was in Utah for a while, but we don't know. This has been a difficult year for our family and we appreciate all the help and support from everyone who knew Gabriel or is touched by his story. There's been some talk that we oppose the shrine and plan to bring legal action against Ruthie Mader, and I want to say for everyone to see, this is not true. We don't pretend to understand everything that has happened, but as long as it's helping people, so much the better. We are ready to put this behind us if we ever can to get on with our lives.

Sincerely,
Bethany Carpenter

—From the Ambient Weekly
July 1991

e l e v e n

Ruthie Mader sat up in bed, watched the sun push itself free of the earth like a giant hothouse flower. The tax debt had weighed on her mind for so long that she felt for it now out of habit, the way the tongue reaches for a notch in the gum, a sour, cracked tooth—but no. In July, the city had voted to purchase ninety acres for the Thomas Mader Recreational Area. The sale had left her with money enough to secure the house and barn, plus the remaining ten acres of land. God was good. And Lucy Kimmeldorf was a genius.

Two weeks after the sale, the Circle had sponsored a victory potluck in her honor. Ruthie placed an open invitation in the *Ambient Weekly*, expecting no more than a hundred people, but by five o'clock that afternoon, there were over four hundred—the line of parked cars stretched to the highway bridge—and most signed their names in the guest book Anna Grey Graf had thought to bring along. Her husband, Bill, had warmed up to the Circle; he even took shifts at the grills with Joe Kimmeldorf, Jeep Curry, and Fred Carpenter, flipping hamburgers and brats. Stan Pranke supervised from a lawn chair, Bill Graf, Sr., and old Pops Carpenter joined him with a six-pack, and every now and then all three of them disappeared in a blast of charcoal smoke. Women unfolded card tables, arranged platters of cold fried chicken and boiled ham and cold cuts, three-bean salads and carrot salads, coleslaw and sauerkraut and finger Jell-O, rolls and chips and sour cream dips, tray after tray of dessert bars. There was sweet lemonade in rented canisters, ice-filled tubs of soda and Pabst. Children raced through the orchard in packs, collecting apples for green-apple fights. Babies slept on blankets spread out in shady rows beside the house. Janey Fields and Danny Hope, just back from their honeymoon, sat beside the babies, and everybody teased them that they better watch it, those things might be contagious. Even Cherish came out of her shell, lifting her head to greet people, chatting with Lisa Marie Kirsch, running for extra serving spoons.

For the first time since that cold night in April—in some ways, it seemed to Ruthie, for the first time since Tom's death—there was a sense of community again. A collective feeling of optimism. When night fell, everyone worked together building a giant bonfire. There were marshmallows and plenty of sticks, and in the restless, searching shadows of the flames, the talk turned quiet, reflective. Alone or in groups, people slipped away to the barn, where they stood before the white stone angel to marvel at what had happened. Some returned to the fire and told of a feeling, a presence, a peacefulness there. Some spoke of other experiences they'd had that ruffled the smooth grain of reason. As soon as the talk turned in this direction, Ruthie saw Cherish rise, make her way back to the house. Soon the light in her bedroom winked on. No doubt she was opening a book, losing herself in the ideas of a stranger. How eager she was to move away from Ambient, to live in a place where no one knew her story, to meet people who would look into her scarred face and accept it as it was, without recalling its former landscape.

And now that day had finally arrived; Ruthie couldn't quite believe it. By noon, Cherish would be settling into a dormitory in Eau Claire, having conversations with people Ruthie would never meet, talking about things that Ruthie, with her outdated high school diploma, would never understand.

Ruthie pulled her knees to her chest, leaned back against the headboard, and closed her eyes to pray. She did not say any particular prayer; she no longer memorized Bible verses. Over the years, she had moved away from the sharp-cornered lines of her schoolgirl catechism, searching for warmer cadences, something more graceful, closer to love. Raising a child had taught her the purest sounds of devotion, how words are merely the residue meaning leaves in our mouths. Monks chanting Latin in brown-robed lines, parents singing nursery rhymes to drowsing children, even the comfort of a standard greeting—*Hi. Hello. How are you? Fine*—the message behind each was constant, unchanging, insistent as a heartbeat. *I'm here. I'm here.* The oldest prayer. Ruthie prayed until she felt herself growing visible, and at that moment she was raised up, becoming—for a brief, brilliant eye blink—larger than she knew herself to be. And that was Faith—the mind's surrender to the stunned and terrified wonder of the heart. Like the moment after Cherish's birth, when she'd reached out to touch that wet, furred skull. Like the moment of Tom's death, when she was in the root cellar, innocently weeding soft apples from the bin, and suddenly felt him standing behind her, one hand in his pocket, and knew. Like the moment in the barn, when she'd first seen the boy bathed in light, smelled the sweetness of his skin. Each time the same whisper: *I'm here, I'm here.* Knowing God would be like such a moment, only stretched into all eternity.

She opened her eyes. Cherish was up; Ruthie could hear her moving around her room, thumping the last of her books into boxes. Since that night on the bridge, she'd suffered from terrible insomnia, which left her glassy-eyed and distracted. She prowled the house with her face tucked low, as if to hide the fading scribble of scars. Anything Ruthie said or did only made things worse. When she tried to explain that when God shuts a door, He opens a window, that even the worst of experiences had the potential for goodness if one only turned them over to the Lord, Cherish merely marked her place in her book with a finger and waited for Ruthie to finish.

"That's one way to look at the world," she'd say, or else, "That's very interesting."

That calm, rational tone. The same tone used by the priest whom the archdiocese sent to investigate the shrine, a plump, kindly man who had already made up his mind. They went over the details again and again. What had the angel looked like? How had Ruthie known what it was? And how much sleep had she had that night? (He apologized, shifted the focus of his inquiries.) The temperature of the boy's skin—would she say it had been room temperature? A little cooler? Warm like a fresh cup of tea? And his coloration—flushed? As in bruised or feverish? As in raw chilled skin? When Ruthie described the odor that had surrounded the body, the priest shook his head in a good-natured way. "Wet hay might have such a smell," he suggested, and then he checked his notes. "You mentioned the boy's damp clothing."

"I know what wet hay smells like," Ruthie said, looking at his soft, city hands. She didn't understand it, either. She still didn't understand. Why had this happened, and why to her? What did it mean? Was she responsible? The same kind of thoughts she'd had after Tom's death. Only then she'd carried those thoughts alone, for even old friends kept their distance—out of shame, perhaps, or else out of guilt. What had happened to Tom might have happened to one of their own loved ones, but it hadn't, and every time they spoke with Ruthie Mader they were glad. And possibly one of them had done it, or known the person who had done it. Everyone was a bit uneasy when the topic snagged itself in the unsuspecting net of conversation. What would you do, if no one had seen? When done was done and there was no going back and changing things anyway? If it had been an accident, a terrible mistake that would cost you everything?

A rooster crowed in the distance, four broken notes like a sob, and the sound drifted in through the open window on a breath of air as warm and moist as her own. Ruthie swung her legs over the edge of the bed and saw Cherish standing in the doorway. "We need to leave by seven," she said.

"It's barely six o'clock."

"It's five after," Cherish said. "I'm going to start loading the truck."

At the potluck, countless people had taken Ruthie aside and told her how much they admired Cherish for getting her life together—some went so far as to say she had been blessed—but Ruthie knew she was more lost now than all those nights she'd sneaked out of the house. Adolescence, like any fever, would have run its course, and if Cherish had been wild, perhaps she couldn't help it, taking after her grandmother the way she did. Gwendolyn had died of lung cancer long before Cherish's birth, but whenever Ruthie looked into her daughter's wide-set eyes, she saw her own mother looking back. That heart-shaped face. That hollowed cheek. That punishing mouth. Gwendolyn was seldom seen without a cigarette lilting from her lips. She spent nearly every weekend at the Hodag, drinking and dancing and flirting with men— there were nights she never came home. She wore low-cut shirts, jangly earrings, stiletto heels that Ruthie was forbidden to try on.

"Don't call me *Mom*," Gwendolyn had said when Ruthie was eight or nine. "It makes me feel old."

But Cherish had been living a quiet life. She'd been working long hours at the library. She'd finished all the books on the Recommended Book List that UW–Eau Claire sent its incoming students. She'd stopped telling lies. If you asked, she would look you right in the face and admit she did not believe in God.

"As a society, we have to move beyond that," she told Ruthie. It was, no doubt, an idea she'd gotten from her reading. "There is no reason to believe that the soul is anything more than what we call memory."

"Then what happens to people when they die?"

"Mom, I don't want to fight about this," Cherish said. "I know religion is a comfort to you, but I just don't believe it anymore."

Ruthie didn't know how to reach her. And now she was leaving, and she was happy to be leaving, and there was nothing to be done except to get up and shower, braid her hair, put on her good dress with the short, cuffed sleeves, even though Cherish had said not to dress up. Clip-on earrings shaped like daisies. Nice white sandals from Penney's. Her Faith cross never left her throat—she would have felt uneasy without it, the way she would have felt had she removed her wedding ring. Suddenly she was hurrying. She wanted to help with the last of the boxes. She wanted to be there with Cherish when she stepped out of her room for the very last time. After today they'd see each other only once a month—perhaps less. And when the holidays arrived, Cherish might decide to go home with a friend. When summer came, she might just find a job in Eau Claire. Ruthie might never again have this opportunity to reach her daughter's heart.

But she found Cherish's room already empty. Bare hangers rang like chimes. The bed was stripped, the desk cleaned out, the shelves robbed of books and clutter. Cracks in the plaster marked the walls in lightning-bolt patterns, and water stains dappled the ceilings. There was a dark spot on the wall where burning wires had nearly started a fire; the light switch beside it was duct-taped into a permanent off position. Now that Ruthie had paid her back taxes, set aside tuition for Cherish, bought a used Ford pickup, a furnace, and a hot-water heater, and exterminated the huge bat colony in the attic, there was little cash left over for all the other things that needed to be done. Somehow the plumbing would have to be replaced. The peeling clapboards needed stripping and painting. The roof leaked; the front porch had rotted through. The kitchen needed appliances—the dishwasher had died years earlier, and only two burners on the stove still worked. Though what would one person need with more than two burners? It was hard to imagine—the small, silent meals. Mornings broken only by the chatter of TV. Life alone.

A book was lying facedown on the nightstand. Ruthie was certain that too much reading was causing Cherish's sleeplessness, but Dr. Kemp said insomnia was a symptom of depression. He said it was important for Ruthie to give Cherish some distance. He said it was important for teens to understand it was OK to hold beliefs that were different from their parents'. Ruthie had nodded when he'd said that. But it wasn't OK; in fact, it was intolerable. It was like being killed. What had ever happened to *Honor thy father and mother?* How else were beliefs to live on, if not through the lives of one's children?

She picked up the book—Nietzsche? *Night*-zee? The biography on the back said that he'd died in an asylum. She tried to read a passage that Cherish had underlined: *The content of our conscience is everything that was during the years of our childhoods regularly demanded of us without reason by people we honored or feared. . . . The belief in authorities is the source of the conscience; it is therefore not the voice of God in the heart of man, but the voice of some men in man.*

She flipped to another page.

. . . there is no longer for you any rewarder and recompenser, no final corrector—there is no longer any reason in what happens, no longer any love in what happens to you—there is no longer any resting place open to your heart where it has only to find and only to seek. . . . And then, at the bottom of the paragraph: *Perhaps it is*

precisely that renunciation which will also lend us the strength by which the renunciation itself can be endured; perhaps man will rise higher and higher from that time when he no longer flows out into God.

She read it several times to be sure she'd understood. How could anybody live in the world, believing something like that?

Footsteps pounded up the stairs; Ruthie kicked the book under the bed just seconds before Cherish came into the room.

"I'm ready whenever you are," Cherish said, looking around the nightstand. "I thought I left a book up here."

Ruthie shook her head. For the first time in months, Cherish's face was flushed with excitement, beautiful still in spite of the scars—perhaps even more beautiful. Ruthie wanted to hold her the way she had when Cherish was still small, feel those sturdy arms around her waist, see the upturned face, its absolute confidence. Nights, they'd said their bedtime prayers together, holding hands across the kitchen table between cooling cups of hot cocoa. There wasn't a question Ruthie couldn't answer. There wasn't a problem Ruthie couldn't solve. And God, like a grand, benevolent giant, was watching out for them both. Or so it had seemed, until now. Until Cherish turned her face away.

"I miss you already," Ruthie said, knowing it was the wrong thing to say.

"I'm not even leaving the state."

"But I worry—"

"I'll be fine." Cherish bounded down the stairs.

They ate a light breakfast before they left. Cherish had already unlocked the door to the shrine, put out the basket of angel pendants and a box of "What to Do in Ambient" brochures, which Lucy replenished from time to time. A raft of swallows glided out into the sunlight, bellies flashing rust. How Ruthie missed the smells and sounds of the sheep, the waxy feel of their fleece, their patient, placid eyes. But she'd sold them to the Farbs, along with the goats, to meet her co-payments on Cherish's medical bills. The chickens had died, one by one, or wandered off. Old Mule had disappeared abruptly—she hated to think he'd been stolen, but clearly there was no sense in keeping animals with so many people coming through. Last weekend alone, there had been sixty-five pilgrims.

"Mom?" Cherish called. She was already sitting in the truck. "If my roommate gets there first, I'll be stuck with the top bunk."

And so that was it. As Ruthie drove down the driveway, toward the J road, she waited for Cherish to look back or, at least, sneak a glance in the rearview mirror. But she didn't, and when they got on the highway, she turned on the radio as if this were any other day, as if they were just going into town to pick up groceries at the Piggly Wiggly. Ruthie sneaked a sideways glance at her daughter. How could a child you had carried inside your own body grow up to become a mystery? They passed the new billboard that marked the edge of the Carpenters' land: I BELIEVE! REMEMBER GABRIEL AT THE RIVER ANGEL SHRINE. They passed what had once been the Faith house. It hadn't taken Roland more than a week to rent it out to an auto parts dealer, and of course they'd whitewashed Cherish and Maya's mural from the walls. It was a shame they'd never finished it. It was a shame that Cherish didn't paint or draw anymore. What would she do with an English degree if, as she claimed, she didn't want to teach? How Ruthie envied Margaret Kirsch, whose daughter was already an assistant manager at the Wal-Mart. Lisa Marie was learning real skills, a life trade. Lisa Marie was staying close to home. Close to her mother.

They turned onto County O, passing the spot where Tom's body had been found, the white cross weathered to the color of sorrow itself, gray as bone. The fields were scorched the color of honey; the horizon shivered with heat. *There is no longer any reason in what happens, no longer any love in what happens to you.*

The sentence had stuck in Ruthie's mind like a terrible song, going round and round. "No wonder that poor man went insane," she said, more to herself than to Cherish.

"Which man?"

"The one who wrote that book."

"Nietzsche." Cherish looked annoyed. "What did you do with it, Mom?" Then she shrugged. "I'll get another copy at the library."

"How can anyone think there's no reason for all that we see?" Ruthie gestured at the brittle fields, at the dust boiling over the highway and the shocked blue heart of the sky. "Somebody did this, somebody made this, just like somebody made us all. If you found a watch lying on the sidewalk, would you think all those intricate pieces had assembled themselves on their own?"

"The world isn't a watch, Mom."

"The things you believe," Ruthie said. "It simply breaks my heart. I wish we could talk about this, sweetheart." They were coming up on I-90/94; she exited onto the cloverleaf and headed west. A highway sign urged people to give themselves a hug-buckle up, and stuck beneath the seat-belt graphic was a river angel bumper sticker: HONK IF YOU BELIEVE! Ruthie truly hated those things, but there wasn't anything she could do about them. People sold them in town along with T-shirts and mugs and pins. Maya Paluski was in Seattle visiting friends for the summer, and she'd sent Ruthie a photo she'd taken of a Jaguar with California tags and THIS CAR PROTECTED BY THE RIVER ANGEL plastered across the bumper.

"Fine," Cherish said. "Let's talk."

"Good," Ruthie said, surprised.

"I'll start," Cherish said. "You say what I believe breaks your heart. But if you believe in what you *say* you believe in, then isn't what *I* believe in simply part of God's will?"

"Oh, honey," Ruthie said. The first sign for Eau Claire appeared: 185 miles. Two crosses stood tall in the mown grass of the easement, fresh pink carnations braided around their necks. "There must have been an accident," she said, trying to change the subject. Talking now would be a mistake; she could see that. They'd only spend the morning fighting. But Cherish wouldn't let it go. She said, "I thought you didn't believe in accidents."

Ruthie looked at her. "What are you talking about?"

"I mean," Cherish said, "you believe that everything is God's will, right? So nothing can be an accident. People die, people live—but either way, it really doesn't matter. So what if two people lost their lives back there. So what if some poor family is grieving. *Give thanks in all circumstances.* How many times in my life have you told me that?" The hot wind rippled through her hair.

"You're twisting my words, and you know it."

"Am I? All right. Let's talk about the carnations, then. What a waste of money!" Ruthie winced; Cherish was mimicking her. "Dead people live with God; they have everything they need. If you're going to give flowers, give them to the living." She dropped back into her regular voice. "You told me that too, remember? Come on, Mom, you wanted to talk. We visited Dad's grave every single Sunday for *years*, and we never once left flowers or pictures or anything. *Anything.* Didn't you care about him? Didn't you love him? Don't you ever miss him?"

Ruthie was stunned. "How can you ask me that?"

"You've never acted like it. You never talk about him. You never even *cried*, not even at the funeral. And whenever I cried, you'd tell me that he'd only been on loan to us anyway and that he really belonged to God, and it was selfish to be unhappy when he was so very, very happy in heaven. Fine, OK, that's what you believe. I guess I can deal with that. But *then* you get after *me* for reading *Nietzsche*. Mom, your ideas are more depressing than anything Nietzsche ever wrote. More fucked up too, if you want to know the truth.''

Ruthie gripped the steering wheel. She said very softly, ''Don't you ever, ever say that word to me.''

''*Fucked up*,'' Cherish said, and she turned up the radio.

One hundred miles to Eau Claire. Gradually, the flat fields rolled themselves into wooded hills, rock formations rising between them, unexpected, ungainly as dinosaurs. The highway cut between granite walls; pink flecks ran through the veins. Seventy-five miles. Another white cross by the roadside: wildflowers dead in a clouded jelly jar, snapshots wrapped in plastic, a pale blue ribbon the color of ice. Someone's life flashed past and was gone, was resurrected as Ruthie imagined the hands which had tied that ribbon, a woman's hands, rough and shaking like her own. And the long weekly drive with the children to place the flowers at the site, and then the longer ride back, tempered with the promise of McDonald's or Dairy Queen, salt and fat and sweetness that fooled nobody's hunger. *Where is Daddy and why has he gone?* The woman's tears brighter than her wedding diamond. The stares of the people in the restaurant. The children hushing themselves after spills. The same scene, week after week.

Ruthie hadn't wanted Cherish to grow up in a house defined by grief. Death was a natural part of God's plan; she didn't want Cherish to fear. If Ruthie needed to cry, she went to her room and shut the door, sobbed into Tom's bathrobe, which still hung from its wobbling hook, feeding the worn flannel into her mouth until she choked on its dust, gagged, spat it out. Ten minutes, fifteen minutes at most, and then it was over, her hair freshly combed, her throat and tongue raw with Listerine. Sundays after Mass, they walked from the church to the cemetery unburdened. No flowers. No photographs. Nothing but a small American flag, which blew away between their visits. Cherish always hunted it down in the ditch that ran alongside the gravestones, returning with the mementos and memorials of others: cards and letters, plastic flowers, angels, saints, and pinwheels. None of that was necessary, Ruthie explained, for Daddy had absolutely everything he needed. "Doesn't he miss us?" Cherish said once, and before the tears could spill over, priming the wetness behind Ruthie's eyes, she replied, "Of course not—he knows we'll join him soon." And yes, she had said it: "It's selfish for us to cry."

Selfish—also human, she realized now. Yet if one weren't careful, grief could take over completely. The way Ruthie had nearly allowed it to do during those terrible months just after Tom's death, a time she'd always hoped Cherish wouldn't remember, would never discover on her own. *Dear Lord*, Ruthie prayed, *tell me what to do*. Forty-six miles. "Cherish," she began, and she turned off the radio. And at last she felt the grace of God assembling the words she needed, placing them one by one, like mints, upon her tongue.

"A week or so after your father's funeral," she said, "I was driving down County O when I saw a car pull up by your father's marker. A little red sporty thing. Something about it made me look twice. When it pulled away, I chased it in that old Ford we had—you remember it? But I couldn't keep up. I turned around and came back home." It had been a long time since Ruthie had talked about that red sports car. Lorna and Jolena and Shelley knew the story. And Maya. The founding members of the Circle of Faith. "But I couldn't stop thinking about it. During the day, while you were in school, I'd bike out to the Neumillers'. I made myself a blind beneath a stand of hickory trees—the cows would gather round, and I'd flap my arms to scare them off—and I waited. The more I thought about it, the more I was absolutely certain that the driver of that sports car was responsible for your father's death. I'd only caught a glimpse of him, but as time passed I began to see him clearly. He was handsome, in his late thirties, with blond hair turning silver and a gold ring on his hand.

He had blue eyes and creases starting around his mouth. A thick neck. A leather watchband. And he was thinking he'd gotten away with something. Maybe even laughing about it—I knew there were people in the world who didn't care what they did. Your grandmother was that way. Once, when I was a kid, she clipped a dog that was crossing the road. It had a silver collar, and I saw it spinning with its jaw smashed open—alive and everything, just badly hurt. But Gwendolyn told me, 'Hang on, baby,' and she shot right out of there, and when we got out to where the Badger State Mall is now, which is where we lived back then, she turned to me and said, 'Looks like we got away with that one.' "

The little dog tumbling end over end. Like a punctured football. Like a knotted-up, worthless rag.

"And if you don't think what goes around comes around," Ruthie said, "let me tell you those words haunted me after Tom's death. It got so I could hear that man's voice in my ear. *Got away with that one*, he'd say. That's when I took Tom's thirty-eight from the attic. You think I'm making this up? I wrapped it in plastic and stashed it in the blind. By then school was out, and I sent you into town every chance I got: summer school, swimming lessons, sleep-overs, church camp. Do you remember?"

Cherish nodded. For once, she seemed to be listening. "I thought you didn't want me around."

"I didn't. All I could think about was that man, how I'd be ready for him the day he came back, and when Stan Pranke stopped by the house one morning, I told him I'd found the suspect, I'd identified him by his little red sports car. And do you know what Stan said? The paint they found on your father's car, on his body—it wasn't red. It was white. From an older-model sedan. It had been in all the papers. And then Stan said he had Tom's thirty-eight and he was going to hang on to it for me, until I felt better, and he hoped that would be soon. That's when I started the Circle of Faith. That's when I turned my anger over to God. And it was like my life was given back to me again."

"I wish you'd told me," Cherish said.

"How could I tell you something like that?" Ruthie said. "I didn't want you feeling like you couldn't have a normal life, like you had to think about him every minute of the day."

"But when you don't talk about someone, you lose the memory. That's when a person is really dead. I can barely remember Dad anymore. . . ."

For a long time, she looked out the window, and Ruthie was afraid she wouldn't say anything more, that their last morning together would be spent in a silence as thick as gauze pressed over a wound. But then she said, "I never told you this, but that night on the bridge? I thought I saw him."

"You saw Tom?" Ruthie's voice rattled over his name.

"He was running toward me like he wanted to save me, and I was so glad to see him because it meant that I was wrong and there was a purpose to everything, we'd go on living forever, just like you'd always said. Something told me, OK, you've seen, now close your eyes. But I had to be certain. I kept my eyes open. Everything was spinning, but I didn't shut my eyes."

"What happened?"

Cherish laughed, a short, bitter sound. "It was only Paul," she said. "That's all I remember—except for you, in the hospital. And I remember thinking, Well, good. She finally knows the truth about me. And I finally know the truth about Dad."

"No," Ruthie said. "Give it another chance."

"I should have closed my eyes," Cherish said. "I can't stop telling myself that—if only I'd closed my eyes. Then I could believe in everything you do. I'd think Dad was in heaven. I'd think some angel rescued Gabriel and that there was a God who could forgive us for what we did."

Gwendolyn's cheekbones. Gwendolyn's face. But Ruthie had

never once seen her mother cry. She gripped her daughter's hand, feeling an overwhelming sense of relief. "You didn't do anything."

"I was there." They were coming into Eau Claire. "Mom, I just want to start over again. I want to get everything right."

"We all want that," Ruthie finally said. "It isn't only you."

They followed the general flow of traffic to the campus, where thousands of parents were already unloading their children in front of a series of box-shaped dorms. "Mine's further down the circle," Cherish said, but there wasn't any way to pull closer, and already they were parked in, people springing from their cars, cutting bicycles and lamps from roof racks. So much commotion—radios blaring, returning students shrieking at the sight of old friends, dorm counselors shouting instructions on bullhorns, and above it all, thousands of parents arguing over the best way to unpack, unload, register. After so many months of dreading the moment of separation from Cherish, Ruthie actually found herself eager to leave. Instead she waited at the car for nearly two hours—"Do not leave your vehicle unattended!" the counselors bellowed—while Cherish got her keys, carried her suitcases up the steps into the building and then, as it turned out, up another four flights of stairs. The roommate was already present—actually, Cherish had two roommates. A counselor had promised a third bed was on the way.

"I don't know where we'll put it," Cherish said. Already she looked at home here, on this campus, with these people—all of them waving hasty goodbyes to crestfallen families, setting off with newfound groups of friends. Even as Cherish checked the truck to make sure she hadn't forgotten anything, someone was hollering, "Hey, Cher? When you're finished, we're going to check out the union!"

"I guess you're all set, then," Ruthie said.

"I guess," Cherish said. "Should I call you tonight?"

"No," Ruthie said, surprising herself. "Take your time, settle in. Call me when you're ready."

"OK." Cherish gave her a quick, tentative hug, and Ruthie smelled the sweet shampoo in her hair.

"I wish I had something I could give you," she said. "A good-bye present."

"Cash?" Cherish said, smiling.

"How about this?" Ruthie said, and she reached up and un-hooked the Faith cross that had hung from her neck since the Circle's first meeting. Cherish took it, watched it dangle from her hand. "It's beautiful," she said, "but it isn't for me. I'm sorry, Mom, I really am."

"I'll wear it for you, then," Ruthie said, and Cherish bent to fasten it back in its place. Then she straightened up, turned around, and walked away.

Driving home, Ruthie forced herself not to think about the empty house. It would be late afternoon by the time she arrived, shadows leaking over the courtyard from the barn. She tried to make plans: She'd have a fried egg sandwich, homemade apple-sauce for dessert. Maybe she'd go down to the cellar, open one of the few bottles of dandelion wine that remained from before Tom's death. She'd call a few Faith members, ask them over to join her. They'd been talking about refurbishing the milk house for their meetings—this might be the time to sketch out some plans. But she kept thinking about Cherish on the bridge, the question Cherish could not stop asking: *What if I'd only closed my eyes?* It was the same question Ruthie had asked herself so many times since that morning in the barn. *What if I'd simply shaken my head, dismissed what I'd seen as exhaustion? What if I'd simply called 911, said only, "I found him, come quickly"?* But the fact was, she had seen. The fact was, she believed. She'd been called to bear witness—to what, she did not know. Perhaps that was what Cherish was trying to do: bear witness to something Ruthie could not see. Maybe the act, in itself, was its own salvation. Hadn't Cherish's book said something like that? Ruthie couldn't remember. She told herself she could always look it up when she got home. But she knew that she wouldn't, at least not now, the way she'd known that Cherish wouldn't accept the cross she'd offered her.

A fried egg sandwich. A glass of Tom's wine. Maybe she wouldn't call anybody. Maybe she'd pull the curtains and sip her wine, and it would be as if Tom were still alive and she was just waiting for him to come home. Cherish would be in the barn, starting chores; there'd be fresh peach ice cream chilling in the freezer. As soon as the Bobcat rattled into the courtyard, she'd stick a stuffed summer squash in the oven, a tray of corn muffins to go with it. She'd greet Tom with a kiss, and they'd put on their boots and smocks and go out to the barn together, dreaming even then of the time when he could finally quit the post office and work the farm full time. How happy he would have been to see the land preserved for others to enjoy in his name. How proud he would have been to see Cherish on this day, and how unfair— Ruthie caught herself, tried, but could not block the thought— how wrong, dear Lord, that he couldn't have been there, just this once, to see her walk away so steadily, to wave along with the other parents shouting, "Goodbye! Goodbye!"

coda

What I remember most about the River Angel Shrine is how dark it was inside, and the dance of the candles in their little glass cups, and the animal odor of the old wooden floors. There was snow on the ground, though not much. I sat in a folding chair, listening to the music of the pigeons in the eaves. Every now and then, one would launch into the dusky air, flap-flap-flapping between the rafters. There was a single shaft of light slicing down from the apex of the barn, illuminating the cold face of the statue—an ugly face, I thought, with its pupilless eyes, its thin-lipped mouth. The stony curve of each wing ended in a knifelike point. It was said the boy's ashes were buried here. I imagined how it would be to lie on my back in this barn, on a night much colder than this day, encircled by the warm breathing of sheep.

I got up and walked around, fingering mementos others had left. A few stuffed animals, a plastic rosary, pack after pack of cigarettes. Mostly, there were photographs, and one in particular caught my eye. A newborn infant—boy or girl, I couldn't tell— who already wore the wise and faraway look of the dead.

back were the words *Remember me*. I walked out
   house across the courtyard looked abandoned,
   woodsmoke from the fireplace, and there were
   owels and sheets hanging from the clothesline. I left a dollar donation, took a little gold angel from the basket. Then I put it back. Then I picked it up again, slipped it into the pocket of my jeans. Another car came slowly up the driveway. Two women were inside. As I drove away, I noticed they had Minnesota tags. One of the women waved.

Later, I found the bridge. The spot the boy had fallen from was marked with a small white cross, and there were a dozen faded plastic bouquets, some of them partially buried in snow, that had been pushed off the highway by plows. I wished I had thought to bring something with me. I walked onto the bridge, looked out over the railing. The water was a clear, cold blue, and I could see the public park, the empty swings rocking just a little, as if occupied by ghosts.

I don't know what I expected to see, there at the bridge or, earlier, in the barn. Several weeks passed before I discovered the little gold angel I'd tucked in my pocket. Now it hangs above my writing desk from a piece of fishing line. The gold is flaking from its back and wings. Why do I keep it? I cannot pretend to believe that transcendence lies beyond the mind, that the soul is more than memory, which is neither fiction nor fact, but a country all its own. Still, as I type these words, the vibrations cause the angel to tremble on its slender thread, and how eager I am to forget, if only for a moment, that I am the source of its fear. I visit the shrines. I walk into the churches, the temples and mosques, the tent revivals and palm reader's shops, and even, once, a Wiccan ceremony in a starlit field of wheat. My love for this world is great enough, at times, to shatter my heart. But what does it matter? Someday I'll slip beneath its surface without a ripple.

And yet I pray for the boy, whom I've chosen to call Gabriel. I pray for the infant in the photograph, its mouth like a tear in a pale piece of cloth. *Remember me.* Remember us. Let the end be more than that unwieldy plunge into ice and darkness. Let there be someone waiting to catch us when we fall.